Eleanor Berry's sixteenth book.

This deep but comical psychological thriller examines the curious relationship between two savagely eccentric doctors, and their sinister connection with a ball of red wool.

They are father and son. Their names are Rowland Rendon and William Rendon. Rowland is a demented Harley Street psychiatrist. William is an angelic-looking, but death-crazy and sex-crazy Hammersmith Hospital pathologist.

When not taking amphetamines, and reading Edgar Allan Poe, he has, among his extreme peculiarities, a penchant for paying prostitutes to sing *God Save the Queen*.

It is impossible for the reader not to love him, and weep for him during his ultimate ruin.

"Despite the sometimes weighty portent of this book, a sense of subtle, dry and powerfully engaging humour reigns throughout its pages. The unexpected twist is stupendous." (Stephen Carson — the *Carolina Sun*).

Other books by Eleanor Berry

Tell us a Sick One Jakey
Never Alone with Rex Malone
The Ruin of Jessie Cavendish
Your Father Died on the Gallows
Robert Maxwell as I Knew Him
Seamus O'Rafferty and Dr Blenkinsop
Alandra Varinia Seed of Sarah
The House of the Mad Doctors
Jaxton the Silver Boy
Someone's Been Done up Harley
O, Hitman, my Hitman!
McArandy was hanged under Tyburn Tree
The Scourging of Poor Little Maggie
The Revenge of Miss Rhoda Buckleshott
The Most Singular Adventures of Eddy Vernon

Some comments.

Never Alone with Rex Malone
("A ribald, ambitious black comedy, a story powerfully told"). *The Daily Mail*

("I was absolutely flabbergasted when I read it!") *Robert Maxwell*

Your Father Died on the Gallows
("A unique display of black humour which somehow fails to depress the reader.") Craig McLittle. *The Rugby Gazette*

Robert Maxwell as I Knew Him
("One of the most amusing books I have read for a long time. Eleanor Berry is an original.") Elisa Seagrave. *The Literary Review*
("Undoubtedly the most amusing book I have read all year.") Julia Llewellyn Smith. *The Times*
("With respect, and I repeat, with very great respect, because I know you are a lady — all you ever do is just go on and on and on and on about this bleeding *bloke*!") *Reggie Kray*

The Scourging of Poor Little Maggie

"This harrowing, tragic and deeply ennobling book, caused me to weep for two days after reading it. I had not experienced this reaction since seeing the film *The Elephant Man*.") Moira McClusky. *The Cork Evening News*.

TAKE IT AWAY, IT'S RED!

To my loyal, childhood friend, REBECCA BARRATT, whose chauffeur entertained me for two hours with one extraordinary anecdote after another, about one of his many psychiatrists, whose name was Dr Rendon. Of note, is the fact that this doctor has no resemblance to anyone bearing the name Rendon, in this book. For ethical reasons, I refrain from giving Rebecca's chauffeur's name.

E.B.

TAKE IT AWAY, IT'S RED!

Eleanor Berry

ARTHUR H. STOCKWELL LTD.
Ilfracombe, Devon

All characters and situations portrayed in this book are imaginary. Any resemblance to persons living or dead is purely coincidental.

British Library Cataloguing in Publication Data.
A catalogue record for this book is available from the British Library.

ISBN 0 7223 3255-6

Printed in England by Arthur H. Stockwell Ltd., Ilfracombe, Devon.

Cover design by Eleanor Berry, Eddy Taylor and Harry Hobbs.

Cover printed in England by Arthur H. Stockwell Ltd., Ilfracombe, Devon.

The date was 12 December, 1993. An inquest was being held in the Westminster Coroner's Court in Horseferry Road, London.

The court was crowded. Only members of the deceased's family and relatives, were able to occupy the small room in which the inquest was taking place.

The Coroner entered the court. He was a dapper, good-looking man, given to no little degree of eccentricity, and was aged about fifty. He had a full head of thick, dark brown hair and was almost six foot tall. The deceased's relatives and girlfriend, an attractive woman with natural copper-coloured hair, ambled lethargically to their feet.

The lack of spontaneity in the movements of most of those present, was caused by the numbness of their grief and their guilt because they had found little time to entertain and socialize with the deceased, so absorbed were they by their own lives.

They had loved him at a distance. His wildness, insanity and childlike, if sometimes frightening, behaviour, fascinated them. His father's persistent cruelty towards him during his childhood, aroused their love, sympathy and compassion, even if they rarely met him, except at weddings and funerals.

"The first hearing this morning, relates to the death of the late William Rendon," said the Coroner, who put on his glasses and opened a file on the desk in front of him.

"William James Victor Rendon was born in St Thomas's Hospital, London on 12th April, 1959, and at the time of his death, was living at 88 Vauxhall Bridge Road, London. He was pronounced dead at 2.00 on the morning of 15th November, 1993, after being taken by ambulance to the Chelsea and Westminster Hospital, London. His occupation was that of doctor.

"At 1.05 on the morning of 15th November, 1993, his girlfriend, Miss Juliet Silverman, let herself into his flat with her latch key, and found him unconscious on the kitchen floor.

"The four gas rings on the stove had been turned on. The smell of leaked gas was so overpowering, that Miss Silverman dragged him by the feet into the hall, and tried to resuscitate him, to no avail.

"She rang emergency services, and at 1.15, an ambulance arrived, as well as two police officers, namely Detective Constable Cranley and PC Goss.

"Paramedics failed to revive him and he was

taken to the Chelsea and Westminster Hospital. Despite Draconian attempts to start his heart, the deceased was pronounced dead at 2.00 that morning.

"Could the first witness, Detective Constable Cranley, please come forward," said the Coroner.

Cranley entered the witness box, and took the Bible oath.

"You are Detective Constable Cranley?" said the Coroner.

"I am, sir."

"Would you please inform the court of your experiences in the early morning of 15th November, 1993.

"They are exactly the same as the facts you have just read out, sir."

"Had you ever had contact with the deceased in his life time?"

"No, sir. My colleague, PC Goss, met him on 11th September, 1993. I am afraid I have nothing further to add."

PC Goss was asked to enter the witness box. He, too, took the Bible oath.

"You are PC Goss?" asked the Coroner.

"Yes, sir."

"Would you mind speaking up, please. This enquiry is a waste of time if the voices of witnesses can't be heard."

"Yes. I am PC Goss," said the witness, this time speaking very loudly, almost to the point of sounding rude.

"I understand you met the deceased late at night on 11th September, 1993. What were the circumstances of this meeting?"

"He was driving the wrong way up Harley Street, which, as you know, is one-way."

"How do you expect me to know it's a one-way street?" asked the Coroner, irritably. "Continue."

"He was driving twenty miles an hour in excess of the speed limit. Also, he had his fog lights on, and his radio was blaring the *March of the Toreadors*, causing a breach of the peace. I pulled him into the side. He wound down his window, looking much the worse for wear. 'What the hell do you want?' he asked. I asked him to turn the music down. In reply, he shouted, 'F-U-C-K you.'

"Do you mean 'fuck'?" asked the Coroner.

"Yes, sir."

"Say, so, then. I don't go round, saying Y-J-W-X-B-A-Z! Continue."

"My colleague, WPC Henry, was with me. I asked the deceased to get out and take a breath test. He was abusive and belligerent and shouted, 'We're not living in Hitler's Germany!'"

A woman sitting at the back of the court, let out a nervous titter.

4

"This is not a laughing matter," said the Coroner. "Did he get out of the car?"

"Yes, with some persuasion. The breath test he submitted was abnormal. A police van took him to the station. He was extremely rude and aggressive throughout the journey and kept shouting that he was a doctor, answering an emergency call.

"His behaviour improved at the station. He was over-talkative, but less rude. He ranted at the desk sergeant about Jack the Ripper."

"Why do you imagine he did that?"

"Because, whatever else he had swallowed, was making him euphoric. He was persistent, manic and authoritarian, and his eyes were glazed and staring. He kept shouting that he knew that Sir William Gull, Queen Victoria's personal surgeon, was Jack the Ripper. He couldn't stop pacing up and down. He said, and these were his exact words, 'Is it true that the Ripperologists at Scotland Yard, are so adamant that their respective views are correct, that the Druitists refuse to sit in the same part of the staff canteen as the Gullists?'

"He even went so far as to suggest that the police arrange for a football match to take place with the Druitists on one team and the Gullists on the other."

The Coroner let out an uncontrolled guffaw. He wondered whether the frenzied supporters of the two respective teams, would be dressed in Victorian clothes, waving carving knives in the air.

"What did the blood test show?"

"It showed he was three and a half times over the legal alcohol limit and that he had 50 mg of amphetamines in his blood. Lab tests showed that he had taken a drug called Dexamphetamine Sulphate. This is a controlled drug and only comes in tablets of 5 mg, which means that he had taken about ten of these in repeated doses. That dosage alone is enough to kill someone easily, unless that person uses the drug habitually."

"Did he say anything about this drug?"

"Yes. He was so high that he confessed, in a very boastful way, that he took Dexedrine, the trade name for Dexamphetamine Sulphate, every day, and could hold any amount of it."

"Did he say he was addicted to it?"

"No, although it would have been impossible for him not to have been addicted, on such high doses every day. He had to wait a long time for the blood test and started shaking and jumping up and down. He said he wanted to go home for more Dexedrine. Yes, on second thoughts, he did say he was addicted, in so many words."

"Well, say so, for God's sake!" snapped the Coroner, adding, "Did you ever see him, again?"

"No, sir."

"Very well. You may stand down. Next time you are asked to give evidence in court, you should make an effort to be more concise and to the point."

"Yes, sir. I'm sorry, sir."

"So am I," said the Coroner, in a rasping tone, adding much more gently, "The next witness I wish to question is Miss Juliet Silverman. Miss Silverman, would you care to come forward, please? If it would make you feel more comfortable, perhaps you would care to give your evidence sitting down."

Juliet was about twenty-five. She walked into the witness box with an air of dignity and composure, although her grief was overtly apparent. She wore a woollen emerald green dress and matching shoes, which complimented her impeccably-groomed, shoulder-length, copper-coloured hair.

"I will be all right standing, sir," she said. Her voice was husky, low and strident, and her accent upper class.

The usher automatically handed her a Bible, assuming, as the first two witnesses had taken the Bible oath, that she, too, would wish to do so.

Her voice was so loud, that Rendon's relatives, and the Coroner, were startled, and jumped.

"No. I'll take the secular oath!" she shouted, angrily, adding, "How do you expect a woman who's lost a lover, to believe there's a God?"

"I understand how much you are suffering, Miss Silverman, but there is really no need to shout in this way, as if the people you are addressing were outside in the street."

"No, sir," said Juliet. She took her chosen oath.

"Would you mind telling the court how long you had known the late William Rendon?" asked the Coroner.

"Two years."

"You were sharing a flat with him throughout most of that period, were you not?"

"Yes, sir."

"Have you any idea why he might have wished to commit suicide?"

"None whatever. He was a strange, rather disturbed person, but the last thing I expected him to do, was end his life. I know his last day alive was unhappy, but not unhappy enough to drive him to suicide."

"When was the last time you saw him, before you found him on the kitchen floor, early on the morning of 15th November?"

"We'd been together most of the day. We always were on Sundays. I went out later. It was already dark."

"Why did you go out?"

"I went to the cinema."

"What film did you see?" asked the Coroner,

who thought that her choice of film, might have some bearing on the case.

"The film was called '*Naked*'. It was a nauseating film about this ghastly, grimy, disgusting man from Manchester. Not only that, a woman was buggered by her landlord in some kitchen."

The Coroner cleared his throat. "I am not interested in what the film was about," he said, irritably. "Also, would you moderate your remarks about the inhabitants of Manchester. My grandmother was born in Manchester."

"I appreciate that," said Juliet. "I didn't get home until very late. I had to go to a pub to recover from the film. Then I walked home. It was so dreadful, I had to stop several times in the street because of my terrible nausea. With the greatest respect, I don't think I'll ever be able to hear a Manchester accent again without emptying my stomach."

"Miss Silverman, while we sympathize with you," said the Coroner, "the court is not in any way concerned with a rambling description of your medical status or your stomach. The fact that you felt sick has nothing whatever to do with the late William Rendon.

"Would you please tell the court concisely, and by Jove, I lay an emphasis on the word, 'concisely', how William behaved throughout

9

Sunday, 14th November?"

Juliet looked lost and flustered.

"Well, it was Remembrance Sunday," she began.

"Of that I am well aware," said the Coroner. "What about it?"

"I was ironing in the front room where the television was. I always like watching the Remembrance ceremony and I turned the volume up. William was in the bedroom, reading *The Lancet*. His flat was well sound-proofed and he could hardly hear anything from the bedroom.

"He came into the room with a cup of coffee in his hand. He looked demented. He started screaming. He shouted, 'No, please, not that! It's too much for me. I can't bear it. Turn it off!' If not those exact words, words to that effect."

"Indeed?" said the Coroner. "Had he recently lost someone who had served?"

"No, I don't think so."

"Have you any idea why the ceremony shown on television disturbed him?"

"None whatever. I asked him to tell me, once he had calmed down and taken some Dexedrine. He said he associated it with something so horrible, he couldn't tell a living soul."

"Was he all right after that?"

"For a short time. We had lunch together in a

French restaurant called *Thierry*'s in the King's Road."

"Then what happened?"

"We were having lunch. We'd had *endives* with cheese, to start with ..."

"I don't want to hear what you ate!" said the Coroner, his voice raised once more. "Was there some unpleasant incident?"

"Yes. A woman came into the restaurant, wearing a bright red overcoat. William started shaking. He had some kind of fit. He was pointing at her, with a look of agony on his face. He kept screaming the words, 'Take it away, it's red!'"

"How very singular! Why do you think he was doing this?"

"It must have been the Speed, oh, sorry, I meant Dexedrine.

"The waiter had told the woman to take her overcoat off. He said the restaurant was well-heated. He seemed offended by the idea of someone wearing an overcoat indoors. She refused to take it off. They had a heated argument. She stormed out. William seemed very distressed.

"I wondered who she was and whether there had been a relationship between them. I thought he knew her. It crossed my mind that he had once robbed her. I wondered whether he owed her a large sum of money in return for drugs she may

11

have given him.

"His reaction terrified me. I couldn't understand what the matter was. I thought, perhaps, the Dexedrine had driven him clinically mad, enough to make him potentially violent. The waiters were flabbergasted."

"So was the red-coated woman, I dare say. How did the other people in the restaurant react to this outburst?"

"They just sat there like a load of cretins waiting for a train. You know how wet and barmy the British are."

"I would thank you to keep your unpatriotic sentiments to yourself, Miss Silverman," said the Coroner. "When and where did you first meet Rendon?"

"He was a Senior Registrar at the Hammersmith Hospital. I was working with him as a medical secretary. Senior Registrar is one rank below consultant."

"In what department?"

"Pathology. That means the analysis of dead bodies. Post mortems. I had to type post mortem reports."

"I may appear to you to be absolutely half-witted, but I am aware what pathology entails, and I also know what a Senior Registrar is," said the Coroner. "How did you manage to get onto friendly terms with Rendon?"

Juliet stretched out her hands, palms downwards, over the edge of the witness box.

"Oh, he often came into my office and talked to me," she said. "He was really friendly."

"What did he talk to you about?"

"He was very jolly. He was always cracking jokes about the stiffs."

"Stiffs?"

"Oh, sorry, I meant dead bodies."

"I don't understand what jokes anyone could wish to make about dead bodies. I wasn't aware that they were a source of merriment. What sort of things did he say?"

"A lot of the bodies were those of alcoholics," said Juliet. "He used to joke about the size and weight of their livers."

"Why do you think he found that so funny?"

"He could make anything grim sound funny. He believed there was a comical side to all things grave. He used that belief in order to survive."

"Is that also your belief?"

"It has to be, hasn't it? If that weren't the case, I'd have topped myself by now."

"What sort of things did he say to you about livers?"

"Well, there was this SHO there with him. He was cutting up stiffs, oh, sorry, dead bodies. He

13

was a bit hung-over. He had two bodies to work on. Both males. One was an alcoholic's. He'd had cirrhosis of the liver. The other was someone who'd died of lung cancer. The post mortem assistant, who'd also had a few too many, picked up this liver, and slapped it onto the scales."

"What liver, dear?"

"I'm just about to tell you, sir.

" 'Two thousand, nine hundred and ninety grams,' the SHO announced.

" 'That's strange,' William called out ..."

"William who?" barked the Coroner, whose concentration had wandered.

"Why, William Rendon, of course."

"Oh, yes, of course. I really do apologize. Please go on."

"So, William said to this SHO: 'If this bloke died of cirrhosis of the liver, how could his liver possibly weigh over two thousand bloody grams? It would be so shrivelled up, it wouldn't weigh more than four hundred grams at most.'

"William came into my office in stitches. The assistant had put the lung cancer victim's liver on the scales by mistake. The hung-over SHO didn't notice."

The Coroner was irritated by the macabre humour, shown in a woman who had recently suffered a bereavement. He considered her behaviour disloyal to the memory of the man who had died, and was unaware of the lengths she had gone through, to hide her grief.

"Young woman," said the Coroner, "would you please refrain from using this court, to show off, by telling bizarre, surreal anecdotes. Kindly keep to the point. This is a serious enquiry, not a comedy show.

"After his visits to your office, how did your relationship progress?"

"He started to take me out to dinner almost every night of the week. I soon moved in with him."

"Did he appear to be in love with you, at this time?" asked the Coroner.

"Yes, he did. He gave me something of a personal and touching nature and told me that it represented his love."

"What was it?"

"It was a poem he had written. It had a pale pink mount and a black frame."

"What sort of poem had he written?"

"The words of the poem itself did not express love. It was a very black-humoured, morbid, macabre poem. It touched me because he knew about my fascination for that sort of thing."

"This gift to you — where is it now?"

"In my handbag. I keep it with me all the time.

My act of doing so, and looking at it every day, is the equivalent of visiting William's grave, and assuaging my guilt for not loving him so passionately at the end of his life."

The Coroner took a sip of water, and leaned forward in his chair.

"Would you mind showing it to me?"

A wave of exhibitionism surged through Juliet. Since the actual wording of the poem did not relate to her personally, she felt no self-consciousness when the opportunity arose for her to shock and revolt the Coroner.

She ran her hand through her hair and tilted her head backwards. She smiled flirtatiously at the Coroner.

"No, sir. I don't mind."

The gift was passed to the Coroner who was initially impressed by William's beautiful, neat, italic handwriting. He held it to the light and adjusted his glasses.

It took him less than five minutes to read the poem. As he did so, the colour gradually drained from his face. He laid it down in front of him and began to retch. When he realized there was no chance of his holding his bile, he left the bench and rushed to the lavatory, while the occupants of the courtroom, gaped at him, aghast. Juliet rested her folded arms on the edge of the witness box, and had a giggling fit.

The Coroner came back into the room, his face drawn and his lips moist.

"I see no reason to circulate this exhibit," he said breathlessly. "Kindly return it to the witness.*

"How did things go after that?" he asked.

"It was difficult at first. I wanted him to take me to Harley Street, and introduce me to his parents. He became evasive. He said his mother and father were dead.

"He wasn't telling the truth. I knew his father wasn't dead. He was a consultant psychiatrist. When I was working as a temporary in a private psychiatric hospital, my boss corresponded with Dr Rendon senior who sometimes rang up. I answered several of his calls."

"Why do you think William lied about his father?"

"I used to think he was ashamed of me."

"Never mind what you used to think. What do you think, now?"

"One night, he was very tired and low. His behaviour was pretty mysterious. He confessed that he had grown to love his father in adult years, and

---

*William Rendon's poem is of such an obscene and disgusting nature, that, for the benefit of readers, depraved enough to wish to see it, it appears in exceptionally small print on a page of its own at the end of this book, and will require the use of a magnifying glass.

17

implied that he didn't want to share him with anyone. Perhaps, there was incest between them, but I never found out," she answered.

"Good Lord! One would hardly expect that kind of behaviour from a psychiatrist. Mind you, I suppose one has to be certified insane before one is allowed to practice as a psychiatrist," remarked the Coroner. "Did Rendon ever take you to the house in Harley Street where he grew up?"

"Yes."

"What happened?"

Juliet was about to burst into tears. She couldn't speak.

"Miss Silverman, are you all right?"

"I think so, sir. This is terribly disturbing."

"Please feel free to continue giving your evidence, sitting down."

"I think I'm all right, sir."

"Would you like some water?"

"I'd prefer a gin and tonic. Oh, sorry, I didn't mean to be flippant. Yes, I would like some water, please."

There was a pause, lasting for five minutes. Juliet took a few sips of the water which had been passed to her. Rendon's relatives, excluding his parents, leant forward on the court's uncomfortable wooden benches.

"Take your time, Miss Silverman," said the

Coroner. "Try to tell the court what happened to you when you and Rendon went to the house in Harley Street."

"He told me there was somewhere in the house he wanted to take me to, a place he and I would have to go to alone.

"He took me up several flights of stairs and showed me a door, leading to an upper landing, which I thought was an attic. He took me up the stairs, to a corridor with its floor covered with linoleum and unlocked the door leading to it. He started to act very strangely. I asked him where he was taking me. He said he wished to show me what he called the nursery wing."

Juliet broke down a second time.

"Go on, Miss Silverman," said the Coroner, gently.

"I'll try, sir, I'll try. It's too morbid and distressing." She took another sip of water.

"Please take your time, Miss Silverman. There is no hurry. All you have to do is tell the truth."

"William and I walked down the corridor. It was unusual for him to show tender, physical affection, except in the privacy of a bedroom. I was surprised when he put his arm round my waist and his head on my shoulder.

"We came to the room on the left, at the end of the corridor. He banged on the door with both hands, and suddenly put on a strange, childish voice. He kept shouting, 'See Nanny! See Nanny!'

"His eyes were rolling about in their sockets like a madman's. I thought perhaps he had been on the drug, again."

"You mean Dexedrine?" asked the Coroner.

"Yes. He'd been using a lot of the stuff every day, because of the pressure of his work. He used the drug to keep himself awake. Other times, he used it for pleasure, to quote his own words, 'to bomb his brains out, to get high enough to hit Mars.'

"He took the pills by the handful. He referred to the drug as 'Mr D.' He said it was his only friend."

"Let's return to the visit to the nursery wing, shall we, Miss Silverman?"

"When no-one answered while he banged on the door, he heaved his weight against it. He had adored his nanny. He had had no security from his parents as a child, although, as I mentioned, he was devoted to his father in adulthood.

"God, aren't psychiatrists ghastly?" remarked the Coroner, spontaneously. He regretted the frivolous nature of the remark and resumed his questioning of Juliet.

"Miss Silverman, you have supplied much evidence that, though harrowing, is not directly related to the death of this thirty-three-year-old man.

If you could keep your answers short and to the point, it would help me with my enquiries, and it would help you by saving you distress. You mustn't regard the simple words 'yes' and 'no' as profanities.

"Could you please bring us all into the nursery, itself," the Coroner continued. "So far, you have supplied enough words to write a book, and you still haven't brought us beyond the corridor," adding, if somewhat inappropriately, "Quite apart from that, the coolers in the mortuary downstairs have broken down, hence the somewhat unpleasant smell, permeating the building. I'm supposed to be seeing the engineers in ten minutes."

"William threw his weight against the door a second time," said Juliet. "It gave way and we went in. There were cobwebs and dust all over the place. The room was wonderfully light. There were two big windows overlooking Harley Street."

"Never mind the cobwebs, dust and light!" shouted the Coroner. "Get to the point, will you."

"William led me over to a green armchair in the corner of the room. He said that this was the chair his nanny had sat in, when she sewed and knitted. He asked me to sit in it."

"I wait with bated breath, Miss Silverman," said the Coroner.

"Then he told me to wait while he took some

things from a cupboard. He came over to me, carrying a grey wig, a ball of bright, red wool, two knitting needles and a white apron with the words 'I love William' embroidered on it in red. He kept telling me red was his favourite colour but he couldn't bear to see it anywhere but in the nursery."

"Why?" asked the Coroner.

"I could never get it out of him. It hurt him too much."

"Was his peculiar attitude towards the colour, red, anything to do with blood?"

"No. Blood is dark red. It was only bright red which effected him."

"Might it have had political associations? Was he, for instance, very Right Wing and averse to Leftist symbols, such as red flags?"

"No. Nothing like that. It was something to do with his childhood. He wouldn't tell me about it." She continued,

"He made me put the apron on. He put the wig on my head and took great pains to adjust it tidily. He put the wool and knitting needles into my hands and ordered me to knit. I don't know how to knit, and I told him so. He said I was to go through the motions of knitting.

"He put on the strange, childish voice again, and knelt on the floor by the armchair.

"He said, 'It's so lovely to be in the nursery

alone with you, again, Nanny. I knew all along you weren't dead. All that's happened is, you once had an old, ailing body. Your soul has fled that body and come into a healthy, strong body. You're going to live forever, Nanny. All I need is you and beloved Mr D.'"

The Coroner looked acutely depressed.

"Lord, save us!" he muttered, adding, "How did you react?"

"...I played his game, to make both our lives worth living. I loved him but I knew he was fucked down the middle."

"Miss Silverman, I would thank you to mind your language! Did Rendon ever do this again?"

"Yes."

"How many times?"

"Just one more time. On the afternoon of Remembrance Day, Sunday 14th November. That was the only other time."

"Did you find anything else about these visits to the nursery, that struck you as being odd? I feel, on hearing you speak, there is something you're holding back."

"There is something else, sir."

"What, precisely?"

"It was ... there was a horrible odour."

"An odour? Of what?"

"Rotten meat."

"What do you mean?"

"There was something up there which I couldn't see. Whatever it was, it had rotted."

"What had?" asked the Coroner, exasperated.

"I've no idea, sir. If I knew, I'd tell you. I didn't notice the odour on the first occasion. Only the last one."

"Did you mention this to him?"

"Yes."

"How did he react?"

"First, he said something about a rat. Then he acted very strangely, again. He suddenly shouted that if I didn't leave the house immediately, I'd be at risk of being killed, and that he might not be able to stop this happening."

"Killed by what? Killed by whom?" rasped the bemused Coroner.

"I don't know. I think he was far iller in mind than he would have had anyone believe."

"All right, I won't question you further about this aspect of the case. No doubt, the police will make the necessary investigations. I'll return to his drug-taking. Was he using Dexedrine every day, until the last day of his life?"

"Yes, I think he was."

"Who was giving it to him?"

"I don't know. Perhaps, he was getting it from the hospital. It's possible he got it from the streets. Maybe, from the Shakespeare pub in Bromley-by-Bow."

"Did you see him taking it?"

"Many times. He didn't even count the pills. He just took them in handfuls."

"Let me refer to the television incident at Vauxhall Bridge Road on Remembrance Sunday," continued the Coroner. "It would appear, would it not, that he was disturbed by the sight of red poppies and wreaths?"

"I can guarantee it was neither poppies nor wreaths which started him off," asserted Juliet.

"Why ever not?"

"Because his television was black and white."

"Remind me, would you," said the Coroner, now completely exhausted, "How old was Rendon when his nanny died?"

"He was eight."

"Did she, by any chance die on Remembrance Sunday?"

"Yes."

"Since he was eight, the year would have been 1967. Given that Rendon had been in the nursery with his nanny before she died, the nanny may well have wanted to watch the ceremony on television. It's very much the sort of thing a nanny would wish to see.

"When you went to the nursery, did you notice

25

a television in the room?"

"Yes, I did. He told me the nanny had died just before the two minute silence. That suggests they had been watching the television, together."

"Given that the year was 1967, the set would have been black and white. Colour televisions were not available in this country until 1968. I recall you said that Rendon's television at Vauxhall Bridge Road was also black and white."

"That is correct."

"So there were two incidents concerning black and white televisions, showing the Remembrance Day Ceremony, in Rendon's life. The second occasion could have reminded him of the first occasion, and tormented him.

"If this were the case, both Remembrance Day Ceremonies and, for some unexplained reason, the colour red, are linked, particularly, if after seeing the parade in his flat, Rendon went to a restaurant and started screaming when he saw someone in red."

Two of William's cousins on his late wife, Anne's side, gave further evidence, and were the only witnesses who knew the details of William's childhood, and the events in his life from the age of eight onwards.

They also knew what had happened to him at a time, when he ran away from home and wandered through the streets of London.

They were the only people who were fully aware of the events perpetrating William's agonizing and horrific association with things which were red. And it had nothing to do with blood or bloodshed or politics. Nor, indeed, did it have a direct connection with the Armistice Day parade. It was more sinister than that.

The Coroner had become paralysed with boredom, disgust and exhaustion by the time they gave their evidence. He found the case too bizarre to retain his interest. He had decided what he would say in his summing up before the two witnesses had spoken.

The Coroner was thirsty and drained a glass of water before beginning the summing up.

"While it is possible, in a man of William Rendon's history of apparent severe mental illness, that he deliberately took his life, one should not assume automatically that this was the cause of his death.

"It is common knowledge that the drug, Dexedrine, or Speed, as it is referred to, is known to be particularly hazardous from a cardiac point of view, when it is abused, to the quite singular extent, that William Rendon abused it. The immediate cause of his death appears to be cardiac failure.

"The turning on of the four gas rings, cannot be

overlooked, and is suggestive of suicide. But we have to take into account, the massive quantity of Dexedrine found in his blood. It had remained in his system, which would indicate that he had been in a mood of euphoria at the time of his collapse.

He could have turned the gas rings on for any number of reasons. One could have been that he was trying to bring extra heat into the flat, and that in his drugged state, it didn't occur to him to find a match to light the gas.

"Another explanation could be that he was so heavily drugged that he might have mistaken the knobs for buttons on a radio.

"There are an interminable number of possible explanations, of which suicide is only one. Now that I have taken all the evidence into account, I don't feel prepared to arrive at an unequivocal conclusion of suicide. I have decided to record an open verdict on this case."

The Coroner, and occupants of the public gallery, rose to their feet. He had already been irritated and frustrated by Juliet Silverman's waffling, long-winded, often irrelevant evidence, by her trying to evoke merriment, and her attempt to describe a film she had seen on 14th November, which had no connection with the case.

As he left the courtroom, and walked down the stairs, a whiff from the uncooled mortuary, hit him straight in the face. He uttered a string of fishwives' expletives.

William Rendon's parents, Rowland and Mary Rendon, met when Rowland was Senior Registrar in Psychiatry at the Maudsley Hospital, in Denmark Hill, London. Mary Cooper was a clinic clerk whose function was to "pull" or assemble the casenotes of mentally-disturbed patients who attended the twice-weekly clinic. Her position, though hard and strenuous, was of the lowest rank in a hospital, short of a cleaner.

If the patients' casenotes could not be found in the cupboard, where they were kept in alphabetical order, she had to walk a long distance to the Medical Records department, and seek out the notes which were in numerical order, each number having six digits.

It was necessary to start with the last two digits, and work her way through the shelves until she found the remaining four.

This pernickety task made her frustrated and dizzy, but, as she had no secretarial skills, the position of clinic clerk, short of that of shop assistant or factory worker, was the only job she could take.

Her parents were poor. They lived in a small,

damp flat in a Victorian house in Wandsworth, overlooking the bleak walls of the prison.

Her father was retired on a small pension. He had been a tailor. Her mother was too disabled with arthritis to work. Mary was the family breadwinner.

Neither of her parents smoked or drank. They had no fear of ill health, but they were deeply religious and considered the intake of tobacco and alcohol to be sinful vices. The father also insisted on saying grace before meals.

Mary was their only child, and they brought her up with the Victorian, puritanical belief that affairs with men, and recreational social pursuits, were evil.

Even when Mary took her first job as a clinic clerk at the Maudsley Hospital, her parents encouraged her to read books of divinity every evening, before having a frugal dinner of sausages, beans and bread and cheese, washed down with tap water.

Her diet lacked vitamins. She had been pale, skinny, nervy and anaemic for most of her life. Her face, which was a greenish shade of white, was framed by thick, curly blonde hair which accentuated her pointed chin. Her eyes were large, round and vulnerable. She was attractive in a bizarre sort of way, like a lost character in a pre-Raphaelite painting, about to expire from tuberculosis.

Both her home circumstances and duties in the hospital, caused her to walk about with her head lowered, in permanent gloom. Her state of mind was even more melancholy, when she had to look for notes in the Medical Records department.

Sometimes, she had to use a ladder to gain access to certain notes. Her anaemia made her feel washed out and giddy and caused her to have fainting attacks. The other clerks were unsympathetic towards her as the drudgery of their duties made them short-tempered. There were times when she asked them to hold the ladder steady for her, having explained that she suffered from fainting and giddy fits.

They refused to help her and regarded her as an oddity and an object of cruel practical jokes and jibes. She was nicknamed 'Swooner'. The derogatory term was used behind her back and eventually to her face.

She was sufficiently strong-willed to persevere at her job, which was better than staying at home with her singularly dull, obsessive parents.

Rowland Rendon came from different social circumstances than Mary. He was a tall, well-built, good-looking man with wavy blonde hair parted in the centre and blue eyes. His parents were wealthy and did not have to work. Rowland inherited a fortune from his father, and only became a doctor through pride, and a desire to earn rank through skill and industry, to keep himself occupied, and to add to his already handsome inheritance.

He was not an only child. He had a sister who was christened Kate Alice. She was five years his junior and he was devoted to her. She died of pneumonia at the age of fourteen.

Kate had golden hair, cascading over her shoulders in ringlets. She was the only person in the world who could make her brother laugh, and was also an accomplished singer and musician. Her talents enchanted Rowland who was devastated by her death. Indeed, he never fully recovered from it and his bitterness and anger, made him increasingly unapproachable over the years.

His parents were idle, and had no ambitions and no wish to occupy their time. This intensified their mourning. They resented the extremity of Rowland's grief and the manner in which he claimed to have a monopoly of it.

Rowland was nineteen when he came home for dinner and was told peremptorily by one of the many servants, that his parents had had to rush to hospital.

They returned to the house at 10.00 that

evening, hysterical. Rowland had no idea that his sister had been ill, as he had been staying with friends. It was his mother who shrieked the tragic news to him. She picked up a pile of plates in the pantry and threw them at the wall, one by one, screaming. Rowland had nightmares about the scene for the rest of his life, and as the memory became more vivid, his treatment of those he had contact with, grew crueller as he got older.

He was graced with almost superhuman intelligence. He trained to become a doctor and, because he only needed four hours' sleep a night, he worked at his studies far longer than his fellow students.

He passed his finals with distinction and became an SHO in Psychiatry, working at Guy's Hospital where he had trained. It was not long before he became a Senior Registrar, and practiced at the Maudsley Hospital.

He finally graduated to the rank of consultant within two years. He applied, successfully, for a post at the red-bricked Waterlow Unit, in a way a psychiatric hospital in itself, attached to the centuries-old Whittington Hospital in Highgate.

Mary was sitting, facing away from the door, in her tiny, windowless office, at the Maudsley Hospital.

She was checking that the notes she had collected, corresponded with the lengthy typed list she had been given.

She knocked one of the files off the desk and was bending over to pick it up. She felt someone's hand fondling her behind. She leapt to her feet, astonished. She felt too weak and tired with her anaemia, to be angry.

Rowland Rendon was standing in front of her. His breath smelt strongly of alcohol and he had a half bottle of whisky in the pocket of his white coat.

Mary had little self respect. She felt honoured by the fact that a good-looking man, of such high rank as Senior Registrar, should be showing any interest in her at all, regardless of the extreme vulgarity of his gesture.

"How are we doing, eh, doll?" he asked, laughing unpleasantly. He had an exaggerated upper class accent.

She was so simple that she mistook his laughter for a sign of friendliness. He was the first man to have made an overture to her and she was flattered. Also, the smell of alcohol on his breath, combined with the bottle of whisky she saw in his pocket, contrasted with the bigoted, puritanical atmosphere in her home, which she dreaded returning to every evening, and hearing her father say grace.

She craved surroundings of drunkenness and

dissipation. The stale smell of alcohol, particularly on a high-ranking doctor's breath, was an elixir to her. Rowland was taken aback by her flirtatious smile.

"Oh, doctor, you took me a bit by surprise!" she said, as she ran her fingers through her blonde curls.

He shut the door and turned the key in the lock.

"By surprise, eh, doll? You seem easy game, what! You didn't react the way other girls do. Most of them slap my face when I do that."

Mary was feeling faint and didn't answer. She continued to stare at Rowland, smiling.

He grabbed her by the arm, and forced his mouth onto hers, gripping her with his left hand and putting his right hand between her legs.

She lost consciousness. When she came round, she took a while to remember what had just happened. Rowland lifted her onto her desk, where she lay on her back. He took the bottle of whisky from his pocket, had a swig and wiped his mouth and chin with the back of his hand.

He held the bottle to her mouth. This time, his laughter was secretive rather than overtly unpleasant. He said,

"There's nothing like whisky if you've just passed out, doll. I knew you'd find it wonderful, all along."

"I get these fainting attacks," said Mary.

"Are you epileptic?"

"I don't know. I'm always tired and weak."

"That's probably due to what you eat. What *do* you eat?"

"I have bread and jam and tea for breakfast. I get some sandwiches from the canteen at lunch and I have sausages, bread and cheese for my evening meal."

"That's a damned stupid diet," said Rowland. "You don't eat any vegetables or proteins. Do you live alone?"

"No. With my parents. I hate it. They say that drinking and smoking are evil. They never talk at meals. They're puritans. My father says grace before we eat."

"Oh, how boring!" said Rowland, adding, "Are you free to have a drink with me after work? By the way, I drive a Bentley, if you're interested."

"Yes, I'm free. It would make a change. Anything to avoid going straight home."

Someone was knocking on the door and turning the handle. Rowland put the whisky back into his pocket and quietly unlocked the door. Mary got off the desk and stood up.

The door was opened by Dr Tobias Shaw, the consultant psychiatrist whom Rowland looked up to and permanently tried to please. They were on first name terms.

"Why was the door locked, Rowland?" asked Shaw, mischievously rather than accusingly.

"No reason, Tobias."

"So you say, old boy, so you say! To get to the point, a paranoid schizophrenic has just been sectioned. He's gone to the Villa*. Oliver Jenkins is the name. He's one of yours. He's been coming to see you quite regularly, hasn't he? He's always on your list."

"That's right, Tobias. I know he's been sectioned. He's not unduly violent, though. He's just a danger to himself."

"How long have you been seeing him?"

"Eighteen months."

"What have you been giving him?"

"100mg of Chlorpromazine three times a day."

"That's quite some dose," said the consultant.

"He's quite some paranoid schizophrenic," said Rowland.

Rowland escorted Mary to his polished brown Bentley. He failed to open the passenger's door for

---

*The Villa is the name given euphemistically to a place in the Maudsley Hospital, where dangerous or violent patients are incarcerated.

her and let himself in on the driver's side.

"I'll take you to one of the pubs," he said abruptly. "Then you can direct me to your parents' place. They won't mind if you're a bit late, will they?"

"Oh, no."

He took her to a local pub and walked with her to the bar, with an arrogant, swaggering gait.

"We'll have two double whiskies, barman."

"Your usual *Bell*'s, sir?"

"Yes."

The barman passed the glasses to them.

"Drink up, will you, girl," the doctor said with sudden urgency. "I haven't got all night."

Mary had already become accustomed to whisky that afternoon. She drained the glass in one go.

"Do you want another?" asked Rowland.

"Oh, I wouldn't say 'no', doctor."

"Cut this ludicrous, rubbishy 'doctor' out, will you. Just say 'Rowland'."

"All right. I'll have another, Rowland."

The second double made her intoxicated. Rowland had to hold her steady as they walked back to the car, which he had parked in a corner of the semi-deserted carpark. He opened one of the rear doors.

"Get in the back, doll," he commanded.

She stared blankly at him.

38

"You thought I didn't mean that, didn't you?"

She continued to stare at him, her huge, questioning eyes infuriating him. His thoughts turned briefly to his beloved sister, Kate. He resented the fact that Mary was alive when Kate was dead.

He turned his head to make sure there was no-one about. He slapped Mary and pushed her violently onto the back seat. He was irritated by her failure to resist, by her tear-filled eyes and her extraordinary stupidity.

He raped her while she lay, screaming. Even his initial entry was hard and rough, and gave her none of the pleasure that she had anticipated in her first sexual act, a thought brought on by her rebellion against her parents.

It was on that night that her son was conceived. Rowland, though not a man of principles, felt vaguely obliged to marry her, although marriage to anyone other than Kate, was obscene to him. It was he who chose the name of the child he hated from the start.

The infant, which he had hoped would be a girl who might inherit Kate's genes, was born at 8.00 on a chilly April morning. He was christened William Victor James.

Rowland hated the idea of having a screaming brat in the house, and hired a sweet-natured, reliable Norland nanny to look after the child. He threw himself vehemently into his work and achieved his ambition to become a consultant.

He moved into a luxurious, multi-storeyed house in Harley Street and practiced there when he was not doing National Health work. He moved his frail, half-witted wife, baby son and nanny, into the Harley Street house.

It was not long before he gave up his National Health work altogether, and worked entirely in Harley Street.

That was when he was able to. He had begun to drink so heavily that there were times when his mentally deranged patients came to see him, and his astounded receptionist found him lying on the floor of his consulting room, in a stupor.

Mary's frailty and mental retardedness worsened. She had hoped in vain that any home, other than that of her parents, would be tolerable. She was too short-sighted and slow-witted to foresee that a Harley Street household, run by a bludgeoning bully, who had raped her and made her pregnant, would make her even more wretched than a damp home overlooking Wandsworth Prison.

Rowland noticed her shaking hands dropping the crockery he had inherited from his mother. He was irritated by the way in which her white face had become heavily lined since the time when he had first met her. Her blonde hair had already gone grey and she had lost her quaint, unusual looks.

He imagined how his sister would have looked at Mary's age, with her milkmaid-fresh complexion, bright blue slanting eyes, and tumbling gold ringlets, combined with her quick wit and musical laugh.

"Why do you have to be dead, Kate, while this ghoulish-looking, clumsy, sickly half-wit remains alive and dull beyond belief at my expense?" he muttered half to himself and half out loud."

Mary was cowering, as if expecting to be beaten for dropping the priceless crockery.

"I'm sorry, Rowland, I didn't hear you," she whispered.

"The bloody crockery you dropped, can't be replaced, you stupid cow!" he shouted.

"I'm so sorry, Rowland, I didn't mean it," she said.

"Like hell you didn't! My beloved sister's dead. I resent the fact that you're here in her place."

Mary was afraid to answer. She knelt on the floor and folded her arms, her head lowered in fear and shame. Neither parent noticed the baby's presence in a cot on the table.

Rowland went over to his wife and dragged her to one side of the room, before gripping her by the hair and swinging her head against the wall. Clumps

41

of her hair came away in his hands. She sobbed silently.

"Look at you, you're half dead already," said Rowland. "Even your hair is in a dreadful condition. When I think of Kate's beautiful gold ringlets and compare them with your frizzled grey bird's nest, I want to be sick. It's true, no-one would have wanted to pull her hair, but if they had, not one strand would have come away in their hand."

William felt wretched, even at the age of one. He lay in his cot, screaming, straining his tiny lungs.

"Can't you shut that damned baby up, woman? Shove your tit in its mouth, for Christ's sake, or are you too sickly to be able to yield any milk?" shouted Rowland.

Mary staggered over to the table, took William from his cot and put his mouth to her breast, rocking backwards and forwards to calm him down. He fell asleep. She laid him in his cot.

"Where the hell's Nanny?" asked Rowland.

"She's had to go to a funeral in Oxfordshire. Her mother's died."

"How dare you allow her to take leave for a whole day!"

"She had to take the day off. First, to travel to Oxfordshire. Then to attend the funeral. After that, she'll have to make another journey back to London."

"As the mistress of this house, you should have exerted what little authority you're capable of showing, and told her to send a bloody wreath, and have done. Who does she think she is, swanning off like that for a whole day when she's in my employ?"

"Of course, I wouldn't normally dare contradict you, Rowland," said Mary, her voice quivering with fear. "It's just that Nanny absolutely adored her mother. Her death was sudden and Nanny was heartbroken when she heard the news. A wreath wouldn't have been enough. She *had* to attend the funeral."

"How did she hear the news?"

"Her father rang up this house."

"What makes you think one of my employees can receive 'phone calls here?"

"There was no other way the news could have reached her."

"There are such things as telegrams."

Rowland's cruelty and bullying had reached such a pitch that Mary felt a fainting attack come on. She pushed her chair away from the table, and put her head between her knees. The blood rushed to her head and she suddenly felt better.

"Is this your usual?" asked Rowland.

"Yes. I'm all right, now."

"A bit of play-acting, shall we say?"

She didn't answer.

"I'll be having a word with Nanny when she comes back from her jolly little jaunt to the country. I don't pay for my staff to go to funerals, whenever it takes their fancy.

"In future, all Nanny's instructions will come directly from me. I will also get a cook, acting as a servant as well, so that you'll have no reason to touch crockery and throw it about. You will stay away from the dining room except for meals. That also applies to the kitchen and the pantry."

"Yes, Rowland."

"As for the brat, you can have access to him if you want. You bore me a son when I wanted a daughter. Just make sure you keep him out of my way. I want him kept in the nursery. If you want to go all the way up there, do so. That's your business. Take him away from this room, now. I can't stand the sight or sound of him."

The nanny's train from Banbury to London had been cancelled. She didn't arrive at Harley Street until 10.00 in the evening. Rowland was in the hall, waiting for her. He had already consumed a whole bottle of whisky.

"Nanny!" he called aggressively.

The nanny was dressed from head to foot in black. She wore black lace gloves, a thin black veil, and carried the ivory-covered prayer book which her mother told her she was to have, if anything happened to her.

The nanny hadn't seen Rowland. Her nerves were already shattered. She jumped.

"Sir?"

"You'd better accompany me to the nursery."

They went upstairs. William was asleep in the room next to the nursery, known as the "night nursery."

"Sit down," said Rowland, as they went into the nursery.

The nanny sat in her customary green armchair in the corner of the room. Rowland remained standing.

"So you took the day off to attend a funeral," he said confrontationally.

The nanny could not forget the sight of her mother's coffin being removed from a hearse, its back window covered with the word MOTHER in different coloured flowers. The memory of the coffin being taken in and out of the church before and after the service, was less painful.

What hurt the nanny most of all, was the lowering of her mother into the grave. The incident was exacerbated by a heavy downpour of rain which soaked her clothes.

By the time she arrived at Harley Street, she realized she had a chest infection. She had a fever and alternated between hot and cold sweats. It hurt her chest even to breathe. She tried to control herself, but was unable to stop her heavy flow of tears, which gave her courage.

"Of course, I had to take the day off. My mother died without warning and I explained all this to Mrs Rendon.

"Anyone in the world has to attend their mother's funeral. It is only right, proper and decent. My mother's death was an earthshattering blow to me and I am shaken enough as it is, without having to be unjustly confronted for attending her funeral," said the plucky nanny, her voice raised in disgust.

Rowland found it hard to be at the receiving end of a ticking off.

"Well, it's just that you were away for the whole day," he said.

"Is that so surprising, sir? My mother was buried in Oxfordshire. How could I be expected to travel there and back, as well as attend the funeral, in less than a day?

"You're a hard, unkind man, sir. You have no compassion for the bereaved. You're downright wicked. Have you ever lost someone you'd loved?"

The psychiatrist had become contrite, within a matter of seconds because someone had dared to stand up to him. That person had also referred to the only thing close to his heart.

Rowland sat down on the less comfortable chair, facing her. She was flabbergasted by the sight of tears in the hard man's eyes.

"Yes, I did, Nanny," he began. "It was years ago. I was only nineteen but I won't forget it to this day. I had a sister. Her name was Kate. I wouldn't want to shock you, Nanny, as you are a lady of the utmost propriety, which is why I engaged you.

"The truth is, I was in love with my sister, so much so that I intended to marry her. She was so beautiful, so witty and so accomplished. I'm afraid she died of pneumonia. I hoped my child would be a girl who might inherit her genes. I never wanted a son."

Rowland wept uncontrollably.

"Oh, sir," said the nanny. "Let me make you a nice cup of tea."

"It's all right, thank you, Nanny. I've behaved unreasonably. I apologize."

As is often the case with babies, the sleeping William sensed what was happening in the nursery. When Rowland confronted the nanny, he had a nightmare and screamed in his sleep because, even at the age of one, he loved her and could not bear

47

to think of her being hurt. As soon as Rowland spoke to her, with what little kindness he possessed, the baby's nightmare came to an end. His dreams became peaceful and pleasant.

Rowland woke up with a hangover the following day, accompanied by the sobering thought about his confession to the nanny about his obsessive and passionate love for his sister. He felt worse than he would have, had he taken his clothes off in front of her. His kindness, under the influence of whisky, had turned to hostility because she knew his secret. He decided to keep out of her way.

Three years passed. William had become a chubby, fair-haired, angel-faced toddler. He feared his father who, when not ignoring him, persistently shouted at him and pushed him out of the way, whenever he crawled into the room, used by patients as a waiting room on weekdays.

Rowland and Mary slept in separate rooms. Rowland's room was large and luxurious and contained a television, video and high-fi equipment. There was also a drinks cabinet and an exercise bicycle with a cinema screen in front of it, which showed idyllic, undulating countryside.

Strangely, there were no pictures on the walls, and no photographs, except for a coloured blown-up picture of Kate, thumping the keys of a harpsichord, her cheeks flushed with excitement and enthusiasm, and her white-toothed smile radiating adolescent joy.

Mary's room was at the other end of a long, gaunt corridor and bore no resemblance to her husband's. It had been occupied by a scullery maid in the nineteenth century. It was tiny, with white-washed walls and a bed not much wider than a stretcher. It faced north, and was cold even in the summer. Rowland had so much contempt for her that he turned down her request for an electric fire in the room. He said the house was so big that it was difficult to maintain, and that electricity had to be rationed.

In the winter, Rowland kept three blow-heaters in his own room and turned them on all day and all night.

Mary did her best to keep out of her husband's way, although she had to suffer his company at meals. She spent nearly all her time in her cold room, and lay in bed, fully dressed.

William found out where she was and came to see her, knowing that, though very quiet, she was neither cruel nor frightening. There were times when he got into the narrow bed with her, but she was so frail, depressed and wretched that she seldom spoke to him, and lay on her back, shaking.

She had developed a violent facial twitch which manifested itself every few seconds. It made her face so disturbingly ugly that it terrified the child.

He didn't go to his mother's room any more, and found complete refuge and peace of mind in the nursery with the nanny. He sat on the floor, playing with his toys, while she sewed and knitted with a permanent expression of serenity on her face.

She was making him a pair of rompers on the sewing machine, and had chosen bright red material.

The child became animated and excited. He got up from the floor and ran over to the nanny. She stopped turning the handle of the old-fashioned machine.

"What is it, my boy?"

William jumped up and down, laughing and pointing at the material.

"Red, Nanny, red! It's red."

"I know it's red, my boy. Is red your favourite colour?"

"Yes! I love red, Nanny. I wish everything was red."

"All right, you shall have what you want. If I don't make your rompers myself, I shall go out and buy red ones, with the money your Daddy gives me. You'll be known as the reddest boy in Harley Street."

For the next few weeks, the nanny dressed William in red. Everything was red, from his rompers, to his overcoat, sweaters, shoes, socks and gloves.

Rowland paid an unexpected visit to the nursery one afternoon, while William was having his rest. The psychiatrist had been drinking heavily and his face was flushed.

"Nanny?".

"Sir?"

"Why is William always wearing red? The colour is really monotonous. I'm sick of seeing him in red. What's all this in aid of?"

"The boy has an absolute passion for red, sir. He's so happy wearing the colour. Since he started, he's had a permanent smile on his face."

"That may well be," said Rowland, "but I have had enough of it. I don't want to see him in red, again. What about royal blue or emerald green?"

"The little lad won't like it, sir."

"Do you think I care whether he likes it or not?" shouted Rowland, making the nanny jump. "He's not in the world in order to have what he wants. He's here to be disciplined, raised by the rod, what!"

"By that, do you mean he's to be a victim of cruelty? He's such a sweet little boy. I don't think I could bear it."

"It is for the father to decide how the child is raised. You're only a nanny. If you're not prepared to obey my orders, you will have to seek employment elsewhere."

"Very well, sir. I will do my best to get him interested in other colours, besides red."

"Kindly do so. If I see him in red one more time, your services will no longer be required in this household."

. William came into the nursery after his rest.

"Daddy's been here, hasn't he, Nanny?"

"Yes, my boy. That, he has."

"What did he want?"

"I'm afraid he says you're not to wear red, any more. He says, if you do, I'll have to go."

"Can't I ever wear red?" bleated the boy.

"Not in front of him, you can't. But he hardly ever comes up here. To keep you happy, I'll wear red, and you can look at me while I knit."

William was only partly satisfied, but came to terms with the fact that at least he could stare at the colour, even if he couldn't wear it.

Two years passed. William was never allowed to have meals with his brutal father and his twitching mother. Nor indeed did he wish to eat with them. Both parents, one harmful, and the other grotesque, but potentially harmless, terrified him and made him tremble in their presence.

It was a warmer than average April day. William had just turned five. His passion for anything red had not diminished, but he was still forbidden to wear the colour, which only increased his fascination for it.

The nanny gave him a rattle in the shape of a W. It was bright red all over and contained noisy plastic beads. They made so much noise when the child shook the rattle, that even the bleeding-hearted nanny regretted having given it to him.

His father was too drunk to remember his son's birthday, but his mother, who was fond of him, despite her disability, gave him a picture book containing paintings of animals. The boy had no interest, either in the book, or in its bizarre-looking donor.

He loved the rattle and was sitting on the nursery floor, shaking it and laughing.

Rowland came into the room. The nanny saw the best in everybody and assumed he had come to give William a birthday present.

"Nanny!" he shouted. His gait was unsteady and he smelt of drink, although it was only 10.00 in the morning.

The nanny put down her knitting and leapt to her feet. At least, she was not wearing red that day. She was wearing black as she was mourning the fourth anniversary of her mother's death.

"Yes, sir?" she said.

"Do you or do you not recall that I will not

tolerate anything red, being in William's possession?"

"You told me he wasn't to wear red, which he isn't. As you can see, his suit is pale pink. You never said he wasn't to play with a red toy."

The nanny had taken a diploma in Psychology before training to look after children. She knew her employer was not only an alcoholic, but was also suffering from a compulsive, obsessive disorder, known in medical jargon as C.O.D. She was aware that it was not uncommon for psychiatrists to be stricken by some form of insanity, and decided to refrain from being out-spoken with Rowland.

"I had no idea the toy would upset you, sir," she said. "After all, it is very small and certainly not tantamount to wearing red."

Rowland didn't listen to her. He was so drunk that he felt nauseated and the nausea increased his demented rage.

He snatched the rattle from the weeping boy's hand.

"No, please, Daddy, don't take my rattle away!"

"Don't you dare address me as 'Daddy'! You will call me 'Father'."

"But it's my birthday, today, Father."

"I curse the very date you were born! You were conceived with neither love, nor joy."

These words were too advanced for William to understand, but he knew of his father's hatred for him which was shown in his ranting voice.

"Please give it back, Father."

Rowland raised one leg onto a chair. He broke the rattle over his knee. So great was his son's pain that he was unable to cry.

Rowland turned to the nanny who was trembling almost as much as her charge's mother.

"Kindly remember, I don't want to see anything red, even in this nursery," said the deranged sadist. "Take this as your last warning."

"All right, sir. I can assure you it won't happen again."

She poured herself a glass of water. William sat on the floor, leaning against her legs. Neither nanny nor charge spoke.

The nanny wondered whether there was a morbid reason behind Rowland's attitude towards red. She concluded that he had found out what his son loved most, and because he despised him for not being a girl, he had embarked on a systematic campaign of revenge towards him, by depriving him of what was dearest to him.

The nanny obeyed Rowland for the next three years. William was eight and still had a compulsive passion for red, inheriting part of his father's obsessive disorder.

Rowland had not been to the nursery for some months. The nanny bought some balls of bright red wool and several spare pairs of knitting needles, so that she could knit William a sweater for him to wear in the nursery.

William was enthralled on watching the nanny, knitting, in the chair opposite him.

"What if Father comes in, Nanny?"

"He's stopped coming, my boy. He's not interested in red things any more. He's not been here for months. He's busy. He's got all his patients to see, and probably rests on Sundays.

William, too, believed his father had no further wish to come to the nursery.

It was Armistice Day in November, 1967. The time was 10.50 a.m. The nanny loved to watch the Whitehall parade and had encouraged William's interest in it as well. She sat, knitting with her eyes on the screen, not looking at her kneedles. The boy was watching the parade, leaning against her legs.

Rowland crept into the room, giving the nanny no time to hide her wool.

"Get up, Nanny," he commanded.

"Please be reasonable, sir. All we're doing is watching the Whitehall parade. We're coming up for the two minute silence. William's enjoying it. I think it's the music he likes, don't you, William?"

"Yes."

"This ceremony is utterly repugnant to me, Nanny. This country would be a happier place, if the Germans had won the war. Hand over the ball of wool, this instant!"

The nanny obeyed. She gave Rowland the wool, as well as the needles on which a large part of William's sweater had been knitted.

The psychiatrist took the wool and needles into the bathroom and put them into an incinerator.

"We're going to your bedroom," he called to the boy.

He ordered his son to lie face downwards on his bed and rolled down his pink trousers. He thrashed him with his bare hands twenty times, breaking the skin.

"Get up. Pull your trousers up and come with me."

"What are you going to do with me?"

"You'll soon find out."

He grabbed William's ear and dragged him into the nursery, where the nanny was standing, crying.

"This is something I want you to witness, William. Nanny, you are to pack your bags immediately and leave this house. You have disobeyed me too many times. You have mollycoddled this spoilt brat and indulged his compulsive whims."

The nanny knew she had nothing to lose.

E

"I think, and always have thought, that *your* behaviour is pretty compulsive, sir," she muttered, adding, "Ever since you told me about your unnatural adoration of your sister, I realized you have a compulsive, obsessive disorder, or C.O.D. as it is known as in your trade."

"How dare you *presume* to use the jargon of my trade, when you are no more than a nanny! You will leave, immediately, with nothing other than a bad reference, should a referee approach me."

The nanny looked at her sad, little charge who stood weeping, silently, his tears falling down his cheeks unchecked, wetting his chin, neck and pale pink suit.

She stood, looking at him with all the love she possessed. Suddenly, she felt a violent pain in the centre of her chest, accompanied by the knowledge that she was gravely unwell. She went deathly pale and her hands went to her throat, as if to put a stop to her illness.

Her legs gave way under her. She fell back dead. As a doctor, Rowland made no attempt to resuscitate her. As a psychiatrist, he showed no interest in his frightened, baffled son, and didn't even speak to him. He had become bored with the situation and left the child alone in the room with the dead woman.

He asked one of his distant relatives to represent

him at the nanny's funeral. He failed, even, to send a wreath.

William knew that his only friend was dead and her body both frightened and fascinated him, which caused him to have an interest in death, both pleasurable and painful, until the end of his life.

He lay down on the floor, by the nanny's side, and held on to the upper part of her body. He had no sense of time, and lay there for as long as he could.

At the end of the parade, *God Save the Queen* was played.

Rowland had returned to the room. He kicked the child in the ribs.

"Leap to your feet when the National Anthem is being played!" he shouted, and left the room as quickly as he had entered it.

William went to his bedroom and put on his grey flannel overcoat, woollen hat and gloves. He ran from the house and got onto the upper deck of a bus, bound for the West End of London, and, because the conductor remained downstairs, he evaded payment of the fare. He jumped out while the bus was still moving and ran into the street, under the delusion that the act of running would ensure his permanent escape from his father.

He reached an area with gay, flickering lights and had no idea where he was.

He was in Soho. The area fascinated him. He wandered round the streets for several hours. Occasionally, he wept about his nanny. He was attracted by an amusement arcade, in which tattered, shabby-looking men jumped excitedly as they played with gaming machines.

William removed his woollen hat because of the heat in the arcade. He did not know how attractive he looked, with his blonde, wavy hair, angel's face and big blue eyes.

He had been standing, staring at the flashing machines for ten minutes. He was startled by someone coming up behind him and tapping him on the shoulder. A man aged about thirty, with long, black hair, parted in the centre, in the standard uniform of hippies in the later sixties, was smiling at him. He had teeth like piano keys and stank like a badger.

The boy's instinctive reaction was of awareness that his nanny would have found him disgusting and would have refused to have him in the nursery. The man's friendly, and seemingly, kindly smile, encouraged him, however, as he thought he was potentially the only friend he had in the world. He had no friends at his school where the other boys shunned him because of his broody behaviour and aloofness.

"What's the problem, eh?" asked the man, as he

leant against a gaming machine, drinking beer from a can. His accent showed neither region nor class.

William was afraid of telling him the truth because he thought the man had a pleasant, caring mien, and would insist on taking him home.

"I ran away from the orphanage, sir. They're so cruel there."

"There's no need to call me 'sir'. It sounds silly and formal," said the man, still smiling. "Everyone knows me as Phil or Philip. You can choose which of those names you want to use. I was at an orphanage, too. Some people there were very cruel. I left when I was fifteen. I did odd jobs here and there. I was a ticket collector on the London underground. After that, I drove a lorry."

None of the information Philip provided, was true, so far. He never went to an orphanage. He came from an upper middle class family, and although his parents were proud of him for winning a scholarship to Eton, they cut him out of their respective Wills when he was expelled for molesting younger boys. He was more embarrassed by his upper class accent, than by his misdemeanours, and effected a neutral middle England brogue.

He was sent to a borstal. Once free, he worked for a high salary, as a well-known newspaper's Moscow correspondent, having taught himself fluent Russian, a language he found particularly easy.

61

The Russian government, then led by Leonid Ilyich Brezhnev, expelled him from Moscow, for reasons which were never disclosed.

He returned to London and was unemployed for a while, before his incarceration in Wormwood Scrubs Prison, for paedophile offences. His full name was known nationally. It was Philip Mark McKenzie, and the story of his crimes covered two pages of *The News of the World*.

His mother's younger sister had died of cancer at the age of twenty-five. She had a particular love for him and left him a modest sum in her Will.

He continued, this time telling the truth.

"My aunt left me some money, enough to live on, but I don't live like a lord. I've got a tiny room round the corner. I can still eat and pay the bills. Your accent's very refined. You sound like little Lord Fauntleroy."

"Who's he, Philip?"

"He's a character out of a book. Now, I've told you my name, aren't you going to tell me yours, or are you too shy?" Where do you come from?"

"My name's William Rendon. I come from London. I've always lived in London."

"That's rather a pretty name, and you're a pretty boy. Pretty boys often have pretty names."

"Do they? I'd never thought of that."

"You say you're from an orphanage. Your

mother and father — have they died?"

"Yes," said the boy, assertively.

"When did that happen?"

"Well, my mother died just after I was born." He paused, as strangers asking him questions about his parents, made him nervous. He added, "My father killed himself. I don't remember either of them. I was a baby when I went to the orphanage."

"Where is this orphanage?" asked Philip.

"I'll tell you as long as you promise not to take me back there. I've no money with me, either. Do you promise?"

Philip crossed his fingers and winked at him.

"...I promise. Scout's honour."

"All right, I'll tell you," said the boy, making up a false name, which the Whitehall parade had reminded him of. "It's called the Orphanage for Children of War Heroes."

"That's a long name. Did you watch the war memorial, today?"

William burst into tears.

"I watched some of it. Then I ran away."

"What? In the middle of it? You're not very patriotic, are you?"

"What does that mean?"

"A patriotic person is someone who loves his country. Do you love your country?"

"I don't know. I don't know anything about this

country. I don't love it and I don't hate it. Anyway, I've never been anywhere else, except London."

"Neither have I. Were all the other children watching the war memorial when you left?"

"Er, yes. That's right. All of them."

"Did no-one ask you where you were going?"

"I said to the bathroom."

"To the bathroom, eh? Are you a boy who likes taking baths?"

"I love baths. I've always had plastic ducks in them."

Philip suddenly looked shifty and conspiratorial.

"Do you like baths with other people?"

"I've never had them with other people. Why do you ask?"

"Just wondered."

"Philip?" said the boy, still liking and trusting the man."

"At your service, William."

"I haven't got any money at all. What am I to do?"

"That's easily solved. If you do certain things for me, you can earn."

"What things? Do you mean, doing your shopping, posting your letters, that sort of thing?"

"Nah! What I'll ask you to do won't be anything like as difficult as that?"

"What do you want me to do?"

"Do you like Chinese food?"

"I've never had it."

"It's nice. When did you last eat?"

"Not since breakfast."

"You must be hungry, then. I'll take you to a Chinese restaurant. I'll even introduce you to the naughtiness of alcohol. Have you ever had alcohol?"

"No. What is it like?"

"It makes you feel lovely and woozy, as if everything you touch will turn to gold."

"If it's as nice as that, I'd like to try it."

"I'm afraid they won't give it to you as you're too young. I'll find a way round that. I'll order a bottle of wine for myself and give you some when the waiters aren't looking."

The more Philip spoke, the more William liked and trusted him. He had never been exposed to illegality and the prospect of being naughty, excited him.

"I do like you most awfully, Philip," he said.

"I like you, as well. When we get back to my humble, little room, I'll teach you things you've never heard about before in your life."

"Do tell me. What things?"

"You'll find out before the night is out."

Philip took William to a cheap Chinese restaurant which he had never visited before. When questioned by an over-inquisitive waiter, puzzled by the sight of a clean, neat boy and a scruffy-looking man, Philip introduced William as his nephew.

Throughout dinner, Philip surreptitiously offered him glasses of wine which intoxicated him and caused him to fall asleep at the table. Philip paid the bill. William was able to walk normally. Only his vision was bleary. His mood was unnaturally elevated as the nausea and violent headache had not yet hit him.

He was excited by the two flights of filthy, narrow, foul-smelling stairs with no bannisters. He tried to decipher the obscene graffiti on the walls, but was unfamiliar with some of the four-letter words which not even his sadistic, depraved father, had uttered in his presence.

Philip produced a key and unlocked his door which was also splashed with graffiti. He led the boy into a cupboard-like room. The room, unlike it's occupant's appearance, was meticulously neat and tidy. A narrow bed with a black, metal head, and bedside table, occupied a corner of the room. The bed was draped with a dirty, but neatly-folded yellow cover.

There was a single gas ring in the other corner. It was well-polished with two upside-down, well-washed mugs precariously balanced on it. There was also a small, empty wardrobe and a well-washed sink with a single tap. There was no bathroom in the building, occupied mainly by impoverished prostitutes. The tenants were expected to wash in a plastic bucket, allocated to each room. There was only one lavatory, on the fourth floor. No-one used it because it was poorly maintained and unhygienic.

William sat on the bed, and bounced up and down. He was intrigued by its creaking mattress. Philip sat down beside him.

"You've been walking about all day and you've had a lot of wine," he said. "The best thing for you to do, is take off your nice, smart clothes and get into bed."

It was the sort of thing that his nanny would have said. He saw Philip as a potential replacement for the woman he had loved so devotedly. He got into bed, expecting his friend to read to him.

Philip picked up an ancient, yellow newspaper from the bedside table. It was *The News of the World* and it dated as far back as the bleak February Friday when a jury unanimously found Philip guilty of paedophilia.

"Do you know what this is, William?"

"It's a newspaper. We've never had that one in the place I ran away from."

"I shouldn't think you have."

"Is it naughty, then?"

67

"I think you could say that, but you seem to like being naughty, don't you?"

"In what way?"

"You wander into amusement arcades, and you not only allow a total stranger to talk to you and take you out to dinner. You actually allow him to take you to his room, without knowing anything about him. He could be a murderer, for all you know."

"But you're not. You're so kind to me."

"You've been lucky. I could be wicked. Don't go off with strange men, again. Promise me that?"

William was on the verge of sleep.

"Yes, I promise," he said.

The boy was confused and bewildered by the events of his night in Philip's room. The man subjected him to lewd, physical advances which struck him as being vaguely pleasurable at first, as well as making him feel instinctively that his new friend was doing something wrong, without his being able to understand why.

Something told him that his nanny would not have approved of what was happening. He was now reasonably sober. He knew that she would not have wanted him to speak to strangers, go out to dinner with them, or accompany them to their rooms.

He remembered her telling him never to do what he had done. Even the stranger himself had reprimanded him. He wondered whether Philip held the same attitude and affection for him, as she had. He thought he probably did but he could not understand the sexual side of Philip's expression of attachment.

He felt increasingly upset and uncomfortable.

"Please, please, don't touch me, sir," he said.

"Come, now, you know my name's Philip. What's all this 'sir' business? We're friends. I like you."

"I know, but I hate it when you touch me. I can't bear it. Please don't. I know Nanny wouldn't have liked it."

"Nanny? You told me you had been in an orphanage all your life. I don't understand."

William rolled over and faced the wall. His hot tears rolled onto the bedclothes.

"What is it, William?"

"I'll tell you the truth if you promise not to hand me over."

"Hand you over to whom?"

"I lied when I told you about the orphanage. My father and mother are alive. My father is a doctor. He lives in Harley Street. He terrifies me because he's always so cruel to me."

"In what way, cruel? You must tell me. I'm your friend. I won't touch you again, Scout's honour. In fact, I'll keep my hands clasped behind my back. Perhaps, I shouldn't have done what I did, but please tell me the truth about who you really are. I won't tell anyone."

"I love red. I love it more than I can say in words."

"Red? What are you talking about? What has this to do with your father?"

"Red means so much to me!"

"All right. I've got a red shirt. Would you like me to wear it, tomorrow?"

"No! It's all been spoilt."

"*What* has?"

"Red. I can't bear to look at it any more. I don't mind seeing red things in the nursery, as long as I don't see them anywhere else."

"Is it something to do with blood? That's it, isn't it, William?"

"No, you don't understand. Nanny died in the middle of the parade. Just before the two minute silence. She loved me so much, she always dressed me in red, to make me happy. My cruel father can't bear it if I'm happy. He told Nanny I was never to wear red again, just because he knows what it means to me.

"Nanny did as she was told. We had this pact. We agreed that I could only wear red and look at red things in the nursery. Nanny gave me a red rattle, shaped like a W for William. My father came to the nursery and smashed it."

"Poor little William!" said Philip. "What else happened?"

"He didn't come up again for a very long time. Nanny bought some balls of bright red wool. She started to knit me a red sweater.

"She was sitting, knitting, watching the parade, a few hours before I met you. My father came into the nursery, again. He was very angry because of what he saw, and he sacked Nanny. She was so shocked, she suddenly died. He beat me so hard before she died."

"What, in front of Nanny?"

"No. He dragged me to my room and beat me. Then he dragged me back to the nursery so that I could watch him sack her.

"He left her, dead. It was so horrible. I ran out of the house and got onto a bus."

"The bus? Was that red, as well?" asked Philip.

"Yes. It made me feel funny and unhappy but it gave me courage. Actually, buses are a darker red than the red that I love. Bright red's the red I really like."

"Poor, poor boy! I'm so very very sorry. I'm afraid there is one thing you must understand. If your parents are alive, and you've run away from them, which you have, I'm breaking the law, letting you stay with me. If I went on, I'd go to prison. I know I promised I wouldn't tell anyone, but this is so serious, now that you've told me the truth, and all this business about red, I've got to take you back to your parents."

"No! No! No!"

"I must, William. It's my responsibility."

"If you take me back, I'll tell everyone you touched me."

"You can if you want. No-one would believe you."

"I've got a feeling you've already been to prison."

"Why do you say that?" asked Philip.

"I just think so. You've been in trouble, before."

"Perhaps that's why I must take you back."

"What if I refuse to say where I live?"

"I'll take you to the nearest police station."

"I'll tell them you touched me," shouted the boy at the top of his voice.

"It's your word against mine. You're a child, and mentally disturbed at that. I'm an adult. Who would they believe?"

A prostitute, using the room next door, had a client with her. The shouted argument between Philip and William, was interfering with her client's ability to perform. He was a stout, gold-toothed Greek. He asked her for his money back. She banged on the wall.

"Bloody hell, you two! Can't you shut up? I'm trying to earn my living, for Christ's sake!"

Philip gently covered William's mouth.

"We'll talk in whispers. You're upsetting other people in the building, shouting like this. Just tell me quietly. Where in Harley Street does your father live? If you don't tell me, I'll look the name Rendon up in the medical directory. In fact, I'll go to a library and do that, anyway, because I know you'll lie to me, in the way you lied about your past."

"All right. It's number 79," said William.

"I'll take you there, as soon as the sun comes up. There's one thing I know. Do you know what that is, William?"

"What?"

"You'd never spill me because I touched you. You're too dependent on me to want to lose me. If I'm not locked up, I'll be here whenever you want to come and see me. I'll be your friend and I shan't ever touch you, again. I give you my word on that."

William closed his eyes. "I'm very tired. I want to go to sleep, now."

"That shows how much you trust me. I'll always be there for you," said the paedophile.

Philip woke William up at dawn and gave him

a mug of hot, sweet tea and biscuits. The boy had a severe hangover.

"Come on. You'll be stronger after breakfast," said Philip. "It's time to get up. I don't want to hand you over, but I must."

William was incapable of getting out of bed. The biscuits were stale and he felt sick.

"I'll tell you what. I'll go out and get you a present. That will get you up," said Philip.

William went to sleep, once more and Philip went out.

"Your present isn't wrapped but it's in my pocket, William. It's for you to pull it out."

The boy put his hand in one pocket which was empty. He tried the other. The pervert had bought him a large, bright red handkerchief.

The boy's whole body went taut. "Take it away, it's red!" he bellowed. The prostitute next door, was woken by his shouting, and banged on the wall, once more.

"I know it's red. That's why I got it for you. You told me you loved it."

"Bright red hurts me, now," said William, ungratefully, "unless I'm in the nursery."

"It won't for long. You'll get used to it. It's for you to hide in your pocket, where your father can't see it."

At 9.00 in the morning, Philip took William on

a crowded bus, bound for Oxford Circus. He walked the weeping boy up Harley Street and rang the bell of number 79.

The receptionist was ill with bronchitis. It was Rendon himself who opened the door, thinking the caller would be his first patient.

Rowland was hoping William had come to harm. He was pleased when he disappeared and never wanted to see him again. He was astonished by the sight of the sobbing, pink-clad boy and the unshaven hippy with him.

"I say, what's all this, then, eh?"

"I've brought your son, home, sir."

"So I see. Where was he, if I might ask?"

"I found him wandering about, crying, at 8.00 o'clock this morning. I asked him where he lived. He gave me this address. You are Dr Rendon, I take it?"

"I am."

"There's something else I have to say, and you're not going to like it."

"Well, get on with it."

"You've been nasty and cruel to him all his life. He could barely sit down on the bus because of the savage beating you gave him, when he hadn't done anything wrong, except for liking things that are red."

"What the hell are you talking about, man?"

rasped the psychiatrist. "What do you know about this problem with red?"

"I'm talking about an organization called the N.S.P.C.C. William knows where I live. If you hurt him again, he's coming to tell me about it. I'll take him to their offices where he'll be examined by a *proper* doctor."

"Kindly mind your own business, you snivelling, unwashed ruffian!"

"You haven't seen the last of me, doctor."

Rowland ignored Philip who walked away with a heavy heart and tears in his eyes. He waited until his adversary was out of sight, and dragged his terrified son into the building. He shook him violently and slapped his face.

"What did you think you were doing, yesterday, when you ran off like that?"

"I couldn't bear what had happened," said the boy. "You beat me. You sacked Nanny who I loved so much."

"Whom I loved so much," corrected Rowland. "You may go on."

"Then it was the way she died. First, she was alive, when we were watching the television. Then, she was dead. I was alone in the room with her."

"Didn't you always like being alone with her? Might that not be the reason I left you there?"

"Not after she'd died, no."

76

"I've got some very good news for you. Do you want to hear it?"

"Yes, Father."

"You're going to spend quite some time in the nursery, now, because I'm going to lock you in. It's the door at the end of the corridor I'm going to lock, so you'll have the whole wing to yourself.

"You will be let out when you go to school, which you will start, again, as from tomorrow. You will be fed, and when your meals arrive, a bell will ring. The landing door will be unlocked and a tray left for you.

"Twenty minutes later, another bell will ring, so that you can hand over your tray. I'm ashamed of you and I don't want you downstairs. There won't be any nanny up there to keep you company. Her body has been removed, and the part of the floor to which she fell, hoovered."

Rowland took his son upstairs. He opened the door, leading to the nursery wing, and pushed him violently, like a hardened criminal. William fell over and Rowland kicked him, refraining from causing him any injury which was not psychological.

"By the way, you'll be responsible for your personal cleanliness, and keeping your clothes in order. You will also dust and hoover the premises once a day," said Rowland.

William went into the nursery. He found it alive with the nanny's presence. He was convinced she was there, even if he couldn't see her. He turned on the television, as she had done the day before. He took the two spare balls of red wool from the cupboard, and gripped them, fearing they would suddenly be snatched from him.

None of the television channels interested him. He sat on the floor with his head resting on the nanny's chair, still holding the balls of wool.

The weather had been fine earlier, but the bleak November sun had vanished behind a cloud. The nanny's spirit seemed to have disappeared, as well. William wept and allowed himself to howl like a wounded wolf. At least, he was consoled by the knowledge that his expression of misery would not be heard.

Neither of Rowland's first two patients had turned up. The 9.00 o'clock patient had failed to explain her absence, and the 10.00 o'clock patient had cancelled at the last minute.

Mary Rendon was sitting in the drawing room at the back of the house. Rowland came in. She had been reading a Mills and Boon book.

"I want to talk to you," he said.

She said nothing. She was frightened.

"Are you familiar with the events of the last two days?" asked Rowland.

"I'm aware William went out of the house. I know the nanny died, just before the two minute silence." As she spoke, one of her eyes opened and shut convulsively, in a rapid, winking motion. Her lips twitched, effecting her whole face. As time had passed, her appearance had deteriorated severely and she looked like a half-dead old woman, crammed with psychotropic drugs.

"That's more or less right," said Rowland, sounding subdued and bored, rather than aggressive. "Do you know about the trouble in relation to the colour, red?" He spoke with exaggerated slowness and clarity, as if talking to a foreigner.

"I've heard you shouting, or raising your voice slightly, I should say, about William's preoccupation with red. I was also told that you sacked the nanny because you caught her knitting him a red sweater in the nursery. I don't really understand what's happened. I think William's terribly unhappy at the moment because of the nanny's death. It's true I could never be a mother to him, so I agreed with your decision to hire a nanny.

"I don't like to say such things, Rowland, but I think you've been a little unkind to William, in not allowing him to wear red. He stopped. You went to the nursery and found red things there. You smashed a rattle and you threw away a ball of wool and knitting needles. Why do you treat the poor boy so sadistically?"

Rowland lost his temper. "I'll tell you why," he snarled. "My sister, Kate, always wore beautiful, red silk dresses whenever she played the harpsichord. If I'd had a daughter, I'd have encouraged her to wear red, but I won't tolerate it in that ghastly boy."

"He may not have worn red to annoy you," said Mary. "But because your sister loved the colour, she may have passed her love for it to William in her genes."

"God, I hate that boy!" shouted Rowland. "I wanted a daughter so that there was a chance of finding Kate's genes in her. I can't bear to think of that little brat inheriting a gene from her."

Mary felt about to receive a blow. She thought carefully what she would say, and said it quietly.

"I've blamed myself all along," she said in unwholesome martyrdom. "I should have been Kate. I'm not good enough for you."

"No, you're bloody well not! I can't even bear looking at you when you make all those horrible, frightened movements. It's your premature age and your obscene twitch which repulse me.

"I wish you'd gone into a mental hospital as opposed to living here, having born me a son, instead of a daughter."

"Does it make any difference?"

"A lot of difference. Why does that brat have to emulate a girl by his love of red clothes?"

"Because the gene was passed from aunt to nephew. It's true William's a boy, but he may still have inherited this passion from Kate."

"Balderdash, woman!" shouted Rowland. "Vain streaks are to be found in a girl, not in a boy."

A temporary receptionist, who had arrived late, came and knocked on Rowland's door.

"Your 12 o'clock patient has arrived. Her name's Lady Geraldine Appleton."

"Thank you." Rowland found the patient outside the waiting room, and treated her with a staggering degree of courtesy, never seen in his treatment of his family.

"I apologize for the wait. Do come in, and my receptionist will bring you coffee. Pretty cold day, isn't it?"

"The first day I've put on my winter coat."

Rowland gave her a charming smile.

"So then, we'd been talking about your relationships with two men, and how their different personalities disturbed you, and made it hard for you to decide which one suited you most."

"Yes."

"Are you perhaps finding it difficult to choose which one you want to live with?"

"Yes. I think you could say that. I'm exhausted

and confused."

"May I make a humble suggestion, Lady Appleton?"

"All right, doctor."

"It's a cold time of the year and last time we met, you told me you had had a bad cold which you couldn't shake off. Why don't you take a holiday in the Caribbean, away from your two suitors. In fact, with your lovely looks, I'm surprised you haven't got more than two. When you come home, your head will be clear and you'll be more able to make your choice. Incidentally, do these men know about each other?"

"No."

"Sensible girl. That's the way to keep it, eh?"

"I feel better for having seen you, again, doctor," said the woman who was tall and thin, with black hair, tumbling onto a see-through, emerald green blouse.

"Good. That's extremely charming of you. Do you know what would make me feel better?"

"No."

"I'll feel better, in this cold weather, when I receive a postcard from you when you're resting in the Caribbean."

"Of course, I'll send you one, if I decide to go there. You're such a nice man, Dr Rendon."

Rowland raised his hands and gave her an

expansive smile.

"Oh, rubbish, Lady Appleton!" he said. "There's no point in being on this earth, if we can't show a bit of kindness, is there?"

Lady Appleton rose from her chair and allowed Rowland to help her on with her mink coat.

"I know you're a psychiatrist and I'm a patient, but do you mind if I ask you a question? I know so little about you as a person."

"Why, yes, of course, Lady Appleton. I know it's the wrong way round, but I'll try to answer. I can't guarantee it, though," said Rowland.

"Are you married? Have you got a family?"

"That's not a very difficult question. The answer is 'yes, I am married.' His pleasant smile was becoming strained. He added, "We've got a son. He's eight years old."

"I didn't know that. What's his name?"

"I can give you his whole name if you want to hear it. It's William James Victor."

"You speak his name as if you were really proud of him."

"I am, Lady Appleton. He's a sweet, enchanting boy. He's so beautiful — handsome just like his father! One could say that I were brimming with pride. I'm afraid my next patient's arrived. I heard the front door being opened. Do, please, look after yourself. Take plenty of vitamins, cut your smoking down, and for God's sake, go somewhere where there's some sun."

"I will, doctor."

They shook hands. She was impressed by his lingering handshake.

"I'm sure you will, Lady Appleton. You're one of my more obedient patients and you've taken my advice before. The best of luck to you."

Rowland had become bored beyond oblivion with his patient and was struggling to remain civil.

"Oh, doctor?"

"Yes, Lady Appleton?"

"Will you give me a repeat prescription for Nembutal? I'm so worked up about these two men, I'm not sleeping."

Rowland walked over to his desk and hurriedly wrote her a prescription with a gold, Parker pen. He turned it over and slapped it on the blotter.

"There you are, Lady Appleton."

"Thank you. You are too kind."

"There's nothing amiss with kindness, as I said, but I'm afraid I've got to suggest, with the greatest reluctance, of course, that you must begin to be on your way. Besides, it's lunch time and the restaurants will start getting full. I want you to eat a decent, nutritious meal, to build yourself up and lower your resistance to germs."

"I'll do that. Goodbye, doctor."

"Goodbye, Lady Appleton. Be sure to look after yourself. Don't forget to send me a card."

There was no "next patient". Rowland went to the cupboard-like reception area and found the girl from the employment agency. She was about twenty, and was wearing a pale blue mini-skirt and a tight-fitting, fluffy white sweater, which was the same colour as her thigh-high, patent boots. She had on golden, brown tights which made her legs look artificially sun-tanned. Her long peroxide hair was swept back from her face in a plait, giving her a distinct, Germanic look which attracted the psychiatrist.

"We haven't met properly, yet," began Rowland, deliberately keeping his distance from her, so as not to be thought too forward. "I expect you know by now, my name's Dr Rowland Rendon. I'm a consultant psychiatrist and I occupy the entire building."

She got up and moved towards him.

"How do you do, doctor? I'm Doris Parsons. Everyone calls me 'Dolly'. I'm from the Atlas Staff Bureau."

"I think Dolly suits you better than Doris. I've always thought Doris suited a much older person than you."

"Thank you," said the girl. "Would you mind telling me what my duties are. No-one's explained them to me."

"That's because there's no-one here," said Rowland. "I'm afraid the duties are quite heavy, and I might as well be absolutely fair to you, and warn you, before you decide they're too much for you. The hours are nine to five, and you will be given a two hour lunch-break, like in France.

"You will have to man the switchboard and type my letters to general practitioners. These letters will be reassuringly short and to the point.

"Just before you go to lunch, you will have to carry the food into the dining room for my wife and myself. This will be until the new maid arrives.

"There will be an additional task for you before your lunch-break, which will be the most taxing of all your tasks."

"Oh? In what way?"

"Well, there's no lift here. You will have to carry a tray of food all the way up to the nursery wing at the top of the house. We keep the door of the nursery corridor locked at all times and you will have your own key."

"That's strange, doctor. I hope you don't mind my saying so." She had a hardly recognizable trace of an Australian accent. "Why must the door be kept locked?"

Rowland offered her a cigarette which she refused. He lit one himself.

"It's because of our boy," Rowland said, hesitantly. "He's got tuberculosis, and, although it's very lonely for him, he has to be kept in isolation. A governess, who has had the disease, comes to the premises, to educate him. She has her own key. Have you had tuberculosis?"

"No, I haven't, but I was vaccinated against it about two months ago."

"That's a relief. It's an exceptionally infectious disease. My wife hasn't had it and she's very frail and sickly."

"I still don't understand why the door has to be locked."

"To prevent my son wandering all over the house. Our cook is also elderly and frail and her immune system is poor. Naturally, the boy wants company. We told him not to leave the nursery wing but he was disobedient and always did so. He wanted his mother and used to run all over the house, looking for her. We could have put him in a clinic, but that would be too cruel, as he hates hospitals."

"How old is he?" asked Dolly.

"He's eight," said Rowland abruptly.

"Who takes him his evening meal?"

87

"Our cook does that. She leaves the tray outside the door and rings a bell. She unlocks the door. My son waits for about a minute and collects the tray. He eats the food and, within twenty minutes, the cook collects the tray from the far end of the nursery wing and locks the door behind her."

Dolly was finding Rowland's monotonous, complicated explanation, tedious.

"What's his name?" she asked.

"William."

"What does he look like?"

"Wavy, blonde hair. Angelic face. Blue eyes. Looks just like his father.

"After his lunch, the tray will remain in the nursery for as long as two hours. When you come back, you unlock the door, and because you have been vaccinated, there's nothing to stop you going to the nursery and meeting William.

"Be warned of one thing. He tells the most fantastic tall stories. That's not unnatural in any boy who has had solitary confinement forced on him, and it would be wrong to blame him. It's not his fault, of course, but he does tell very misleading lies."

"Lies? What sort of lies?" asked Dolly.

"Well, his favourite lie is telling anyone who goes near him, that I am a terrible bully, that I am cruel to him and that I beat him with a leather belt.

Really, Dolly, I ask you!"

"I can't imagine you bullying anyone, Dr Rendon. I can tell you're a gentleman. I can understand how frustrating it is for your son to be isolated, but his continuous lying seems to me to be absolutely intolerable. Don't worry, I won't be taken in by any of it. I'm not a gullible person. I'm a tough egg."

"Come to me, Dolly," said Rowland suddenly.

She was attracted to his wavy, blonde hair, polite manner and educated voice. Most of her previous male friends had been rough, leather-jacketed hooligans, who had smelt of drink and had encouraged spectators to riot at football matches, spurred by a destructive love of violence for its own sake.

She considered Rowland to be sophisticated and gentle in comparison, and allowed him to kiss her.

"It's lunch time, now, Dolly. Everything's ready and Mrs Rendon is sitting in the dining room. The kitchen is down the corridor on the right. All you have to do is collect the food from the cook and bring it into the dining room. I'll introduce you to the cook."

Rowland surprised the neurotic old lady, when going into the kitchen. She had a heavily-lined, bitter face and her appearance was slatternly.

"Mrs Dudley, this young lady is my new

89

secretary and helper. If she gets on with us, and we get on with her, we shall try to persuade her to work here permanently. Her agency sent her here as a temporary. Her name's Dolly Parsons and she seems to be settling down, although she hasn't been with us for long. Dolly, this is Mrs Dudley."

The two women shook hands. Dolly's handshake was firm, to the point of being painful. Mrs Dudley's was weak and clammy. She did not look Dolly in the eye and deliberately failed to say "how do you do?"

Dolly took an instant dislike to Mrs Dudley. Rowland took the young woman into the corridor.

"You mustn't be put off by Mrs Dudley's manner," he said in a pleasant tone. "She is most awfully rude and unfriendly, but she has been with my wife and me for a considerable time. She's a good cook, and that's all that matters. She's never in contact with anyone, except me, when I give her her cheque every month.

"I'm going in, now. You go back and carry the dishes through the other door, there's a good girl."

Dolly was surprised by the abundance of food to be carried from the kitchen into the dining room. There were several first courses, all rich and chosen by Rowland. These were followed by grouse, swede purée, different vegetables and chips, as well as boiled potatoes. There was an elaborate salad and an abnormal number of cheeses. The last course was a combination of chocolate mousse, cream-filled cake and *grand marnier* soufflé, which had flattened and become an omelette. This sickly fare was accompanied by dried figs, dates, nuts and a bowl of fruit.

Dolly was struck by the fact that Rowland made no attempt to introduce her to his sedentary wife. She was also appalled by her shabby clothes and hideous, rhythmical, facial twitch. This had become so pronounced that she bared almost all her teeth, which were a horrible shade of dark brown.

"Thank you, Dolly," said Rowland. "Don't forget to take the tray upstairs, will you?"

"No, Dr Rendon."

Dolly noticed there was only one plate on the child's tray. It had a tin cover. There was a piece of hard, unbuttered bread and a glass of water. She lifted the plate's cover out of curiosity and found a single piece of Spam, a ring of beetroot and a tiny, boiled potato, enough to keep the boy alive, and no more.

She wondered whether this was a diet prescribed for children with tuberculosis, and concluded that it must be, as she could not imagine the seemingly, kindly Rowland deliberately starving his son.

As she walked down the narrow corridor leading to the nursery, she was surprised to hear a rustling noise. She thought at first it was the sound of rats. She came closer to the room and heard a child running.

The door was slightly ajar. She opened it by leaning against it. The child was opening a cupboard in the corner of the room, and throwing two balls of red wool into it with a desperate sense of urgency. He looked smaller than his eight years. He had on a pair of pale blue trousers and a matching sweater. His thick, curly blonde hair was dishevelled. His smile, which had once lit up his face, was transformed into a look of intense gloom. The only prominent feature of his face, was a pair of huge, pleading blue eyes, one of which had been blackened by a blow.

"Hullo, I'm Dolly. Your father said your name was William. He's a nice man. Where would you like me to put your tray?"

William walked over to the green chair in the corner of the room, where he used to sit, leaning against the nanny's legs.

"On the table to the right of this chair, please," he said with unparalleled solemnity.

Dolly did as she was asked. William ate the Spam, beetroot and potato so fast that she was hardly able to see him bringing his fork to his mouth.

"You were hungry, weren't you, William?"

"I am always hungry."

"I hear you've got tuberculosis."

"What's that?"

"It's an illness. The person suffering from it coughs all the time and brings up blood."

"I haven't got a cough."

"I don't understand. Of course, you've got a cough, and a fever and you feel ill. You certainly don't look well."

"I haven't got a cough or fever. I feel well, but I'm hungry all the time. They're not giving me enough to eat."

"Why are you locked in like this?"

"Father said I was to be locked in."

"Why?"

"He hates me so much. I've never understood why. I've never done wrong. I've tried so hard to please him."

Dolly looked even more baffled than when she had entered the nursery.

"When I came in with your lunch, I saw you throwing two balls of wool into the cupboard. Do you hide things in the wool?"

"Hide what? Oh, you mean food. No, I don't."

"What do you hide in that wool? You certainly didn't want me to see what you were doing."

The sympathetic tone of her voice caused him to cry. He put his arms round her waist.

"What's the matter, you poor boy?"

"I was hiding the wool because, when I heard you coming, I thought you were Father."

"Come on, William, what do you keep in those balls of wool? If you don't tell me, I'll have to unravel them. I suspect you keep naughty tablets in there. If you don't tell me the truth, I'll have no choice but to unravel them."

"What does 'unravel' mean?"

"It means undoing them to find out what's in the middle of them."

"You can do that if you want, as long as you don't take the wool away."

Dolly was exasperated, as well as having her maternal instinct aroused by the miserable, pathetic boy.

"You've got a black eye," she said, suddenly. "What happened?"

"Father hit me because I ran away."

"I won't hear a word against your father. He's a nice, decent, kind man. He said you told fibs about him bullying you, when he hasn't done so. He said you told others that he beat you with a leather belt. I don't believe he's ever hurt you. Show me the wounds."

William rolled down his trousers and briefs. There were deep, freshly delivered welts on his behind. Some of the blood had got onto his clothing.

"Who on earth did this to you?" asked Dolly. "I suspect it was that cook. She looks nasty enough. Was it her?"

"No."

"Was it your mother, then? I refuse to believe it was your father."

"It *was* Father."

"I don't believe you."

"It wasn't the cook. It wasn't Mother. It was Father."

Dolly was in a state of extreme confusion. Her role was made more difficult because of her instinctive liking for Rowland. She decided that, if she found out for certain that he was the culprit, she would continue to show affection for him, as well as providing love and companionship for his son, with a view to betraying her employer.

"I want you to tell me about this wool," she said. "There's a connection between the wool and your father. If you don't tell me, I can't become your friend and I can't help you. You do want me to help you, don't you?"

"Yes. I think I can see you as my friend. I made another friend when I ran away. He's such a nice man. He took me to his room and we went to bed together."

"*What?*"

"Well, he touched me, but when I told him not to, he stopped."

"Have you told anyone this?"

"No, but I love him. If I can escape from here, I'll go to him because I want to live with him."

"You'll never be able to do that," said Dolly.

"Why?"

"I can't say why. There are some things I can't explain to you."

"He takes *The News of the World*," said the boy, conspiratorially.

"I'm not interested in what newspapers he reads. Besides, only dreadfully simple people take *The News of the World*. What's his name?"

"Philip."

"Philip who?"

"I don't know his surname, but he's so kind."

"All right, all right, never mind that for the moment. You're to tell me about the wool."

William paused for at least a minute. His body seemed to shrivel as his soul withdrew into its shell.

"The wool is red," he whispered. "And it's only in this room that I can bear to see it."

"Yes, I know the wool is red. I saw it when you put it away. You'll have to do better than that if you want me to help you."

"I told Philip the whole truth about Father, Nanny and the wool, and about things that are red, of course."

"Then you must tell me everything you told Philip. I'll come over and sit in that nice, green chair and you can sit on my knee."

"I don't want us to sit in that chair. That's where I sat with Nanny. Can we sit in the other chair?"

"Yes. I don't see why not. I want you to tell me the whole story. You will give me every detail there is. If you leave anything out, you won't be able to see me as your friend. Take your time. I've got another hour before I go on duty."

William sobbed for ten minutes. Eventually, he told Dolly everything he had told Philip, including Rowland's words to Philip when he brought his son home.

"Do you feel better, now?" asked Dolly.

"Yes, I think I do."

"You only think it?"

"I know I do. You will come and see me, won't you? You *will* go on being my friend? I know I'll be a bit happier if I've got a friend."

"It's all right, William. I'll always be your friend. You know that."

"Is all this going to hurt me for the rest of my life?"

"Not if I have anything to do with it. I promise never to wear red, except when I come to this room."

"You know very well I can't get out of here, but I do love it in here," said William. "It means so much to me to sit here with Nanny. I can't see her, of course, but I know she's here, and it doesn't hurt me to see red things in here, like it does outside.

"So you said, William. I'll be back, tomorrow."

Dolly continued to work for Rowland, and had been in his employ for three months. She loved seeing William when she brought his lunch to the nursery. Rowland was powerfully attracted to her and suggested she take the post permanently.

It was just after 5.00 o'clock one Wednesday afternoon. She had left her chair and was putting on her coat.

Rowland came towards her. She turned to face him, flirtatiously, for the sake of the child. He kissed her and pushed her gently to the floor.

Twenty minutes passed. He said,

"Mary, my wife, that is, has gone to bed. It's her usual hypochondriasis. Are you doing anything this evening?"

"No. I was going to wash my hair and get an early night."

"Your hair looks clean enough to me. Why don't you come up for a drink?"

She did as he asked. That evening, she was wearing a black suede mini-skirt, her tight, white sweater and white boots.

"Well, you beautiful piece of work, what will you have?"

"Double gin and tonic."

He had the same. They drained their glasses and had more.

"How are you getting on with that William?" asked Rowland.

"OK. He's difficult to get to know. He never says anything."

"Oh, doesn't he?"

"No. He eats his lunch very quickly, so much so that I'm able to take the tray away, almost before I've delivered it. I hope you won't mind me saying this. He never complains, of course, but I really do think he'd like to eat more than what is provided. He's so hungry."

"Well, he's got a condition, Dolly. Since he had his adenoids scraped, he blew out like a barrel. If he has anything in excess of his diet, he risks blowing out again and that would slow down his metabolism, and might even effect his heart later on in life.

"Has he ever talked to you about my beating and bullying him?"

"No. He's never mentioned that."

"Has he ever said anything to you about his nanny?"

"The one who died?"

"Yes. Does he ever talk about her?"

"No. As a matter of fact, he's never mentioned her."

"Does he talk to you about anything?"

"As I said, he's a solemn little boy, forever enveloped in the silence of the grave."

"Does he refer to things that are red?" asked Rowland suspiciously.

"Red? No. But I really do think he should have a little more to eat, like a bar of chocolate at the end of his lunch. I noticed he had a black eye the first day I met him."

"I know," said Rowland. "That was delivered by the man who picked him up in the street, when he tried to run away."

"Surely, there's no need to lock him in when I have evidence that he does not have tuberculosis, or even the mildest cough or fever. He's definitely not infectious. There's nothing wrong with him, except his hunger."

"We've got to keep him disciplined," said Rowland. "After all, I want him to be a doctor and get into a teaching hospital such as the Hammersmith or Guy's. As I've been through the echelons of the medical profession, it is only right that my son must be made to do the same.

"He's left with two alternatives, either going into Medicine and enjoying a colossal inheritance from me, or going into another trade and having no inherited wealth at all."

"Do you know of any potential medical trainees, who have to be locked up by their fathers in order to learn discipline?" she asked. "I'm humbly suggesting that, without your knowing it, and without his saying anything, harm is being done to this boy. It's true, he's never mentioned any acts of cruelty, but I think he really does need fattening up. Why can't you have him down for meals — if only for him to make contact with you and his mother? He can always go back to the nursery afterwards."

"I'll think that one over, if I may," said Rowland. "It's not easy to concentrate when I'm looking at your magnificent legs. Perhaps, I should talk to him a bit more and let him know of my wish that he go into the medical profession. I agree he shouldn't sit in the nursery all day, but he likes to."

"If he likes it so much, why is he locked in? Also, I hope you don't mind me asking, but why were you so insistent that he had tuberculosis, when he has neither a cough nor a fever?"

Rowland had become relaxed by the gin. Had he had nothing to drink, he would have found Dolly interfering and intrusive, and may even have sacked her. He lay back on his armchair, some of the gin still in his glass.

"I understand your reasons for being so curious," he said. "The boy's a wayward little fellow. I've no idea what area of London he ended up in, that day he ran off. When he came back, he was clinging to a most insalubrious-looking man, a real Dickensian street rogue. That man could have given him drugs. I dread to think what else he could have done.

"As for the tuberculosis, he's been near another boy who's got it. I may have been wrong to tell you he actually had the disease, but I was overwrought because he keeps wandering off. We were worried sick that day he ran off. We thought he'd been murdered.

"Our nanny died suddenly. She had a heart attack. Yes, Dolly, I was over-dramatizing. It's not that William actually has tuberculosis, but he is in quarantine for it, and the quarantine period for that disease is pretty long.

"It's true, I've spoken to him a bit sharply in the past," he added, "and sometimes I feel rather guilty if I've done so unprovoked.

"Shall we try having lunch downstairs, tomorrow? I'd like you to dine with us, too, if you are free."

"I'd love that, Rowland. You mustn't spoil me."

Once more, the doctor kissed her on the mouth. Once more, he pulled her to the floor. She was satisfied with his performance as a lover, and despite her suspicions of his cruelty to his son, the liaison with the psychiatrist continued to excite her.

"William will have finished eating, Dolly. Shall we go up to the nursery together?"

"I'd like that, as long as we don't do anything naughty up there."

"You rude little girl!" said Rowland. He pushed a stray lock of peroxide hair from her forehead and kissed her cheek. "It's you I should have married," he said. "You're so like my sister."

"Your sister? I didn't know you had a sister. What's her name?"

"Kate. Her full name was Kate Alice. She died of pneumonia when she was only fourteen. I absolutely doted on her. She had the same golden hair and peach-like skin as yourself."

"You must miss her terribly. I'm sorry."

The lovers went into the nursery. William was sitting, leaning against the nanny's chair. He clung to the chair as if protecting himself from the blows he expected his father to deliver.

"Hullo. How's William?" said Dolly.

"I am all right."

"I am all right, what?" said Rowland.

"Sorry, I meant, I am all right, thank you."

Rowland went over to the table in the centre of the room. He saw a nearly completed jigsaw of Hieronymous Bosch's *Hay Wagon*, showing only its central panel.

"Was it you who did all this?" he asked.

"Well, it was me and Nanny."

"Nanny and I."

The father turned his head away from the son.

"Oh, Miss Parsons, would you mind leaving us alone for a moment? There's a letter on the tape that needs to be done urgently. It's addressed to Dr Powell."

"Very good, Dr Rendon. I'll go down straight away."

She did not go down. She walked briskly to the end of the corridor, removed her boots and walked silently back to the nursery door which was closed.

"Last Monday, your teacher gave you some verses to learn from *Alice Through the Looking Glass*," said Rowland.

"Yes, that's right, Father."

"You were asked to learn the first six verses of *The Walrus and the Carpenter*. Go to your satchel and bring me the book."

William did so. He had not learned the verses. He was terrified. Rowland opened the book and found the poem.

"Don't waste time, boy. Recite what you

104

have learned."

William looked blankly at Rowland.

"'*The sun was shining on the sea*'," he began, like an animal on its way to the slaughterhouse. A long silence reigned.

"Well, go on, boy, let's hear the rest of it."

"'*The sun was shining on the sea*'," repeated the child, his voice hoarse. He wrapped his arms round himself and backed away from his father. Rowland advanced towards him.

"So you think that's the whole poem, do you?" he said. "I'm waiting for the rest."

William went into a corner, sat on the floor and curled up into a ball, to make the ensuing blows less painful.

"'*The sun was shining on the sea*'," he whispered, as if these words were a passport to a land in which there would be no cruelty and no pain.

"Don't try my patience! I pay an arm and a leg for your education."

"I haven't done it, yet, Father. I'm afraid I was doing my jigsaw puzzle."

"In other words, you've been disobedient."

"I'm afraid I have, Father."

"Do you know what this means?"

"Yes, Father."

"Roll down your trousers."

105

H

Rowland pushed him face-downwards on one of the upright chairs surrounding the table. He took off his belt and lashed the boy until his arm was stiff. William did not scream like a healthy child receiving a beating. The punishment was so violent that he let out stifled, bird-like bleats. He got up from the chair and forced himself to stand up straight.

Rowland picked up *The Hay Wagon* and dragged its meticulously placed pieces apart. He threw them into their box which he closed and put under his arm.

When Dolly heard him coming towards the door, she left the nursery wing. She had made a decision to marry Rowland who would have been pleased to divorce his wife. She knew that the only way to protect William would be to marry the sadistic psychiatrist.

Rowland, Mary, Dolly and William were seated round the dining room table. Reproductions of some of Hogarth's grosser paintings, peered down upon the uncomfortably silent quartet.

The cook brought the lunch into the dining room. It was similar in quantity and richness, to the food brought in the previous day.

"How's that arthritis of yours, these days, Mrs

Dudley?" asked Rowland affably, in order to impress Dolly.

"It's about the same. It never improves. It just gets worse, but thank you so much for asking, sir." There was a shudder in her voice. Dolly noticed that she smelt strongly of body odour.

"I'm so sorry," said Rowland. "I appreciate how hard you work, preparing all these beautiful dishes, but in your determination to give me pleasure, I feel you should not get over-anxious."

"I like doing what I have to do, and doing it well."

Rowland was bored with the conversation. He looked at William, who was sitting with his head bowed, like a dog about to be whipped. The beetroot and cream soup was too rich for him. He pushed his spoon round his plate.

"Someone said, and I won't say who, that you were hungry all the time and that I wasn't giving you enough to eat," remarked Rowland, in an uncharacteristically pleasant tone. "Here you are, with almost all the food in the world in front of you, and you have no appetite. What does it all mean, eh, my boy?"

"I'm very sorry, Father. I'm afraid I want to be sick," said William. "Would you excuse me, please?"

"Why, yes," replied the father, baffled.

The boy rushed from the room. Mary Rendon fiddled with her prematurely grey hair and slid her shaking hand down the back of her frumpish, brown, woollen dress.

Dolly observed her appearance and habits. She wondered why Rowland had married her. Rowland caught her eye, knowing, instinctively, what she was thinking. He winked at her and smiled. She returned his smile.

William came back to the room, his face pale and his lips moist. He wondered what form of cruelty his father would inflict on him, next. He climbed up onto his chair.

"I'm sorry I was sick, Father," he muttered.

Rowland ignored him. He entered into a laboured conversation with Dolly about various subjects in which he had no interest. He felt that she would find at least sixty per cent of them reasonably inspiring. He referred to such topics as restaurants, pubs, different kinds of alcohol, plays, films, books, travel, and indoor and outdoor games.

She was flattered by his efforts to entertain her, but found his conversation unnaturally stiff and stilted. She told him she enjoyed tennis, frequented French restaurants and liked to visit France because of the food.

"Is France the only country you like?" asked Rowland. "I would have thought a lady with your flair and style would prefer Italy."

Dolly allowed him to refill her wine glass with *Chardonnay*, his favourite white wine. She said,

"I don't feel comfortable about going to Italy. The natives are OK but I can't make head or tail of the *lire*. It seems as if a note for nine hundred thousand *lire* amounts to little more than a shilling. If ever I go to Italy, I just insist on paying all these blighters in pounds. I don't speak the language, but I find I get understood if I shout in English and add 'O' onto everything."

Rowland felt at ease and peace with himself. He refilled his glass, drained it, and filled it once more. He had had a quarter of a bottle of whisky earlier, and felt pleasantly inebriated.

"I say, you really do have an astonishing way of expressing yourself," he remarked, his speech mildly slurred. "I think you're probably one of the funniest women I've ever met."

He drank the glass of wine and poured out more. His mood changed abruptly. He had been cheerful and jocular, and suddenly became restless and brooding. During such moods, he invariably spoke of his sister, Kate.

"Oh, Dolly, you're getting more and more like my beloved Kate, every day. She was vivacious and funny, just like you. You'll never believe what she did once, not long before she went down with the pneumonia which killed her."

Dolly leant across the table and fixed Rowland with the mischievous smile which excited him.

"Oh, do tell me what she did."

"She had a crush on a famous actor. She read in a newspaper that the actor had had to withdraw from his play in the West End, because he was ill and had to go to hospital.

"Kate looked up the number of every hospital in London, both National Health and private. Then, she rang each hospital, one by one. It took her at least two days, but she was determined to find him. That's how gutsy she was. Once she set herself a task, she never gave up.

"She found the actor in the end. He was in a private hospital in north London. She rang up, and asked to be put through to the Charge Nurse looking after him.

"Kate told the woman she was the private secretary of a world-famous film director, who wished to communicate with him urgently. The Nurse believed her and connected her.

"She was a bit coy, when speaking to the actor at first. But she put on an adult's voice, and said the film director had with him the screenplay of a film about Christ, and that this actor was being sought to play the leading role. She told the actor that the director had asked her to bring a copy of the script to the hospital.

"The actor was enthusiastic about it, and said he wished to read it. Kate went round to the hospital, wearing a tight dress and a brassière stuffed with tissues.

"She asked where he was. This time, she said she was his daughter. She went straight into his room, and found him lying on his bed, smoking a cigarette.

"Oh, Dolly, you'll never believe how bold and feisty and brazen she was! She shouted, 'I'm not leaving your room until I've had my way with you!'

"The man got off lightly, though. Kate's voice was heard from the corridor. She was ordered to leave. Although she was only fourteen, she had the mind and spirit of a twenty-year-old. She was so advanced for her years, so clever, so beautiful and so radiant."

Dolly enjoyed being compared with Kate, particularly as Rowland had said she resembled her. She looked briefly across the table at Mary who was fiendishly wringing her hands. Her twitch was as bad as ever, if not fractionally worse. The right hand side of her face jerked spasmodically, and hot tears rolled unchecked down her withered cheeks onto her skinny, sinewy neck.

Dolly found her repellant and was nauseated every time she looked at her. At the same time, she

111

pitied her. She feared she herself might lose her looks on reaching Mary's age, and was guilty about her thoughts towards the unfortunate, older woman.

The glasses of wine had made her more benevolent than she was when sober. Her cynical pity changed to endearment. She knew she would be called upon to replace Mary and wondered, with some concern, where she would go and who would look after her.

Dolly was a tough and resilient woman. She reasoned that Mary's future and welfare were no concern of hers. Mary had nothing to look forward to, whereas William, to whom Dolly had dedicated herself, had at least two-thirds of his life ahead of him, and was in need of protection until he reached manhood.

Rowland had been silent for at least ten minutes. He fixed his hideous, broken wife with a hostile stare.

"I do wish you'd get out, woman!" he bellowed. "You are such an obscene freak, I can't bear looking at you."

Mary obeyed, like a dying dog called to heel. Dolly hoped he wouldn't ask her to leave the room as well, as the prospect of leaving William alone with his father, frightened her. She turned to William.

"I'm so sorry you were sick at lunch," she

began. "Was there any part of the meal you enjoyed?"

William felt safer when Dolly was in the room. He said,

"I was better after I was sick, thank you. I liked the sausages and fried potatoes most. I also liked the bread and butter pudding."

"All right, Dolly, old girl," said Rowland. "I'm afraid I'm going to send you back to your desk."

"Just before I go back, can I go up to the nursery with William?" requested Dolly.

"Whatever for? He knows his own way up."

"Ah, but I'm carrying the key. I locked the door as a precaution. He can't get in without me."

"All right, all right," said Rowland. "These lunches can't go on for ever. Go on, take him up. I've got someone coming in ten minutes."

Four years passed. Mary mysteriously disappeared, and her body was found floating in the Thames, following an intensive police search. She had been crying every night during the week before she died, and had struggled to blink back her tears during the day.

Dolly was convinced she had deliberately killed herself, but felt no guilt because of her obligation to William.

Rowland was noticeably pleased. Two days after

113

Mary's death, he took Dolly to a registry office and married her.

Rowland and Dolly were sitting in the dining room, having a cooked breakfast. Rowland had put on two stone in weight, but Dolly, who had the appetite of a sparrow that day, had kept both her figure and her fresh looks.

William had just turned twelve. He remained graced with an innocent, beautific face. He was a bit happier, following the disappearance of his plain, gloomy mother. He trusted Dolly who was able to spend longer hours in the nursery with him, as Rowland had hired another secretary.

It was his birthday that day, and the prospect of spending time in Dolly's company, and receiving a gift-wrapped present from her, filled him with an optimism which he could not remember feeling for a considerable time.

He washed and groomed himself. He put on a clean white sweater and freshly-laundered bright blue trousers. He ran down the stairs, two at a time and went into the dining room. Rowland was smoking a cigar. He was studying a copy of *The Lancet*, studiously underlining passages about masturbation. Dolly was eating scrambled eggs.

William went to the hot plate. He lifted the solid silver covers of each dish one by one, and put them back noisily. The last dish he uncovered was full of over-cooked sausages. He liked sausages, particularly when they were burnt. He picked one up and crammed it into his mouth and allowed the silver cover to fall onto the dish, making a clattering noise.

Rowland threw *The Lancet* onto the floor. Dolly looked up suddenly, and hoped her husband would refrain from being unkind to William on his birthday.

"William!" Rowland bellowed. "You will kindly go upstairs until you can behave in a civilized manner!"*

The boy's mood changed dramatically from happiness to the despair which had broken him for as far back as he could remember.

He no longer felt like eating the sausage in his mouth. He removed the chewed pieces and held them in the palm of his hand.

"Yes, Father," he said, respectfully. He lowered his head and left the room, shutting the door, quietly. He had taken a marathon amount of abuse during the first twelve years of his life, but had never remembered anyone, even his father, hurting him on his birthday, except on the occasion when

---

*By the most gracious courtesy of Sir Winston Churchill's description of an incident during his early life.

It is to be noted that no other incidents in this book are in any way, be it directly, or indirectly, related to him.

his red rattle had been broken in his early years.

"Darling, don't you think you were being a bit harsh? You were right, of course. He was making a lot of noise, but he looks up to you. He's such a sensitive boy."

"Rubbish, Dolly! If he eats in the dining room, he should show some elementary manners."

"No-one is made of iron. If you spoke to me like that, I'd think you didn't care for me at all," said Dolly.

"I say, do you really think that?"

"I do think that. Also, it's his birthday, today. I was going to give him his present after breakfast."

"His birthday, eh? I'd forgotten that."

"Why don't you go and talk to him — after you've finished breakfast?"

"I won't go when I've finished. I'll go now," said Rowland.

"Oh, darling, that *would* be nice."

William was sitting at the nursery table, with his left hand supporting his chin. He was filling in a jigsaw puzzle with his right hand. The paintings of Hieronymous Bosch had a therapeutic effect on him. Their detailed, weird, surreal pessimism held a warped fascination for him. Tormented though he was already, he liked to ogle the paintings, in order

116

that he might become more so. He was working on the *Temptation of St. Anthony.*

He suddenly saw his father, at the other side of the table. Rowland walked round to him.

"William?" he began.

"Yes, Father?"

"I say, I didn't realize it was your birthday, today. I always had it in mind that you were a June baby."

William said nothing. He yearned for his father to say something pleasant to him. Rowland handed him an unwrapped gold watch.

"Oh, it's beautiful, Father! Thank you."

"Try it on for size."

William did so. The watch was too big for him. He pushed it further up his arm.

"It's lovely."

"Are you sure? If it's too loose, I can always take it back and have it reduced in size."

"Oh, no. It fits me perfectly. Thank you so much. I know I displeased you earlier, but I'm happier now."

"William, there's something else I want to talk to you about. Perhaps I was a bit unkind to you at breakfast. It's usual for children to get upset when their parents shout at them, but that doesn't mean they don't care for them. I do care for you. I care very much, and I want you to understand that."

117

Rowland bent over to look at the picture on the table.

"I say, aren't you a bit short of blue pieces for the sky?"

It was a Saturday and Rowland was not working. He sat down alongside his son and helped him to finish filling in the pieces.

"It looks good, doesn't it, William?"

Rowland and William talked for a few minutes before Rowland left the room. William felt so overjoyed that he wept. He waited for his father to go down the corridor and open and close the door at the end.

He went back to the age of eight. He rushed to the cupboard and seized the two sacred balls of red wool and clutched them in each hand. He went over to the chair in which his nanny used to sit, and knelt in front of it, staring at the unoccupied space, convinced the nanny was still there.

"Nanny!" he shouted. A voice in his head answered. It was his nanny's voice.

"Oh, Nanny, Father *talked* to me! It was wonderful. He was so kind. He gave me a beautiful gold watch and he even helped me with the jigsaw puzzle."

Rowland's outbursts of kindness increased over the

years. Dolly had melted much of his brutality. The boy could bear his almost loveless life, because of Dolly's devotion and companionship. She was also able to control Rowland, to no little extent, due to her prettiness, pertness, sense of humour and nocturnal performance.

If she told him he had been particularly unpleasant towards his son, he frequently deferred to her, and was kind to him.

William still spent all his spare time in the nursery, sometimes alone, sometimes with Dolly.

He was fifteen. He was sitting at the table, smiling. He was painting a pine forest. He had managed to make the trees a rich shade of dark green, showing the glare of the sun lighting their foliage.

The only strange thing about the picture, was the sky, from which the summer sun was meant to shine. It was not an azure blue, but bright red. The sky had been crudely filled with black penned images of death. The sight of tombstones, coffins and gibbets looked absurdly out of place above a glowing, dark green forest.

He looked up from his work, and saw his father the other side of the table. He was flushed in the face and drunk, but on this occasion, the alcohol had made him affable.

"William?"

"Yes, Father."

"You've taken up painting, I see. I say, you certainly haven't given up your extraordinary obsession about red."

"It's such a mood-elevating colour, Father."

William was relieved that this was another occasion on which his father appeared to be kind and friendly. He inadvertently blurted out a treasured secret, which caused him unbearable pain, because he did not understand it himself.

"It's only up here in the nursery that I'm able to love and appreciate the colour. When I'm in this room, looking at it, I feel I'm in Paradise, but if I'm anywhere else, it haunts me."

"Why?" asked Rowland.

"Maybe, it's due to my memory of Nanny's death. I associate her with it because she always gave me red things, and there were times when I could get away with wearing red in here, where I thought it unlikely that you would find me."

Rowland remembered his son's passionate love of red, but his excessive daily consumption of alcohol, had dulled a lot of his brain cells. This was one of a few occasions when his long-term memory failed to serve him.

"I don't know what you're talking about, William. Why on earth would I have forbidden you to wear red? Why would I have gone so far as to order you not to have red things?"

The son suddenly despised, rather than feared the father. He knew that his partial loss of memory had deprived him of some of his conscience and anything associated with it.

"Do you really not remember, Father? Don't you remember beating me with your belt?"

"Come, William, I never beat you."

"Don't you remember sacking Nanny because you caught her knitting a red sweater on Remembrance Day, when she fell to the floor, dead?"

"No, William. You're making all this up. You're mad."

"Don't you remember saying you wished you'd never had a son, because you wanted a daughter?"

"No. I think you're telling a pack of wounding lies. I've always loved you."

"That's not true, Father. The mental and physical wounds you inflicted on me, will never heal."

"All right, William, all right. If I've been unkind to you, I really am sorry."

"Isn't it a bit late to say you're sorry? The damage has already been done. Once I'm out of this room, I can't bear to see red things without being tortured. It's only here that I can tolerate and love it, because so much love was once bestowed on me

121

J

here, never anywhere else."

Rowland sat down at the table, opposite William.

"As a psychiatrist, I am reluctant to psycho-analyse my own son, but I'd like you to be treated by one of my colleagues. What you have just said, about your attitude towards red, shows you have a deep-rooted psychosis. None of the things you say, make any sense, whatever."

"The first thing I'll tell him is what a sadistic father I have," said William.

"You don't realize how hurtful your accusations are," said Rowland. "I've never willingly harmed you."

"Oh, haven't you? Don't you remember what happened on that Remembrance Day?"

"Which one? There's one every year. There have been a lot of them since you were little."

"The one we had the day Nanny died after you fired her. It was then that you said the country would be a happier place, had the Germans won the War."

"I never said that. Nor did I even think it."

"You should never have conceived me!" shouted William.

"Try to understand. I do apportion some of the blame to my insensitive behaviour, although it's not what you described. When you were born, I was not quite prepared for fatherhood. I was young and foolish. Your mother became pregnant, and I had to marry her because I would never dishonour a lady, even if I didn't love her."

"You could have forced her to abort, Father. My past and present lives have not been tolerable, because of you."

Rowland stretched out his arms in an expansive gesture and rested his hands at the back of his head.

"Really, William, this conversation is repetitive beyond belief and is getting us nowhere. Not only that, it's time we discussed your future.

"I specifically want you to go into Medicine. I want you to get yourself into medical school, and qualify to become a doctor, just as I did. Of all avenues, the medical profession is the finest and noblest.

"Perhaps you have it in mind to choose another trade. What do you think?"

"I haven't thought about a career, yet. I've got to take my 'O' levels and 'A' levels first.

"What subjects are you doing 'O' levels in?"

"English language and literature, Latin, Greek, French, Physics, Chemistry and Biology."

"The last three will be the most useful to you. How do you feel about going into Medicine?"

"I haven't made up my mind. First, I've got to sort myself out about red," said William vaguely.

"I don't want to hear any more of this dotty talk about red! The situation is this, and I'll put it to you, plainly. If you qualify as a doctor, half of my inheritance, namely moneys, goods and chattels, will be passed onto you in my Will. The other half will go to Dolly. If you don't choose Medicine, but go into a different field, you will inherit nothing. In other words, you'll be on your own. Which sounds more attractive — the obligation to work exceptionally hard as a doctor, and be rich, or to work, say, as a barrister or a stockbroker, and have nothing to turn to, if you fall flat on your face? Which of these sounds more sensible?"

"Well, the trade where the money is, of course, Father," said William, abruptly.

"Good. You're saying, in fact, that you'll be happy to go into Medicine?"

"As I said, I want to take the most financially secure option. Besides, I've always had an interest in matters related to Medicine."

"Oh, what matters have you had an interest in?"

"I'm fascinated by death and disease, Father." said the youth, spontaneously, failing to look his father in the face.

"Why?"

"Perhaps, because I saw Nanny die when I was eight. I suffered so much that I made myself find death more pleasurable than painful."

Rowland lost his temper. He was not prepared to be reminded of his previous cruelty towards his son, a second time.

"Are you daring to criticize the manner in which I raised you, yet again?" he shouted.

"I've just told you about your cruelty, and it would be painful to return to the subject. However, I agree that the idea of my going into Medicine, is the best one."

William passed his 'O' levels and had high grades in all the subjects. The same applied to his 'A' levels in Physics, Chemistry and Biology. William moved into a house in central London, but was allowed to keep the key to his father's house.

By the time he entered the Hammersmith Hospital Medical School, he had become an alcoholic, like his father, and smoked three packets of *Benson and Hedges* cigarettes a day. He drank, not for pleasure, but as an antidote to his unlifting, disturbed moods, and the acute melancholy fits that they caused. Whether rightly or wrongly, he believed that the drink sharpened his concentration and shed his inhibitions.

The memory of his childhood continued to cause him recurrent attacks of despondency, but, when he remembered to, he found a temporary solution to the problems which bright red caused him.

He wore dark glasses, which created the illusion that all bright red things were dark red.

When questioned by his lecturers and peers, he told them that he had a medical condition effecting his eyes. His charming, gentle, affable manner endeared his questioners to him. They accepted his word and respected his industry and stoicism.

It did not take him long to find out how overpoweringly attractive were his wavy, gold-blonde hair and big, blue, tormented, bloodshot eyes which he flaunted on occasions when he took his dark glasses off. His eyes, combined with the innocence and vulnerability of his facial expression, made him irresistible to women. He had developed a markedly high sex drive, and could take a woman to his bed whenever he wanted, which was almost every night of the week.

He got on well with his fellow students. They shared with him a passion for abandoned drinking after their studies, and even during their lunch breaks.

William found it irritating that the nearest pub to the Hammersmith Hospital, The Pavilion, was about two miles away. The two roads leading to it, were bleak, drab and depressing. William felt particularly downhearted during these journeys. His mood was flattened even more by the sight of a disused football pitch, its trampled surface covered by mud and puddles.

This, combined with piles of autumn leaves on the pavement, and a permanently grey sky, made him want to run to the place where alcohol would obliterate his misery and turn it, if only temporarily, to joy.

It was an evening in early October at the start of his first year at medical school. He went to The Pavilion, accompanied by three male medical students, whom he hardly knew, and a young woman called Sarah.

The three men were unattractive. One of them was sallow-complexioned, with oily, shoulder-length hair. The two others had foul breath and disfiguring acne.

Sarah appeared to be attached to the man with the shoulder-length hair. She leant heavily against him, holding his arm as they walked.

She was tall and slim, with shiny, nut-brown hair, swept back in a slide, and freckles covering most of her face. Her only unflattering feature, was a pair of expressionless, upward-slanting, greenish eyes, which looked like dead fish on a slab.

The Pavilion was nearly empty. The five medical students went up to one of the bars.

William was the only one who ordered a neat double whisky. The others had pints of dark-coloured beer. They sat down at a nearby table.

William ignored the long-haired medical student, who sat next to Sarah with his arm round her. He noticed that there was nothing red in his surroundings, and took his sun-glasses off. He drained his glass of whisky, which dispelled his black mood. He sat on Sarah's other side. He gave her time to observe his good looks, and leant against her, smiling.

"Don't you find it disgraceful that there's no pub nearer the hospital than this?" he said.

She liked the spontaneous nature of his question, and, apart from his looks, she was attracted to his soft voice and educated accent.

"I can't say I enjoy the walk much, particularly at this gloomy time of year," she said. He found her voice unusual. It was high-pitched, loud and nasal. Though not particularly alluring, it intrigued him.

"Where are you from, Sarah? Are you Canadian?"

"No." She let out a shrill, musical laugh. "I'm from Bismarck, North Dakota."

"What made you want to come to a medical school in London?"

"I've been in London for ten years, and I've

always wanted to be a doctor. I don't like my home town. I come from a large, compulsively social family. They're all noisy and claustrophobic. I wanted to get away from them all, as far as I could. Away from them, away from the States."

"Surely, your family aren't as bad as that. How many brothers and sisters have you got?"

"Four sisters and a brother. All older than me," said Sarah. She was often bored when questioned about her siblings.

"Is your father a doctor?"

"No. He's a lawyer."

The long-haired man on Sarah's other side, leant forward, to speak to William. His name was Alfie Gillmore.

"Do you normally go round poaching other people's women, Rendon?" He had a trace of a London East End accent, which, it was clear, he was trying desperately hard to shed.

"A lady has the right to speak to anyone she chooses. She's a person, not a chattel," said William.

"She's my girl. I'd thank you to stop chatting her up."

"It's for you to decide, Sarah," said William. "Do you want me to go on speaking to you, or would you like me to shut up and go away?"

"You're right. I am no-one's property," she

said. "You're too arrogant and possessive, Alfie. I'd much rather talk to William."

Gillmore rose to his feet, and drained his glass which he banged on the table. "I'm off, now," he said. "As for you, Sarah, I'll look for my fun, elsewhere. I can see you've made your decision."

The two students facing William, Gillmore and Sarah, did not particularly like Gillmore, whom they considered petty, dirty, aggressive and quarrelsome. They were amused by his stormy exit from the room.

William went to the bar to buy everyone another drink, and order a neat, double whisky for himself. He went back to the table and sat next to Sarah.

"I *am* sorry about that," he said. "I wouldn't want to come between two people going out, together. Is the gentleman very important to you?"

"No. I wouldn't say so. Nor is he a gentleman. He's very selfish and demanding. We'd only been together for three weeks. He's a slob."

"I do hope you wouldn't say anything like that about me. I'm not selfish. I'm not demanding."

"I know. He's different to you. I was going to end it, anyway, but I couldn't bring myself to, until now. I felt like someone on the diving board unable to jump in the water to have a last swim, before changing for dinner. You came up behind me and prompted me."

130

William drained his second glass of whisky.

"I love your analogy," he said. "You've got style. You've got class. That man doesn't deserve you, but I think I do. Are you free, tonight?"

"Well, I was going to go pub-crawling with Alfie," said Sarah.

"But he's gone. That leaves you free to come out to dinner with me. That is, if you want to. There's no rule to say you've got to."

"I do want to. Alfie had been taking me to some dreadful places. He never gave me dinner, once. The only time he gave me something to eat, was when he bought me lunch in the dismal hospital canteen."

"It sounds as if he had been a rivetting, exciting, imaginative companion. I'm sure you were heart-broken when he walked out, just now."

"Oh, without any shadow of doubt. It was so bad I felt like ending my life."

William felt heartened. A sense of humour in a woman, was vital to him in a relationship. He took Sarah's arm, and walked her back to the hospital, where he had parked his Jensen. He opened the door for her, something Gillmore had never done, when she got into his scratched, heavily-dented Triumph.

"I bet that Gillmore fellow never opened the door for you, like this," said William.

"If he had, he would have found it difficult. The passenger's door was so dented, it wouldn't open. If you wanted to get in, you had to climb over the driver's seat."

"What sort of car does the bastard drive?"

"A Triumph."

"Not so nice as a Jensen, eh?"

William drove the Jensen onto the dual carriageway, leading to central London. He put on a cassette of Rachmaninov's Second Piano Concerto. The music had a relaxing effect on both driver and passenger.

They had gone through Hyde Park and reached Knightsbridge.

"What sort of food do you like, Sarah?"

"Anything, as long as it's not Indian."

"You must have some preference."

"Well, I like Italian food."

William parked the Jensen badly. Most of the car occupied the pavement, and was rammed, almost at right angles to it, between two other parked cars.

He held her hand and escorted her to a nearly empty restaurant called *Mamma Mia*, which played operatic arias over a loudspeaker.

They drank a bottle of *Chardonnay* in silence, broken eventually by William.

"So you say, your father's a lawyer?"

"Yes. That's right."

"Is he a nice man?"

"I think so," she said stiltedly. William knew the question had unnerved her. She added, "He once wanted to go into politics, but things didn't work out. To go into politics, you have to be a decent liar. If you don't know how to lie convincingly, you can't possibly be a professional politician."

William laughed.

"There's nothing I love more than a witty woman," he said.

Neither spoke for the rest of dinner. They drank a second bottle of *Chardonnay* and stared at each other.

"I'm afraid I can't drive, now," said William. "We'll have to ask these people to get us a taxi. I don't want to pressurize or embarrass you, and if you say 'no', I shan't be offended. Do you want to go home, or would you prefer to stay with me?"

"I want to stay with you."

"Do you live alone?"

"No. I share with another woman."

"Another woman? That's strange."

"We hardly ever see each other."

"What's the point of living with her, then?"

"It helps with the rent."

"Oh? I had the impression you were from a

wealthy family. I didn't know you'd need to share, to pay the rent."

Sarah was so ashamed, that she broke into a heavy sweat.

"Well, it's this way. I've always been a bit self-conscious about my family's wealth. I don't like talking about it because I don't want to sound ostentatious. It's not true. I do live alone. I only told you I shared because I wanted to hide the truth. I didn't want you to know I was rich."

"Why, Sarah?"

"Because, these days, a woman is hated if she's rich, particularly if her wealth is unearned. Somehow, Alfie found out. He got rather nasty about it, and showed me up in front of his friends."

"I always knew Gillmore was a bastard. I'm not, though. I don't mind your being rich. I like you for what you are. Not only that, I'm rich, too."

William asked the taxi driver to go to a three storey house, 26 Rutland Gate. He owned the whole house. The walls of every room were covered with Impressionist paintings, Daumiers, Bonnards, a Turner and a few Victorian narrative pictures. At least his father had kept his promise. He had given his son a large sum of money, because he had agreed to go to medical school.

In William's bedroom, occupied by a four-poster bed, was a solitary photograph of his nanny. Sarah was captivated by her benign, serene and benevolent features.

"Is it your mother?" she asked.

"No. It's my nanny. She died," he said in a staccato tone. "My mother died some years later. She had some nerve-related illness," he added, awkwardly.

Sarah felt shy, which he sensed instantly.

"Would you like me to take off your clothes?" he asked.

"All right."

"There's no need to be shy with me. I'm sure Gillmore was always belittling you about this sort of thing."

She stood like a department store dummy, while he undressed her, delicately folding up her garments, as if they were sacred.

They got into bed, and lay on their backs.

"Don't feel you've got to do anything, just to be polite. I'm sure Gillmore pushed you about, and treated you like a prostitute," he said.

"Why do you keep referring to him?"

"Because I'm jealous of him. He's not nearly good enough for you."

"I'm glad he's gone. You've never told me anything about your family, William."

William spoke in jerks, like a petrol car whose tank had been filled with diesel.

135

"I have no brothers or sisters. My mother is dead, as I said. I have a few cousins whom I don't see much of, but I'm very fond of them. My father is alive," he said, in a low voice, as if as an afterthought.

"What's your father like?"

William turned away from her and told her the story of his wretched life. He was so terrified of losing her, that he refrained from making any references to his peculiar attitude towards things which were red.

"I'm so very sorry," she said. "What is your father's profession?"

"He's a Harley Street psychiatrist."

"Never!"

"It's true, he is. He married again after my mother died. The lady's much younger than he is. She's always very nice to me. Her name's Dolly."

"Is she pretty?"

"Yes. Very."

"Have you ever been naughty with her?"

"God Almighty, no! I wouldn't dare. Are you jealous?"

"Of course. In the same way you are of Gillmore."

"You sound very wide awake. Has the effect of the wine worn off?"

"I think it has."

"I'm not sleepy, either. I don't want you to feel you are obliged to give me pleasure, just because I took you out to dinner."

"Oh, it's all right."

"I am completely ready," he said assertively, his conversation taking a turn for the vulgar."

"Good."

"Do you have a preference for any particular style?"

"You sound the epitome of a Harley Street psychiatrist's son! If you really want to know, I like it very rough."

"Sarah, you're an American in every sense of the word."

Neither of them slept that night. They had too much to say to each other. William smoked continuously. By the time it was light, Sarah was talking about her planned addition of clothes to her wardrobe.

"What colours do you think suit me best?" she asked.

"You'd look wonderful in any colour. Any colour except red," he said, urgently.

"Why red?"

"It just wouldn't go with your complexion."

"Do you think so? In that case, I promise I'll never wear red."

They romped once more before it was time to

get up. William's habit of smoking compulsively throughout the rough sex acts, fascinated and attracted Sarah.

Gillmore was militantly opposed to smokers. His self-righteousness about cigarettes was abhorrent, even to non-smokers. Sarah had not expected Gillmore to storm out of The Pavilion, and had kept a hidden packet of *Consulate* cigarettes in the bottom of her handbag.

The lovers smoked a cigarette each, before getting out of bed.

It was a sunny, crisp morning, and the dew shone on the fallen autumn leaves, making them pretty, rather than gloom-inspiring, unlike their appearance the previous evening. Both William and Sarah were wearing white coats, even before arriving at the hospital. They wished to give passers-by the impression that they were erudite in the field of medicine. Somehow, their white coats made them look sexually attractive.

William felt uncharacteristically peaceful and contented as he walked to the hospital with Sarah holding his arm.

Their lecture, about fluctuations of liver enzymes, was due to begin in half an hour. They were surprised to find Gillmore and the two foul-complexioned medical students, sitting, cramped together on a wooden bench, also in white coats.

The three men were looking indifferently at an imposing, unprepossessing work of modern art near the hospital entrance.

The two men sitting on either side of Gillmore, were called Perry Jackson and Alexander Miller. They considered themselves social misfits and were unwilling to approach women because of their disfiguring acne. They sought out Gillmore's company because he appeared to be the only person who was able to put up with their drab, lukewarm personalities.

Gillmore was tolerant of them because of their physical unattractiveness. They were no threat to him where women were concerned. He knew that if a woman approached the three of them together, she would be likely to make conversational overtures to him, not his companions. He was aware that his sallow, sultry, Indian look appealed to Bohemian women in particular, and was complacent about his smooth, unblemished skin.

He sprung to his feet as William and Sarah walked through the hospital gates.

"A word with you, Rendon, if you don't mind," he said, unpleasantly. His London East End accent was more marked than he usually allowed it to be.

William lit a cigarette, with a smart, gold lighter, bearing the initials W.R. on it.

"If you wish," he said. "Where do you want us

to have this private interchange?"

"Over there under them, I mean, those trees on the left where the taxis come in, and you can put that cigarette out while you're about it."

"I won't. It's you who wanted us to talk, not me. Stop pushing people around. You'll get yourself disliked." He cursed himself for never having had the courage to say this to his father.

Gillmore didn't answer. The two men walked over to the area shaded by trees. They stood between two waiting taxis, one of whose drivers was chewing gum and reading *The Sun* newspaper.

William leant against the wall, still smoking, blowing rings contemptuously into Gillmore's face.

"What do you want?" he asked, angrily.

"Are you Rowland Rendon's son — the Harley Street shrink?"

"I am."

"You close to him?"

"Your question is unclear. Be a bit more coherent and I might decide to answer it."

"How close are you to your shrink father, Rendon? You're spoiled, so I'd assume you'd be close to him. He's given you all these material goods, hasn't he?"

"Looks like it, doesn't it?"

"OK, then. Just how close are you?"

William knew Gillmore was thinking of incest,

and found his question repellant.

"Well, I sleep on the top floor, and he sleeps on the first floor. To reach that distance from the outside of the building, a crow would have to fly about twenty feet. I trust that answers your question"

"He's got oodles of money, hasn't he?"

"What's that got to do with you?"

"Everything. He's a right, privileged bastard. He must be if his son can afford to drive a Jensen."

William hated this man, not because of his inverted snobbery, but because of his intense jealousy of him. He was jealous of him because he was poor. He was tough, and resilient and had absolutely nothing to lose.

Despite his unhappy childhood, William had been raised in a wealthy household. There was a possible but unlikely risk of his material possessions and wealth being taken away from him, which would leave him with none of the spiritual resources existing with the other man.

His jealousy had turned to savage and inveterate hatred. Just as Gillmore had bitterly, indirectly alluded to his own poverty, William deliberately over-flaunted his own riches, which, despite the convenience and extreme pleasure they afforded him, cruelly weighed upon his soul, like shackles.

"You're right. He is," said William. "The only

141

problem is, my chauffeur's off sick this week. Otherwise, he would be driving the charming Jensen, himself."

"You swank bugger!"

"Take me as you find me, Gillmore."

Gillmore leant against the wall, as well, his weight on his right leg and his left foot crossing it.

"Did that tart, Sarah, tell you to give it to her rough?" he asked.

William had no idea what he was doing, but he knew, instinctively, that he had inherited some of the worst of his father's genes. He turned to Gillmore and reached into his pocket. An ivory-handled flick-knife, its blade over six inches long, suddenly leapt into his hand.

He unlocked the safety catch and pushed the button. He eased the blade back into its handle and pressed the button once more. *Click hooitt. Click hooit.*

It was only the fear of seeing the bright redness of superficially-shed blood, which reminded him that the blade was pressing against Gillmore's throat. Had he been wearing his dark glasses, he would have thought nothing of severing his jugular artery. His proneness to vindictive violence and inability to foresee his actions, made him aware that an umbilical cord would tie him to his father until the end of his life.

Not only was his father responsible for his pathological streak. He was also indirectly responsible for the fact that he had to wear sunglasses almost all the time, even when the weather was dire and overcast.

Gillmore interrupted his disagreeable thoughts.

"Are you raving mad, mate?"

"No. I bitterly resent your referring to Sarah as a 'tart'.

"She is," said Gillmore.

"I'm prepared to have a fair fight with you about it."

"If you insist. We'll meet on the disused football pitch early tomorrow morning. Fists only. No weapons."

"OK. Once the fight is over, I order you never ever to come anywhere near me, again."

As he spoke, William observed the sombre walls of Wormwood Scrubs Jail, adjacent to the Hammersmith Hospital. The sight of the prison, its tall walls topped with barbed wire, sickened and terrified him even more than things which were red.

It was raining early the following morning. William and Gillmore were on the football pitch, both wearing dark-coloured track-suits.

William was backed by Miller, who had grown

to dislike Gillmore. Gillmore was supported by Jackson, who had become impressed by his brightness and who deferred to him.

Both the backers failed to realize they would be splashed by the mud on the sodden grass, and wore white coats, to be ready for the first lecture of the day, this time about ovarian cancer.

Sarah was present on the football pitch. Gillmore had begun to repulse her. She had seen William threatening him with a knife and loved him even more, for doing so. A man pressing a knife against another man's throat in defence of her honour, thrilled and excited her.

William had had no training in physical combat, but he had, apart from his father's less fortunate genes, inherited the older man's muscularity and extraordinary strength.

Gillmore, on the other hand, had an unfit and feeble physique.

The two men lunged at each other. William was excited by Sarah's shouts and cheers.

Gillmore knew that William was the strongest of the two. He kicked his opponent in the genitals.

It took William a few minutes to recover. Rage multiplied his strength. He punched Gillmore in the jaw, knocking him out.

Jackson rushed over to him and carried out what he assumed to be a professional surface examination.

"It's all right. He's in sinus rhythm. His JVP* is not raised," he announced.

Miller advanced towards William and congratulated him, before embracing him with an enthusiasm which embarrassed him.

Sarah ran towards William and kissed him on the lips. This, too, distressed him as his repressed upbringing had made him averse to public displays of affection.

The five students sauntered along to the hospital. Jackson and Miller were unaware that the bottoms of their white coats were covered with mud. William felt intensely depressed. Gillmore knew he had lost the respect of the two other male students, as well as what he had assumed was Sarah's love, which had in fact been no more than mild physical attraction, mixed with contempt.

The lecture on ovarian cancer was delivered by Professor Alec Singleton, a short, stout, sixty-year-old with thin, silvery hair.

He spoke of a case of a fifty-two-year-old woman, who had suffered intense stomach pains for two years before being given an appointment to see a specialist.

Professor Singleton's intonation was lack-lustre and monotonous. He lost the interest of all his

*Jugular venous pressure.

145

students, except for William, the only student who listened animatedly and took notes.

The Professor sounded like a hung-over, agnostic priest. He described how the patient's cancer had spread from the ovary to the small and large bowel, and the pelvis. It was thought that she would die, but all her tumours were obliterated by an intensive course of chemotherapy.

Singleton noticed that Gillmore, sitting in the front row, had fallen asleep.

"Am I boring you, Mr Gillmore?" he asked.

"Oh, no, sir!"

"In that case, would you please wake up. What have I been talking about?"

"Ovarian cancer, sir."

"Would you care to enlighten me, further?"

"Yes. You were talking about a lady who had it, sir."

"Where?"

"In an ovary, sir."

"I think you're capable of giving me a more intelligent answer than that."

"I'm sorry, sir."

"Where did it progress?"

"Well, all over the body, sir."

"Might I ask why you chose to come to medical school?"

"To train to be a doctor, sir."

146

Jackson and Miller tittered.

"In that case, why have you not been listening?"

"Because I was hit earlier this morning, sir."

"Hit? By whom?"

"Rendon, sir."

"I'd like to remind you that you are no longer in a preparatory school. If you are not prepared to listen and learn in an adult manner, I suggest you embark on another trade."

Jackson and Miller, both sitting in the back row, were the last to leave the lecture hall.

"Mr Jackson and Mr Miller, may I have a word with you?" said the Professor.

The two students were subservient and respectful by nature. They stood still.

"Why are your coats in this filthy, disgusting condition?"

Jackson and Miller looked at the fronts of their coats and fixed the Professor with a bemused stare.

"I don't understand, sir," said Jackson.

"Turn round, both of you."

The young men obeyed.

"Take your coats off and look at the backs of them. They are a shattering, thundering disgrace."

When the men removed their coats, they held them in the air and scrutinized them.

"We're sorry, sir," said Jackson, the only student prepared to speak.

147

"Why are they in this revolting state?" asked the Professor.

"We were on the football pitch."

"Why were you wearing white coats on a football pitch?"

"Well, we didn't know we were going to get muddy."

"What were you doing there?"

"We were referee-ing a fight, sir."

"A fight between whom?"

"Rendon and Gillmore, sir."

"Why were they fighting?"

"They were fighting over a woman, sir."

The Professor's facial expression changed from one of irritation, to amusement. He slapped his thigh and let out a guffaw.

"Why the hell didn't you say so?" he shouted.

William and Sarah were lively and animated after their studies that day. They went to his house in Rutland Gate, lay on the four-poster bed and drank gin and tonic.

William had had six double gins, but felt nothing. She had just finished her third single and felt pleasantly drunk.

"I've got an evening paper, here. I want to go to the cinema, tonight," she announced, with a degree of petulance which delighted him.

"All right. Is there anything in particular you want to see?"

"Not really. I just want to go for the sake of going."

"I only like black and white films," said William.

"Why?"

"I like old films. Also, I prefer to leave colours to the imagination. I don't like them being imposed on me," he said, cautiously.

The idea of having to put on dark glasses in front of her, in a cinema, showing anything red, terrified him. He decided that, if pushed, he would make an excuse about having recurrent migraines.

"That's an extraordinary view to take," she said, "but it attracts me to you more because you're not of the norm. *Some Like it Hot* is on at the Classic in Baker Street. That's in black and white."

"Are you quite sure of that?"

"Yes, quite sure."

William took her to Baker Street in the Jensen. He was not worried about the possibility of being breathalysed, as the gin had had no effect on him.

The queue outside the cinema was surprisingly long, and it was raining heavily.

"I really don't think I can sit this out," she said, rather irritably. "Why don't we find somewhere in Leicester Square?"

He wanted to go home, but was afraid of losing her love.

"OK, I don't mind."

"Do you think there are any black and white films in Leicester Square?" she asked.

"I doubt it, but I don't mind seeing something in colour."

They went into the first cinema they could find, without a queue outside it, because the film showing had already started. William had become so exhausted that he failed to take in the title of the film they would be seeing.

They went to the ticket office. The gin had begun to intoxicate him.

"What film are we seeing?" he asked.

"*The Krays.*"

"You mean the Kray twins?"

"That's right. You don't mind, do you? I love violence."

"No, no, not at all."

"I find those two so attractive," she said, "but not nearly as attractive as you, of course," she added as a hasty afterthought. "They were heroic men while they were free. They protected old people, women and children."

"Oh, did they?"

"You look awfully strange. Are you all right?"

150

"Why, yes. Whatever you enjoy, automatically gives me pleasure."

They went into the crowded auditorium. Apart from the light from the film, which was showing the twins' high-spirited aunt, Rose, knocking over a petrified SHO* on a hospital ward, the cinema was pitch dark.

"Usherette!" screamed Sarah.

"Whatever's the matter?" he asked.

"There's supposed to be a bloody usherette, here! I can't see where I'm going."

William had not brought his dark glasses with him, as he thought he would be seeing *Some Like it Hot*. He knew there would be bloodshed during the film, and closed his eyes.

The film was showing the twins impaling a seedy-looking troublemaker's hands to a billiard table, with long, sharp knives. There was bright, red blood everywhere which excited Sarah. She tapped William on the shoulder.

"Look, William! What's wrong? Your eyes are tight shut."

"I'm sorry. It's the blood."

"But you're a medical student. How is it you can't stand the sight of blood? You just wait till the end, when dear old Reggie stabs Jack the Hat McVitie to death, with the pale light of the moon

---

*SHO — Senior House Officer. Euphemism for a junior doctor.

151

shining wistfully on his blood-spattered stiletto. That's justice for you, all right."

William thought briefly of the Bosch painting, depicting the temptation of St Antony. He saw himself as the man with a hill growing out of his back, and arrows raining in on him when he was unable to put up a defence.

He thought obsessively about the events in the nursery on Remembrance Sunday, when he was eight years old. The more he tried to expel the thoughts, the more vehemently they scourged him. He repeated the same words he used, as instinctively as the act of raising his arm to lessen the glare of the sun. He knelt on the floor between the seats and banged his fists against his head, while startled viewers turned round and gaped at him.

"Take it away, it's red! Take it away, it's red!"

Sarah assumed he was having a fit, brought on by exhaustion and sleep deprivation. She put her arms round him.

"Come on, William. I'll take you home."

He allowed her to lead him into the street like a dog. She guided him to the underground carpark nearby, and took the keys of the Jensen from his pocket. She unlocked the doors and pushed him gently into the passenger's seat.

"It's all right, now. We're going home."

"What happened? I can't remember a thing."

"We were seeing a film about the Kray twins."

"Who?"

"The Kray twins, dear."

"Are they anything to do with ovarian cancer?"

"No, of course they're not, you fool! You'll remember in a few minutes. You had some sort of fit. I thought it was epilepsy. I'm calling the doctor out when we get home."

"Have you any idea what I did?"

"Yes. You had a screaming fit. You kept shouting the words 'Take it away, it's red!'"

William began to shake. Sarah put on his seat belt. She did not have a driving licence, and when she turned on the ignition, putting the automatic gear into reverse, she drove very badly, crashing into other parked cars as she did so, and had hysterical giggles.

They queued to pay the carpark attendant. William suddenly became alert and put his hands round her throat in a vice-like grip.

"You killed me, Father! You murdered me in cold blood! You never allowed me to live! Not since she died, and you locked me in for all that time like a dog. You wouldn't even give me enough to eat."

Sarah not only ran the risk of being prosecuted for driving without a licence. She also feared for her life. She grabbed William's genitalia which

L

caused him to relax his grip. She slapped his face. "Who am I?" she shouted. He failed to answer. "I'm your girlfriend. I am not your father. I'm Sarah. Do you understand, now? I'm Sarah, and I'm taking you home."

He had come to his senses by the time Sarah guided him upstairs to his room. She undressed him and helped him into bed.

"Don't get a doctor out," he said.

"Are you sure you're feeling better?"

"Yes. Much better. Get in with me."

"Don't you think we ought to do something about your seeing a psychiatrist?"

"No. One day I'll take you to my father's house, 79 Harley Street. I'll be able to tell you everything, then and show you something you ought to see. So far, I've only told you half the story."

"What more is there to tell me?"

"There's one more thing. Something you ought to see. Information you need to know."

"About what?"

"About red."

"Red? You've mentioned that before. You told me never to wear red."

"I know."

"Did your father lock you in a red room, like in *Jane Eyre*?"

"No, nothing like that. It was something much

worse. That's why I often wear dark glasses. There are red things all over the place, bright red things."

"All right, all right. I don't want to hear anything else. There's no lecture until tomorrow afternoon. You will take me to your father's house in the morning, and you will show me whatever it is that's been troubling you like this."

Sarah brought him filtered coffee and bread and honey the next morning.

"We go, today," she said, sounding like someone in the WRENS.

"Very well. It will be painful, but it's something you need to know. I've got two keys, one to the front door, the other to the place I'll be taking you to."

"Yes, I'm sure you have. When you've finished breakfast, and had a few cigarettes, you will be getting up, showering, dressing and getting ready for us to go to Harley Street."

William went to the bathroom. He took three blue Valium pills (the stronger ones) and six amphetamines, unaware that the latter would fail to work, so soon after he had eaten. At least, the Valium gave him the strength to walk Sarah to the dented Jensen which had crashed into a few cars the night before.

They belted themselves in.

"What are all these dents doing on the

car?" he asked.

"Dents? Oh, they must have been caused by careless drivers when it was parked."

"I just can't tolerate this. This is a beautiful car. I've only had it for four weeks. When someone hits a car, they're supposed to leave a note of their name and address on the windscreen."

His anger, tetchily emanating from his horrifying childhood experiences, moved Sarah who wanted to take him on her knee and caress him.

"This is no time to get cross, dear. The dents aren't serious. We can get them evened out. Also, there are no scratches."

"I think the Valium's beginning to take effect, now," he said. "I feel easier about things, the dents, the drive, and, of course, the destination," he added in a lowered voice.

He drove up Park Lane, round Marble Arch, into the bottom of Wimpole Street and into Harley Street.

William drove a short distance down the street and parked his dented Jensen in a small, gravelly slipway outside number 79. He got out and went to the passenger side.

"Let me help you out, Sarah. You do look particularly pretty today, in your lovely white dress. I hope this business won't take long."

He embraced her and she felt his tears

on her cheek.

He opened the door with his latch key. He noted the time was 10.30 a.m. It was a Thursday, when his father would most likely be seeing patients.

"Come, Sarah, you won't feel anything. The things you'll hear and see will be a sort of exorcism. When it's over, provided you do a certain thing I tell you to do, I know I'll find complete peace and happiness, and so will you. Once we've qualified, I want to marry you, and you'll have beautiful, happy children. We'll go back to the Garden of Eden and will live in Paradise on earth. There'll be an end to the suffering, an end to the pain, very soon."

"What are you going to ask me to do? That particular thing, what will it be?"

"It will be a lovely and easy thing. It will take about five minutes?"

Sarah was both curious and bewildered.

"I don't feel like having sex on these premises," she announced assertively, her voice echoing, as she walked over the marble floor.

William was amused.

"You really must keep your voice down, Sarah! You've no idea who might be listening. No. It won't be sex."

They turned the corner to the secretary's tiny office. There was no-one there. William thought she might be on sick leave. Dolly was no-where in sight, either. She was two months' pregnant with Rowland's child, and had gone for a walk in Regent's Park, with a bag-full of bread crusts to feed the ducks.

"I've no idea where Father and Dolly are," said William. "I had an idea Father would be seeing patients this morning. Some of them may have cancelled, because of this germ going round. Come with me to the back-rooms, the rooms the family use. It's possible we'll find Father, there, reading."

He sensed Sarah's unease, and her unwillingness to meet Rowland.

"He won't hurt you because you're a woman," he said. "He's always had a roving eye for the ladies. My only fear is he might try to nick you, and I couldn't possibly allow that."

Sarah hurriedly sat down in an upright seventeenth century chair, behind the secretary's. It was the chair Rowland used when he dictated letters and reports.

Her face had turned white, as if she had either seen or felt a sense of evil, so extreme, it was not of this world.

"Oh, Sarah, whatever is the matter?"

"I'm psychic. I know something terrible is going to happen in here. This is a ghastly house. It does not like people."

"Don't you trust me? You've got me here with you, haven't you? Don't you feel safe with me?"

"Please can we leave?"

"Not until you've seen what you must see, and done what you must do. Once that's happened, we'll be as free as satiated gulls, soaring over the Dover Cliffs into the beautiful clear sky. Get up and take my arm."

"Help me!"

"I am helping you. Aren't you well?"

"No. I've suddenly become very depressed. I've never felt like this before, except when I was ten, and I saw my mother's dog being put to sleep. Please can we go?"

"I've got an idea," he said. "I've got a bottle of amphetamines in my pocket. You only need to take two. As you had no breakfast, they'll work very quickly and change you entirely. You'll be back to your old self. You'll feel wonderful, and the feeling will continue for the rest of the day."

"All right. I'll take them. I'd do anything to get out of this mood."

He gave her the two pills.

"Where can I wash them down?"

"Just go across the room. There's a cloakroom facing you.

"I'm not going in there alone, William."

He eased her to one of the basins and

turned on the tap.

"Their working time varies," he said. "I should think they'll work for you in about fifteen minutes. We'll go back and sit in the secretary's office until they do. You shall sit in the big, wooden chair, as you're the lady, and it's the special chair, i.e., the consultant's chair. I shall sit on the secretary's chair and stare at your beautiful legs."

She said nothing and rocked backwards and forwards.

"While we're waiting, I'll tell you a joke," said William. "There's nothing like humour to relax someone. A mental patient said to his psychiatrist 'Oh, God, I'm just racked by obsessions!' 'Are you indeed?' replied the psychiatrist. 'I'm obsessed by racks.'"

The amphetamines hit Sarah very suddenly. She didn't find the joke amusing, but let out a guffaw of relief because her intense psychological suffering had disappeared.

Neither she, nor William's other friends and acquaintances, were fully aware of his chronic, unlifting agony. He was normally jolly and laughing and charming on the surface. His eyes, which had seen so much pain, sparkled warmly and were capable, even, of deceiving a professional clairvoyant.

It was only his frequent use of alcohol and

amphetamines which allowed him short breaks from his incarceration in hell, where his soul soaked unwaveringly, in sulphuric acid.

There were few occasions when he enjoyed mild relief from his suffering. On "better", days, he felt like a lifer, surrounded by darkness, who had been given a treat, and allowed to look fleetingly through a hole at the blue sky outside the jail.

It was a joy for him to witness Sarah's immediate watershed of euphoria, as well as being a relief for him, not to have to pamper her when she was tough and high.

"You seem a lot better, already, after taking Mr D."

"Mr D?"

"The two amphetamines you took are known as Dexedrine, or, if you want it in full, Dexamphetamine Sulphate. I call it 'Mr D'. Others call it 'Speed'."

"How do you get it?"

"There are two ways. If you're a fool, you get it from the streets, where you have no idea how much you're buying, or, indeed, whether it's mixed with ground glass, powder, or anything else which could kill you.

"I get it from my doctor. He's known as a 'sporting doctor'."

"Is that because he's keen on sports?"

"No. It means he's prepared to dole out a bit of the jolly old recreational medication. He's understanding about the exhaustion and stress, people in the medical profession go through. His name's Dr Malcolm Killjoy. That's a funny name for a sporting doctor, isn't it?"

William continued to feel nauseated and sick of life, as he spoke to Sarah in this cosy, jolly manner. She failed to recognize his mood.

He took the bottle out of his pocket a second time and took a handful of Dexedrine, which he threw into his mouth, and chewed before swallowing. He knew he would have to wait in the surroundings which sickened and depressed him. He wanted to get through the procedure and take Sarah home.

"Time's getting on, Sarah," he said. "We've wasted time, hanging about, talking. Let's go through to the back rooms and find Father. I'm going to guess what he'll be reading. His preferred journals are *The Lancet*, *The British Medical Journal* or *The British Journal of Psychiatry*. I've got a feeling it will be the last of these. Father's always had an interest in public exhibitionism and an eclectic approach to its management. There's often coverage of it in that journal."

They were walking down a dark, narrow corridor. Its oak-panelled walls were scratched, and worm-ridden and radiated an atmosphere of psychological despair and decay of some years' duration.

Sarah was immune to it. Her fear, unease and edginess, had been drowned by the drug.

"That last journal, William, does it give graphic descriptions of masturbation?"

"For Christ's sake, keep your voice down! If Father's in the back room, he'll hear every word."

She remembered the tail end of a long poem she had been made to learn by heart in her teens, for giggling, during the playing of *The Stars and Stripes*. This was at a formal ceremony on the lawn of her father's house, when the Attorney General was visiting. She raised her voice theatrically.

> "*And his eyes have all the seeming of a demon that is dreaming...*"

"Do, please be quiet," said William. "I've asked you nicely."

William knocked on a heavy oak door but got no answer.

"Father," he called.

There was still no answer so he opened the door and beckoned Sarah in.

Rowland was not reading. He was lying on a bolstered Empire sofa, with his head tilted over its

163

back, facing the ceiling. His cheeks were an unhealthy shade of purple. An empty whisky bottle was lying near him on the floor.

William was ashamed and nauseated. Not once in his life, had he been able to let his right hand know what his left hand was doing.

He felt that Sarah's presence in the company of a member of his family, would help him overcome this handicap. Had Rowland been alert and studying, he hoped, with uncharacteristic optimism, that a goal might have been reached, once father and mistress had shaken hands.

Sarah recognized his thoughts and his pain. Although the pills had made her disinhibited, she remained thoughtful and intuitive, contrasting with her exhibitionism in the corridor.

The drug made her reach out to William, and she knew that the only way she could break through his misery, would be through the use of outlandish humour, which would fly straight into the eye of his neurosis, like the splitting of an atom.

She gave an exaggerated imitation of Scarlett O'Hara's voice.

"Why, fiddle-de-dee and great balls of fire! If that ain't ya cute old, apple-cheeked, cotton-pickin' Pappa! 'Aint he just the itssiest, bitsiest, darlingest Harley Street shrinki-winky you ever did see?"

Rowland was too intoxicated to know who his

164

visitors were but he heard some of their words. He drawled senselessly in his stupor.

"Wake up, Dolly! Are these patients? Someone's been reciting poetry. Sort it out, will you. I'll be awake in a minute. There's an American here, somewhere, isn't there?"

"Let's get out of here," said William. "That joke of yours came in the right place at the right time. It's made me stronger. Come on, I'm taking you up, now. It will soon be over, for both of us."

"Where are we going?"

"Right up to the top of the house."

He put his arm round her shoulder and guided her to the steep steps which led to the door of the nursery wing.

He unlocked the door. He took Sarah up another flight of steps, covered, like the narrow corridor's floor, in linoleum.

Sarah was still immune to fear but her intellect was razor-sharp. She could smell and feel the waves of concentrated evil, pressing in on her, without daunting or nauseating her.

"Are you all right?" he asked.

"Thanks to Mr D. I'm not scared, but I can feel something very nasty."

He guided her to the bedroom, with twin beds, one used by his nanny, the other, his own.

"I'm sorry, Sarah. I'm so worn out, I feel I'm

about to die. I'll lie down on the bed I used to sleep in. I can't take you to the other room until Mr D. kicks in. He's bloody slow, today. It's the bread and honey which held him up, blast it!"

William lay on the bed, his feet side by side, his left arm crossing his chest, like a corpse. He chain-smoked with his right hand. Sarah knelt in front of him, feeling like a priest, taking Last Rites.

"It won't be long, now, Sarah."

His eyes flooded with tears which rolled down his cheeks, unchecked.

"Do you believe in a Supreme Being?" she asked, suddenly.

"No."

He undid the top two buttons of his shirt and loosened his tie.

"Take my cock," he said...

They lay on their backs. He was smiling. It was not his auto-pilot smile, but a radiant smile of unsuppressed joy.

"Mr D.'s kicked in," he said. "There's a basin in the corner if you want to clean up. Don't take too long. We've still got the worst ahead of us, before the best."

They dressed and went into the corridor, with their arms round each other's waists. The door leading to the room William wished to show Sarah, was at the end of the corridor on the left. He tightened his grasp round her waist, as he turned the handle of the door. A strange, high-pitched rasp, startling Sarah, came into his voice. "See Nanny! See Nanny!"

He thought at first the door was locked and that he might have to force it open. It was only stiff and didn't take long to give way under his weight.

The cold, damp room had not been cleaned for many years. The green carpet was dusty and the ceilings covered with cobwebs. A fire no longer blazed in the grate, as it had before the nanny died. The television, which had shown the Remembrance Sunday parade, the last thing she saw before her death, was covered with half an inch of dust.

William tried to turn the set on. It was out of use because of the damp and the passage of time.

The only features of the room devoid of its gaping sadness, were two large windows, covering the wall behind the table. The sun shone straight through them, lighting the room.

Sarah's Dexedrine had reached its highest peak by now. She felt she was in Heaven, but behind her happiness, was the suspicion that it's vaults would suddenly give way beneath her. This was because the evil in this room, more pronounced than any other room in the house, was breathing against her face, hair and skin, in its sinister attempt to break through the Dexedrine.

She was determined to do whatever William wished, before it wore off, and hurriedly tried to humour him with another of her, somewhat unfunny, Southern Belle jokes.

"Gee, William, isn't this just the sweetest, dinkiest room you ever did see?"

This time, the tanked-up, tormented godless desperado thought the joke was hilarious. He banged his fist on the table and cackled like a hyena giving birth.

She felt cold, low-spirited and frightened once more.

"I'm not feeling so good, now, William. Can we get it over with?"

"Yes. We'll start, now. I told you it wouldn't take long, provided you do exactly as I say."

He opened the cupboard and took out the bright, red balls of wool and knitting needles.

"Look, Sarah. They're bright red. They're beautiful. The trouble is, I can't bear to look at bright red things, anywhere but this room, hence my need to wear dark glasses all the time. They make me see a darker red. That doesn't bother me. I can only enjoy the full, radiant colour, in this room, because this is my Room of Love."

"*I* love you, William."

"I know you do. But this is so deep-rooted. Sometimes, when things are bad, I let myself into the house and come up to this room, and I hold these balls of wool. They comfort me because they were the ones my nanny was using the day she died. I feel her in here, now. I come and talk to her, sometimes. I know she's here, although I can't see her."

"Why can't you take the wool away? I'm sure your nanny's spirit would come with you as well, that is, whenever you get out the wool. If you kept it with you, surely you wouldn't go off your head, and start screaming your head off during films about the Krays."

"That was because the blood was bright red. I hadn't brought my sun-glasses. I can tolerate dark red. It's only bright red which tortures me."

"William, don't use the glasses, bring the wool, and your nanny's love with it!"

"It's not so simple. Although I know she's in this room, I would sometimes like to be able to see her, sitting in the green armchair in the corner, knitting."

"If you really tried, you could make her *appear* before you."

"Oh, Sarah, I've tried! I've tried!"

"There must be a way round this."

A strange expression came into William's eyes. His Dexedrine was still working.

"There is, Sarah. That's what made me bring

M

you here, because you're the epitome of everything on earth that's good."

"What *can* I do, William? I'd do anything to make you happier."

William's voice took on a bizarre, commanding tone.

"Take the wool, Sarah."

She did as she was told.

"There are two other things I want you to take from the cupboard."

"All right."

"First, there's a grey wig."

"Wig," said Sarah, slapping it into William's hands, like a surgeon's assistant.

"There's also a plastic apron, with the words 'I love William' embroidered on it."

Sarah repeated the procedure, struggling to shake off her gloom.

"Apron," she said, still in operating theatre mode.

"I want you to coil your hair on top of your head and pull the wig down over it. After that, I want you to put the apron on. Then you must take up one of the balls of wool and knitting needles. Go over to the chair and sit in it. That's all I want you to do, just to help me find sanity. I'll come and sit at your feet and rest my head against your legs."

Sarah stood motionless and burst into tears.

"Whatever's the matter? I don't want to see you crying," said William.

"William, please try to understand! I love you, but that doesn't mean I have to do everything you say."

"What do you mean?"

"I'm so very sorry. I just can't do what you've asked me to do."

"Why, Sarah? It would mean so much to me."

"I can't! What you are asking of me is neither healthy, nor normal. It's unwholesome. Besides, you'd be sitting at my feet, believing I was someone else, someone now dead. It's as if I didn't have any identity. If you want me to go on loving you, you must know me as Sarah. It's rather hurtful of you to wish to turn me into a dead woman from the past.

"I know how much you loved her, but she is dead. The least I can expect of you is that you love me more than any other woman."

"Oh, Sarah, I wish it could be as simple as that. Of course, I love you more than anyone else, but all I want is to get rid of my insanity. So far, this seems the only way. I promise I won't ask you twice. Please, Sarah? I shouldn't have to go down on my knees and beg you.

"If you refused, I know something ghastly would happen to us both. If you complied, I would be cured and you would be happy."

171

"Well, I do refuse," she said, suddenly angry. "And nothing ghastly will happen to either of us."

Without warning, he put his hands round her neck as he had in the underground carpark.

"What the hell are you doing, William?"

"You really have *got* to do as I say. Say you will, and I'll forget your treacherous, cruel behaviour."

"Will you take your hands away? When have I been cruel or treacherous?"

He did so. "I've something to tell you, William?" she said. Her voice remained steadied by the drug, although its general effect had worn off. It was temporary stupidity, rather than courage, which caused her words to be overtly candid.

"I'm afraid I'm going to have to leave you, William, for the sake of my personal safety. Please take me back to your house, so that I can pack my belongings and go back to the place where I used to live."

His hands went to her throat, once more.

"I can't have you leaving me, Sarah. I'd rather have you dead, than free to be taken by another man. I have no choice but to kill you. That way, I can come up here and see you and Nanny together as one.

She widened her mouth, about to scream for help.

"No one will hear you at the top of the house," said William.

As he spoke, he tightened his grip on her throat, while her eyes protruded from their sockets, making her look ugly. Within a few minutes, she was dead.

William let her body fall to the floor, and rolled it into a ball. He tied her arms and made them hug her bent legs, with some thick, coarse string from the cupboard he kept the wool in.

He was in a trance and his mind and actions were divided, as if his brain had been cut in half. He dragged the body to the corner of the room and pushed it into the small alcove behind his nanny's chair. He pulled the chair closer to the alcove. He retrieved Sarah's handbag from the bedroom and threw it into the alcove as well. Once he had done these things, it was as if a light in his mind had been turned out.

His thoughts were now centred entirely on the lecture he would be attending that afternoon. Another lecturer, Professor Thompson, would be addressing his students on kidney function. He suddenly became tired. He sat at the table with his head in his hands, thinking about kidneys and the phenomenal boringness of renal medicine.

He heard slow, laboured footsteps in the corridor, coming closer and closer to the nursery. They were those of his father.

"Hullo, William," said Rowland affably. "I had some idea I'd find you up here. Dolly and the cook have often witnessed your regular little pilgrimages to the nursery."

"It's nice to see you again, Father." William was devoid of fear and tension because, at that moment, his mind had temporarily erased his deed. "How did you know I was up here?"

"I was having a rest downstairs. I haven't got any patients this morning. I was too sleepy to make an effort to say 'hullo' to you. I heard two voices. One was yours. The other's was a young lady's. American accent, I seem to recall. So you've got a sweetheart, I see."

William's mind was still preoccupied with the lecture he would be attending on renal function. He had no memory of his bringing Sarah to the house.

"Oh, she's one of my girlfriends," he said.

"One of them, eh, you cheeky bugger? I hope you haven't broken the American lady's heart."

"Not at all, Father, just her neck. Whoops! Just one of my little jokes, Father. She's secure enough in mind. She knows I like her more than the others."

"Her stay in the house was pretty short-lived. Did you throw her out or something?"

"No. She wanted to go. She said she wanted to get some shopping over and done with."

174

"Have neither of you got any work to do?"

"There aren't any lectures this morning. I'm going to the one at 2.00 this afternoon."

"What is it on?"

"Kidney function and causes of renal failure."

"Who's giving it?"

"Dr Thompson. He's the consultant in renal medicine at the Hammersmith."

"Not Dr Ben Thompson, is it?"

"That's right. Do you know him?"

"Yes. Not very well. I had to send one of my lithium patients to him. A lady patient. Saw him privately. She took an immediate dislike to him. In fact, she was adamant in her expression of hatred towards him. She said he was cold, disinterested and unsympathetic. He didn't even bother to follow her up after her first consultation."

"I'd be interested to know if it's the same man," said William. "Have you ever seen him face to face?"

"I have indeed. I often bump into him at the Royal Society of Medicine."

"What does he look like, Father?"

"He's about five foot, ten inches tall. He wears a toupée. From the front, he looks like a weather-beaten old bulldog. He has a permanent, disfiguring rash on his cheeks which makes him look as if he's had a skin graft. He wears inelegant glasses, jammed onto his face and most of his teeth are missing. That doesn't matter, though, because he never smiles. He reminds me of the leading necrophiliac in the film, *The Texas Chainsaw Massacre*." He speaks with the breathy intonation that Marilyn Monroe might have had, had she had a sex change operation. Over all, he's pretty common."

William laughed. His father's entire personality had changed since his marriage to Dolly. His former loathing for his son had gradually turned to paternal affection, and finally to guilt-infested love."

"I like your description, Father. You've got a way with words, particularly towards those you dislike. Perhaps you should have been a writer."

"I wouldn't have the patience for that. That kind of occupation would be much too arduous for me. Once I pick up a pen, I find it difficult to write things down, except prescriptions."

William was silent. He thought deeply about the extraordinary metamorphosis in his father's behaviour towards him. He remembered the beatings, the bullying, the crushing jibes, the near starvation and the cruelty he had had to suffer from his hands as a child.

He wondered whether his backward, mentally-handicapped mother, with her disconcerting facial

176

twitch, had caused him to vent his misery on his helpless son. A short wave of bitterness and resentment surged through his mind.

Then, he remembered his father's peace of mind and contentment, beginning after his second marriage. Dolly had mellowed him beyond recognition. They had all their meals with William. Rowland was often talkative, pleasant and uncharacteristically full of life and laughter.

He never failed to draw his adolescent son into the conversation and made his growing feelings of affection increasingly more apparent. Although he indulged in heavy drinking, the habit improved the genial tone of his conversation and installed a new gentleness within him.

William understood his father's former unhappiness. He, too, resented his mother's lack of vanity and her inability to perform as a mother.

He watched his father, sitting on the other side of the table, smiling, as if proud of his clever, industrious son. He felt confused by the two conflicting modes of behaviour, but was inundated with the love of the older man.

Some disturbed and unpleasant thoughts passed through his mind as he thought of Sarah. He wondered where she was, and instinctively knew that she had been exposed to danger. He had no idea that he had murdered her, but he longed to find her and make sure that no harm had come to her.

Rowland looked at the two balls of bright red wool on the table.

"You haven't taken up knitting, have you, by any chance, my boy? Be sure never to do that in front of a woman. She'd think you were the most awful sissy!"

The young man knew his mind was struggling to overcome something unpleasant. He was even more concerned by the fact that he did not fully understand the contents of his head. He was frightened. Suddenly, he burst into tears.

"Why, William, old fellow, whatever is the matter?"

"I don't know, Father. I'm confused and frightened but I don't know why."

"Nothing I said just now, eh? Are you hurt because I said women would be likely to think that men who knitted were sissies?"

"No, Father."

"It's your favourite girlfriend, isn't it? The American lady. Is it something she said to you?"

"It's something to do with her but it isn't anything she said to me."

"She's been going with other young men? Is that it? I'm not a consultant psychiatrist for nothing."

"No. It's not that, either. I can't remember when I last saw her. I feel something may have happened to her."

"I can tell you when you were both together. It was an hour or two ago. You came to see me when I was resting. In my semi-conscious state, I heard her being extremely impertinent to me. She had a Northern American voice, but she said something decidedly rude in an improvised accent of the deep South. She's been in this house, all right. She probably told you she was going off to catch up on things, and left, but you were too distracted to listen. I'm sure you didn't bring her up here. This room is sacred to you. You only come here in private."

"I don't know. My mind's gone blank. Perhaps, I've got a brain tumour."

"Don't be so damned silly! You were so preoccupied with your renal lecture, you got absent-minded. It's possible you didn't even have the courtesy to kiss her goodbye."

The son looked at the father and the father looked at the son. The father was also becoming tearful and broke the silence.

"William, my boy?" he began.

"Father?"

"Let's both go and sit in the green armchair in the corner, where you and Nanny used to sit."

William suddenly recalled Philip, the paedophile he had met in Soho as a child. He remembered his

179

own words, "Please don't touch me, sir," as vividly as if the incident had occurred recently. Part of him yearned for the love his father had denied him in childhood. The other part was revolted by the threat of close physical association with anyone other than a woman.

He forced himself to accept close proximity to his father, since, he reasoned, a father's love was right and proper and a paedophile's was not.

"All right, Father," he said, after some thought.

The chair was only just wide enough to hold the two grown men. An onlooker would have found their appearance bizarre and comical.

The father put his arms round the son's waist. The son deeply regretted the fact that he had been born British, and hence considered it a form of indecent exposure to show emotion, and even more obscene to have physical contact which was not sexual in nature. His entire body was taut in his father's arms, like that of a cat sensing danger.

"Try to relax a bit, my boy," said Rowland. "I know it's hard for you. We, British, despise intimacy, but even so, I can't do any work on your demented psyche, unless you let yourself go."

William tried to relax his muscles as best he could. He felt sleepy. He was addicted to Dexedrine and longed for more.

"I don't know how to say this," began Rowland.

"I will never forgive myself, as long as I live, for the things I did to you when you were little. I don't think I was fully normal when I was doing these things. My mind was so severely disturbed that I failed to recognize the difference between kindness and cruelty. As opposites, they are closer to each other than is imagined."

Rowland was puzzled by the unexpected improvement in his memory and intellectual faculties. During his previous conversation with his son, his mind had been muddled and confused, due to an excessive alcohol intake. Although he had had a lot to drink before visiting his son on the day of his lecture, his intake had been less, and he was pleasantly surprised by his mental alacrity.

He continued, "I wanted to make you tough and resilient. The more brutally I punished you, the more I wanted you to become completely invulnerable. I wanted you to be like me, strong, ruthless and heartless, incapable of humiliation, fear and pain.

"It was always my wish that you train to be a doctor because medicine is the noblest profession of all. It is also the toughest and most competitive profession, perhaps short of being in the Marines or the French Foreign Legion."

Rowland felt out of breath. He paused before talking, once more.

"I punished you on occasions when you didn't deserve it. I never wanted you to think chastisement was unfair. I just wanted you to become immune to it.

"That time when your teacher had asked you to learn *The Walrus and the Carpenter*, and you had worked on your jigsaw puzzle instead, the punishment I inflicted was gravely disproportionate to the crime. I wanted you to have a hide of solid iron, so that no-one would be able to hurt you in adulthood.

"When I came to this room to hurt you, I wanted your sweet, innocent face to haunt and injure me for the rest of my days.

"I hated your mother, William, not because she was wicked, which she was not, but because she had neither vanity, femininity, wit, nor guts. I lived in fear that you would inherit her pathetic genes. I had to make you immune, and at the same time, to make myself suffer because I hated myself so much."

"Why did you hate yourself, Father?" asked William, who was on the verge of drifting into a secure, comfortable sleep, radiantly safe with the knowledge that his father loved him so dearly.

"I think you know this, already," said Rowland. "When I was nineteen, my sister, Kate, died of pneumonia at the age of fourteen. I adored that girl, and I believe I still do. I was very angry about her death, and it took me a considerable time, longer than the norm, to recover from it. I hated myself for not being able to contain my sorrow. I thought it was unmanly and unnatural to grieve for more than a year. I couldn't stop thinking about her, though. I even dreamed about her. How repulsively effete my attitude was for all those years!"

"But it's only natural for a brother to love a sister, Father."

"Not the way I did, my boy. I didn't take her death the way a strong person would. The grief was so bad that it twisted my brain. I hurt your mother, but that was easy, as she was a puddingy lump, such an obscene freak of nature. It wasn't easy to hurt you, William. I used to cry, once I'd left the nursery wing. I couldn't bear what I was doing, and it was because I couldn't bear it, that I went on doing it."

Although Dexedrine withdrawal is reputedly unpleasant, the drowsiness that it entails, had a peculiarly comforting effect on William.

"Do you remember Remembrance Sunday, Father? Do you remember leaving me alone with Nanny after she died? Do you remember locking me up in the nursery wing? Do you remember feeding me with next to nothing?"

Rowland wanted to sob openly and howl like a

lost wolf. It was his Britishness which prevented him from doing so, and it was his shame of his nationality which intensified his guilt.

"Of course, I remember those events, William. A lot of the trouble started when I discovered your passion for things which were red. I took them away from you, to deprive you of what you loved most.

"Your suffering was horrendous, but mine was even worse. My sister, Kate, had a passion for red. It was her favourite colour. Your love for it reminded me of her even more, when I wanted to forget her.

"I half wanted Nanny to die. I could tell that she was frail and that her health would suffer if I drove her away from you. I felt you needed a serious bereavement at your young age, to make you immune to loss for the rest of your life.

"I think I've said it all, now. I've certainly tried. Do you feel you can forgive me?"

By now, the two men had lost control of themselves and were weeping like a pair of premenstrual housemaids. William was the first to break the unnervingly long silence.

"Of course, I forgive you, Father. I'm not vindictive, and never have been. Your confession has taken a weight off me. I had no idea how much you cared for me. It's your confession which has

184

given me strength, though, not your cruelty when I was small. When I have children, I'll bring them up differently. It is love which gives strength, not unkindness, but I accept you were misguided, and at that time of your life your vision was distorted."

Rowland was startled by a knock coming from behind the chair. It was as if someone had kicked the chair.

"Did you notice that, William?" He sounded alarmed.

"Notice what, Father?"

"Something banged against the back of the chair just then."

"Are you sure? I'll go and have a look."

William went to the back of the chair, pushed against the alcove.

"Whatever it is, it's in the alcove, Father. You'll have to get up so that I can move the chair."

Rowland rose to his feet and stood behind his son."

"Maybe, it's rats," he said.

William pushed the chair forward. The weight of Sarah's trussed-up body, had been too heavy for the string which bound her. She was lying flat on her back, with one of her shoes loosened.

"I say, there's a dead woman in here," remarked Rowland, mildly.

The sight of Sarah's body strangely dispelled

185

William's fears about her safety. His gradual awareness of what he had done, soothed him by providing him with the knowledge that Sarah was indeed safe. Even in death, she was permanently available for him.

"Looks like it, doesn't it, Father?" he said after a pause. He realized he had murdered her because she had refused to dress up as the nanny, and sit in the armchair, knitting.

"How the hell did she get up here?" asked Rowland.

"Oh, I brought her up here with me," said William, casually. "I needed a real life replacement for Nanny. I asked her to put on a grey wig and apron, and sit here, knitting."

"*Knitting*?" exclaimed Rowland. "Before you told her to sit here, knitting, did you do anything else to her or ask any favours of her?"

"Yes. I lay down on the bed next door and I asked her to take my cock."

"Can we really not manage without that vulgar word?" said Rowland. "Anything else?"

William almost felt like flirting with his father, who had become a heroic, God-like figure to him. He looked him coquettishly in the eye, with intent to shock him.

"Yes. Once I got hard, I fucked her."

Rowland cleared his throat in an exaggerated,

186

theatrical manner.

"Oh, William, we are two, respectable well-brought-up men from illustrious backgrounds! Could you please take a grip on yourself, and refrain from the use of such utterly disgusting language. Kindly explain yourself, again, in a civilized and salubrious manner."

"I'm sorry. What I meant to say was, once I had become physically roused, I had sexual intercourse with her."

"Good. Those words sound infinitely more acceptable. Let's get back to the knitting. Did she do what you so curiously asked her to?"

"No, she didn't. That's where the trouble started. I killed her because she refused to do what I wanted her to."

"Good Lord! Have you done this to any other women?"

"No, Father. Just this one."

"Do you intend to continue this practice?"

"I do hope not, Father. Dead bodies are such dreadful commodities."

"I don't quite understand when you say you hope not. What I want to know is, is this likely to happen up here, again? You must remember that I am a respectable Harley Street psychiatrist. I'm most averse to having a mortuary on my premises. I do have a reputation to keep up in this street."

"Well, I understand, Father."

"Who was this woman, anyway?

"Her name was Sarah."

"Sarah who?"

"I can't remember her surname, to tell you the truth. She was American."

"You really are an eccentric boy!"

"I suppose I am, Father."

"Has she got friends or relations in England?"

"All her relatives are in North Dakota. That's in the northern part of America."

"I haven't just fallen off a lorry!" barked Rowland. "Even I know where North Dakota is. Is she the woman who was so damned impertinent while I was resting? She was insolent enough to call me the 'itssiest, bitsiest, darlingest Harley Street shrinki-winky'. That was her, wasn't it?"

"Yes, Father."

"She must have had some friends in England."

"She was training at the Hammersmith with me. She had no real friends that I know of. Just another lover. She didn't see him any more, not after I started taking her out."

"I see. You bumped him off, too, did you?"

"No, I didn't do that, Father." He paused. "Oh, he's a Communist," he added, nonsensically.

"Are you sure she has no-one, who is likely to ask where she is?"

"Pretty sure."

Rowland took his pipe from his pocket and lit it. He walked across the room, and back again to the armchair.

"There's only one way to deal with this problem, William."

"Oh?"

"There's no way either of us can afford to be seen, carrying a dead body from a smart Harley Street residence, and slinging it into the boot of a car."

"No, indeed, Father."

"All we can do is leave her here to rot and be sure the nursery wing is kept locked at all times. I'm the only person, apart from you, who has a key. Even Dolly hasn't got one."

"That seems the best solution," said William, now bored with the situation.

"Are you coming up here, again?"

"Yes. Certainly in the immediate future, for my own purposes."

"For what purposes?"

"Necrophilia, Father."

Rowland sat in the armchair, once more and inhaled the smoke from his pipe.

"In a way, I'm pleased about this business," he said.

"Why?"

189

"Because at last, I've been properly punished for my crimes against you as a child. I'm responsible for what you've turned out to be, and I'm therefore going to cover up for you. I do not intend to call the police. Nor, indeed, do I intend to discuss this matter with anyone else, not even Dolly."

"That's damned sporting of you, Father."

"My poor, poor little schizophrenic boy! I'm the only person in the world you can talk to, now. I will always be here for you."

Rowland got up. The two raving madmen embraced, and made fleeting eye contact, which strengthened the new bond between them.

"A sane person cannot help a madman," said the psychiatrist. "Only another madman can."

The father and son walked downstairs. Rowland's patient had just arrived. William wandered absent-mindedly into the waiting room, where an elderly couple and two lean homosexuals, were sitting. The younger men were talking intimately in whispers. The leanest of the pair had been reading *Crime and Punishment*, one of William's favourite books. He had left the book open on the arm of his stiff, wooden chair.

William felt temporarily exorcized. It was as if his guilt for Sarah's murder, had been so extensively unloaded on to his father, that he was again unaware of what had happened to her. He had a vague notion that she would be there for him, although he knew that she had mysteriously gone "missing", and he had no recollection of her having visited the house. He was filled with hope that he would find her again.

His symptoms of Dexedrine withdrawal, still troubled him, but he had enough of the drug in his system to keep his spirits artificially raised.

A glowing ray of autumn sun shone through the window, into the waiting room. The homosexual had picked up his book once more. He was too vain to wear glasses and used a magnifying glass, mouthing the words intently as he read them.

William went up to him and sat aggressively astride him. The homosexual thought he was going to make a pass at him.

"I say, when you read that book, do you ever get fantasies about being buggered by Raskolnikov on the floor of his garret?" shouted William.

He felt disappointed when the man ignored him.

He went out into the street and hailed a taxi. He had suddenly become so disturbed by Sarah's disappearance that he decided to go to the police in person.

He walked out into the middle of the street, waving his arms in the air like a cuckolded Frenchman. A taxi-driver screeched to a halt and rammed his front wheel onto the pavement.

"No common sense! It's all the same with them bloody doctors. Where to?"

"Marylebone Police Station," said William, urgently.

"Can't you walk that distance? It's only the other side of Cavendish Square."

"That's too far for me to walk. I'm not up to it."

"Oh? Are you feeling sick?"

"No!"

"I say that, because if you are sick, I'll be off the road for two days."

"I'm not going to be sick!"

William took out his mobile telephone. Now that he had developed a strong love for his father, he became morbidly and illogically afraid of losing him. He wanted to be assured that his father was all right, and not strained enough after their intimate conversation, to have a heart attack.

He leant forward, pulled up the aerial and dialled his father's secretary's number. It was engaged. William became paranoid due to the Dexedrine withdrawal. He panicked because he assumed automatically that his father had been taken ill and that his secretary was calling for an ambulance.

He dialled the number again. This time, it rang once and stopped because the signal was poor. The

Dexedrine withdrawal had reached such a high peak that he was having palpitations.

He emptied another handful of the pills into the palm of his hand. He chewed them up and swallowed them.

"Pull into the side, driver!" he shouted.

"All right, all right. Keep your hair on, Guv'nor."

He got out of the taxi and onto the pavement.

"Hey! You haven't paid me. The fare's two pounds fifty."

"I'm coming back in. I'm trying to get a signal on my mobile!" shouted William. "Have you got a mobile 'phone I can use?"

"No. Are you getting back in, or aren't you?"

"I'll get back in when I've got a signal. I've got to make sure my father's all right. I've become so attached to him, now. That is to say, after I made my confession. I told him the most dreadful things — things I wouldn't repeat to a living soul!" he shouted, thinking he was speaking normally. "He means everything in the world to me." He did not care what the taxi driver thought of his eccentricity.

He banged on the window, "What about you?" he shouted. "Do you think my father's all right? Do you think he may have been taken ill?"

"How the fucking hell should I know?"

The driver was particularly bad-tempered

because he realized that his right front tyre had been punctured when he hit the curb to avoid William. He found his passenger's behaviour hysterical and irritating.

He engaged first gear and began to move slowly down the congested street.

"You can't just go off and leave me like this!" bellowed William. "Why are you persecuting me? What have I done to you?"

The driver put his foot on the brake and locked the doors with an automatic device. He looked at William in his mirror, and noticed that he was sweating profusely and had an insane glint in his eyes.

"I hope I never have to drive you again. You're a certified, bleeding basket case!" shouted the driver.

William walked the rest of the way to the police station. The extra dose of Dexedrine had had a calming effect on him. The withdrawal symptoms had disappeared. He was able to speak calmly and lucidly to the police, although he ran into difficulty when he described Sarah as his "girlfriend", without knowing her surname.

"Do you usually sleep with women without knowing their surnames?" asked one of the police officers.

William started shouting again, without

his knowledge.

"Nearly all the time. I need women. I get nightmares, if I have to go for as long as twenty-four hours without one. Surnames are not important to me, and never have been in any relationship, as long as I can keep my cock on the move."

"In that case, sir, there's nothing we can do to help you."

"I'm terribly upset," said William.

"Why?"

"Because a taxi driver called me a 'certified bleeding basket case'."

"I'd be prepared to call that an understatement," said the police officer.

William arrived fifteen minutes late for Dr Ben Thompson's lecture on kidney function. The lecture hall was almost empty, because Thompson's strange, breathy voice had a nauseating effect on many of his students. He was wearing a white coat two sizes too small for him, and looked ridiculous.

William entered the room, looking harassed and flustered.

"Nice of you to drop in, Mr Rendon."

"I'm so sorry I'm late. I was with my girl-friend. She disappeared and I couldn't find her," said William, genuinely believing he was telling the truth.

"I dare say she's fed up because you're always late when you take her out. Perhaps, she considers that rude."

"I got held up. I was able to have a long talk with Father. Then, there was the problem with congested roads. I did all I could to weave the Jensen in and out of the traffic."

William's verbose delivery of unsolicited information, and interruption of his lecture irritated Thompson.

"I'm not interested in why you're late!" he shouted. "Sit down and shut up!"

"Perhaps I should run a smaller car. A Jensen can be murder in traffic."

"I don't want to hear another word about your blasted, bloody Jensen!" rasped Thompson. "With your kind permission, I'd like to continue my lecture."

The students left the room when the lecture was over. Thompson's tedious intonation had made them sleepy.

"Mr Rendon? called Thompson.

"Sir?"

"Have you any comments about my lecture?"

"Yes. Perhaps you mentioned this before I came in. If you did not, you should have covered the ways in which certain drugs can have a harmful effect on renal function, Lithium, for instance."

Thompson was startled by the young man's impertinence. "That has not made me any the wiser," he said.

"The wiser, I dare say not. Only better informed."

Though more intelligent than his contemporaries, William was neglectful of his studies. His thoughts were centred on women, and his new, almost sacred attachment to his father.

It was a Sunday morning, ten days after Sarah's death. He was due to have lunch with his father and stepmother. He let himself in to number 79 Harley Street, and found Rowland and Dolly sitting in the back room. Rowland was reading a medical journal, and Dolly was working on some tapestry, depicting a gruesome Hogarth drawing of a surgeon experimenting on a conscious patient.

"Hullo, my boy!" said Rowland.

"Hullo, Father. I'm relieved to see you looking so well. Hullo, Dolly. Your tapestry is most appropriate for a medical household."

"How are you keeping, William?" she said. "I hope all the pretty girls aren't distracting you from your studies."

"No, of course not."

"Don't believe a word of it, Dolly," said Rowland. "Can I have a word with you in private, outside in the hall?"

"Of course, Father."

The two men went over to the area, occupied by the secretary during the week.

"I'm most anxious to know what the situation is in relation to your women," said Rowland.

William invariably remembered his murdering side when with his father.

"At the moment, I'm having a different woman every night. If I don't, I feel really peculiar. I go with prostitutes most of the time. It's only women I fall in love with, whom I bring to the nursery wing, if that's what you're worried about."

"For God's sake, boy, have you been taking any others up there, since you and I had that long conversation?"

"I haven't brought any of them up, since. Well, I don't think I have. I'm trying to discipline myself not to take a woman I love, up there."

"Or a woman you don't love, either, I hope?"

"I will try so very hard not to, Father."

"I say that, because if you kill another woman up there, and I find out, I'll have to cement in the door leading to the nursery wing."

William felt a brief surge of anger towards his father. He resented Rowland's threat to deprive him of access to the Room of Love, where he could look at bright red things, without pain. He remembered the occasion when his father had smashed the red rattle he had so loved. He turned to Rowland.

"'*The sun was shining on the sea*', Father! Do you remember that? The first line of *The Walrus and the Carpenter*?"

"There's no need to shout," said Rowland. "That was one occasion which caused me so much shame and guilt, that my feelings surpassed the terrible physical pain I inflicted on you. However much I say 'sorry' to you, my boy, I don't think all the 'sorries' in the world will ever wash my crimes from my hands."

There was a pause. Rowland put more tobacco into his pipe and lit it. William pulled heavily on his *Benson and Hedges* cigarette.

"I feel we need to address the subject of your women, once more," said Rowland.

"What about them?"

"I don't quite understand why you need to have a woman every single night. Why should this be necessary? Not even the most sexually obsessed man in the world would require one every night. Are there any nights when you can do without?"

"No. I need the sex act and the climax at least

once a night. It relieves all my tension."

Rowland tapped his pipe on the edge of his secretary's computer keys.

"What the blazes are you going to do, if you catch a socking good venereal disease, or even AIDS?" he asked.

"I use a condom, Father."

"Good lad!"

Rowland sat down on the secretary's swivel chair. Until then, the two men had been standing.

"We need to talk quite seriously about the problems we both encounter, when you are tempted to take women to the nursery. I'm under the impression that you really can't control yourself, when a woman refuses to comply with your bizarre requests, regarding, well, knitting, wool and all that sort of thing.

"I go up there at least once a day to check that you haven't left a body up there, since the day you killed Sarah, the American. When I went up this morning, I was relieved to see that hers was the only body in the room.

"I live in terror that you are going to indulge repeatedly in this hobby, each time being unable to control yourself. Although I stay awake at night, worrying about you, I can't see a solution, other than cementing the door to the nursery wing."

"Oh, Father, you couldn't possibly do that! You

told me you'd only do that, if you found another body there. You can't block my path to my Room of Love."

Rowland got up, walked across the hall and back to the secretary's area.

"I just don't think I can tolerate the idea of one murder after another being committed in my house," he said. "If the police found out, this whole business would be splashed all over *The News of the World*. It really would create a most squalid impression. Not only that, I would be accused of being an accessory to the fact that this has been going on.

"If you get into this situation again, which I fear you will, because of the mental illness my cruelty has caused you, perhaps I can suggest a different plan.

"Say, you take a woman up there, and you love her, and she refuses to do what you want. I'd prefer it if you took her away and murdered her in your own house. That way, I would not be involved.

"If I were to be thrown into Wormwood Scrubs, it wouldn't be fair on Dolly, and certainly not on my patients who are totally dependent on me."

William considered his father's words.

"The trouble is, I don't even know I'm doing it, Father," he said. "One moment, I hear her say she refuses to do what I want. The next moment, I find

201

her dead on the floor. Then I hide her body and my mind goes blank."

"You know you have schizophrenia, don't you?"

"Do I? When things get out of hand, something in my head shuts down. My memory goes. Once I leave this house, I feel as if I've just woken up. I didn't remember taking Sarah to the nursery. All I knew was that she'd gone away. I think I may have been up there again since our conversation, but I must have been alone."

"How do you know you were alone?"

"Because you said you'd only found one body up there. Had I taken a woman, who refused to co-operate, I'd have killed her, and you would have found her. It's possible I may have taken someone there and she might have complied, which would have meant she'd walked away, free."

"Can you remember any of your visits since we talked?" asked Rowland.

"Now that I'm with you, I can remember things better. I think I went there once or twice."

"Did you occupy yourself in any way, or did you just sit there, staring into space?"

"No," said William, quietly. "I went to Sarah."

Rowland was more traumatized than his son. He was reminded yet again that he was responsible for changing an innocent child into a monster. The notion of suicide crossed his mind, but he knew he had to live, in order to protect his wife and son. It pained him to ask his next question, which was almost harder for him, than the act of gouging out an eye.

. "What do you mean, when you say you went to Sarah?" he asked.

"I took her maggot-infested body in my arms, regardless of the terrible smell. I discharged myself on her."

Rowland sat down on the swivel chair once more. He thought he was going to faint and covered his face with his hands.

"Go to the drawing room and bring down a bottle of whisky with two glasses. Hurry!"

William did as he was told. He filled half of each glass with neat whisky. They both drank like stranded men in a desert, deprived of water, and refilled their glasses. Rowland was the first to speak.

"You've got to have psychiatric treatment, my boy," he said. "I'm afraid there's no-one I can send you to, because I'm too ashamed. I'll treat you, myself. My duty to you comes before my duty to my patients. We'll need to talk for an hour each day. Does 7.00 in the evening suit you?"

"That's all right. I'm not usually doing anything, then."

"I suggest we talk in the nursery, on a purely

professional basis. You'll need medication as well, as your condition is very severe. It will mean your having to take a combination of Haloperidol and Chlorpromazine before you go to bed. The combined doses of these will induce deep sleep, undisturbed by nightmares."

"Will that interfere with my sex life?" asked William.

"You've got sex on the brain. I don't believe you think of any other subject from one day to the next."

The father and son continued to drink. Rowland turned his head away from William, and started to cry.

"Oh, please don't, Father. It's wrong to chastise yourself like this. Your guilt is far greater than is reasonable. All that matters is that I've come to see you as an equal and have forgiven you. If you go on punishing yourself, your suffering is going to hurt me far more than anything you did in the past."

"I'm so glad I've lived long enough to make up for what I did. I'll get you well. I promise that," said Rowland.

"What's going on? You two have been out here for nearly three quarters of an hour!" They did not notice Dolly walking towards them. She was wearing a loose, bright blue silk dress.

"What's this bottle of whisky doing

here?" she asked.

"No reason," said Rowland, his speech slightly slurred. "We were having a talk about William's studies at the Hammersmith."

"I'm pleased you're discussing that. I'm under the impression that William spends all his time chasing women, and very little time on his studies, as I said, earlier."

"You know that's not true, Dolly," said William.

"My God, you're both drunk!" shouted Dolly. "Lunch is ready. It's disgraceful of you to be drinking as early as this."

"We're sorry, Dolly," said Rowland.

They sat down and started their first course, consisting of liver pâté and toast.

"Dolly and I have something very important to tell you, William," said Rowland.

"Oh, what's that?"

"Dolly's going to have a baby. The scan has shown it will be a girl."

William spread some pâté, nearly half an inch thick, onto his toast.

"Congratulations to you, both. When will she be born?"

"In about March," said Rowland, self-consciously. "We think she'll be a Pisces. It's a pretty stable, reliable sign, eh, Dolly."

William disliked the idea of having a younger sibling. He had begun to delight in his father's companionship, and the idea that his father's love would be directed towards another, depressed him. He put the toast he was about to eat back on his plate and lowered his head.

"What are you going to call her?" he asked.

"We've decided on Kate Alice."

"Aren't you pleased, William?" asked Dolly.

"Of course, I'm pleased."

"No, you aren't," said Rowland. "You fear she'll get all my attention and that you'll be left out. You're afraid I'll stop loving you. You are mistaken. She won't have the same unhappy childhood that you had, so I'll still owe you more than I'll owe her. You have my word on that. We're going to get you well, and see you smiling and laughing, right, Dolly?"

Dolly looked at William's sad, untrusting face, affectionately.

"We're both on your side, William, dear," she said.

William and Rowland had been going to the nursery on a nightly basis, and spent an hour each time, talking. They sat on either side of the table, drinking whisky and smoking.

Their conversations were similar to their exchanges since Sarah's death. They were painful, repetitive and not entirely devoid of grim humour. It was the combination of alcohol and occasional merriment which made these conversations bearable.

William's words alternated between rage and devotion, the latter being more dominant. Rowland's were tearfully-expressed and guilt-ridden, and at the same time, saturated with a love which was almost incestuous.

William was taking regular doses of Haloperidol and Chlorpromazine. These prevented his insomnia and nightmares and relaxed him a little, but dulled his intellect. He got on with his studies, and it was only because of his once sharp mind, that he was able to produce satisfactory essays which he wrote on auto-pilot.

His excessive womanizing remained as before, but he was less demanding of the physical attributes of women. He was content to perform only once nightly. In the past, the women had been woken with demands for rough sex, once they had fallen asleep. Under the drugs, he held them securely and went to sleep himself, without making continuous, nervous conversation to them.

He met a girl called Anne, at another lecture, delivered by Dr Ben Thompson.

The lecture room was crowded. William and Anne were sitting in the back row. She looked similar to Sarah and had long dark hair. She was sewing, aware that Thompson was unable to see what she was doing.

William opened the whispered conversation.

"What are you making?"

"I'm embroidering my father's initials on a handkerchief. It's his birthday next week."

"It's pretty. Does your father live in London?"

"He lives in NW3 — Hampstead."

"Alone?"

"With my mother and my two sisters."

"Older than you?"

"Both younger."

"Do you boss them around?"

"I used to. They won't stand for it, now."

"What's your name?"

"Anne. Anne Brenchley."

" Mine's William Rendon. What's your father's profession?"

"He's a dentist."

"What, in H. Street?"

"H? Oh, you mean Harley Street? That's right. Number 17. We've talked enough about me. What about you?"

"I'm an only child. My mother's dead. My stepmother lives with my father, now. He's a psychiatrist, also in H. Street."

"Do you live at home?"

"No. I've got a house of my own in Knightsbridge."

"Do you like your father and stepmother?"

"I get on well with both of them. I'm very close to my father. I confide in him."

"I bet you don't confide in him about your sex life."

"Yes, I do."

"That's a bit bizarre, isn't it?"

"Yes, it is, but my father and I are both pretty bizarre."

Anne didn't answer. She continued to sew and held her work up to the light.

"Have you got a lover?" asked William.

"No. I live at home. My parents won't allow any of us to have men, sleeping overnight in the house."

"I can understand that," said William. "My father says I can't bring women to the house, either."

"Ah, but you've got a house of your own."

"What do you do when you're not studying medicine?" he asked.

"I like making my own clothes."

"Oh? Do you like knitting?"

"Yes. I knitted the sweater I'm wearing."

William observed the sweater. It was bottle green, with patterned orange fish at the end of the sleeves, neck and waist. It looked as if it had come from an Oxfam shop.

"It's very colourful. Did you do the whole thing, yourself?"

"Yes. I worked on it on and off. It took me a few months."

William and Anne were eating lunch in the Hammersmith Hospital canteen, which is notorious for poor quality food and dour lighting. They introduced themselves.

"This place reminds me of the horrible canteen in the novel, *1984*," said Anne.

"I know that book well. I know exactly what you mean. I'm thinking of that scene when Syme expresses enthusiasm for public hangings. Don't you find it outrageous that hospital canteens aren't licensed?"

"It is outrageous," she said. "We all need alcohol with our food. In France, you even get it in prisons."

"I've got something here you'll like," said William. "Drink your water, close your eyes and pass me your empty glass."

He took a bottle of vodka from the pocket of his white coat and filled half of her glass with it.

"Drink it," he commanded.

She did as she was told. She swallowed it in one go. He poured her some more, and had some himself.

"Have you got any lectures this afternoon, Anne?"

"No."

"Would you like to come back to my house in Knightsbridge?"

"Do you live alone, there?"

"Of course."

Anne looked through the *Evening Standard* and said she wanted to see a TV production of the film, *The Wicked Lady*.

"I don't know it," he said. "What is it about?"

"It's set in the Eighteenth Century and there's a long public execution at the end. You said something about that in the canteen."

They took off their clothes and got into bed. William pulled Anne's head towards him and pushed his tongue into her mouth. He entered her gently and became increasingly rough. The act finished within twenty minutes when she screamed in ecstasy.

They slept until 6.00 that evening, when it was time for William to get up and see his father for his 7.00 o'clock consultation in the nursery.

"What's the hurry, William?"

"Oh, I'm afraid I've got an appointment

at 7.00 o'clock."

"That's not very civil! So she's as fascinating as that, is she?"

"You've got it all wrong, Anne. I have my therapy every evening at 7.00 o'clock for an hour each time."

"What therapy is that?"

"Oh, I have to see my psychiatrist, that's all."

"Can't you ring him up and cancel?"

"I couldn't possibly do that. I've been a bit ill, and I've got to turn up every evening, without fail."

"I'm sorry you've been ill."

"It's nothing serious. I think the psychiatrist is much iller than I am."

"That's often the case. What do you talk to him about?"

"Last time, we referred to the poem, *The Walrus and the Carpenter*," he said, spontaneously.

"I know that one. I can recite the whole of it if you want."

William turned his back to her as he put on his jacket.

"I would terribly rather you didn't," he said.

Rowland was waiting for William in the hall. Dolly was feeling sick and had gone upstairs to lie down.

"You're nice and punctual, my boy. Shall we go up?"

The two men were sitting opposite each other on either side of the table in the nursery. A bottle of whisky and two glasses stood between them.

"So, then, my boy, tell me about the women you've had since we last met."

"There's only been one, Father."

"Oh, there has, has there? Is that hampton of yours working all right?"

"Oh, indeed it is," replied William, flushing. "Her name's Anne. She's got long dark hair."

"Like Sarah, eh?"

"I'm sorry?"

"'Sarah', I said. Wake up, boy! The decomposing biddy behind the chair, stinking the whole bloody corridor out!"

"Oh, yes, Sarah. Anne's like her to look at."

"You like 'em with long dark hair, don't you?"

"Yes."

"Take some whisky, boy."

William obeyed.

"Do you intend to bring her up here, and put her through all this knitting rubbish?"

"I haven't had that in mind, Father."

"If you have any ideas about that, will you promise to tell me right away?"

"I promise."

213

William returned to his house. He found Anne standing in front of a mirror, brushing her long, dark hair.

"Your hair looks nice and glossy," he said.

She didn't answer. She smiled at him.

"Would you like me to cook dinner here? We could eat and watch a video," he said.

"What can you cook?"

"I'm afraid I'm not very good. I can do you a cheese omelette and some salad. Or, I could give you *spaghetti bolagnaise.*"

"I'd prefer cheese omelette."

Anne lay on her back on William's bed while he went to the kitchen. He was not an accomplished cook and the omelette he made was unpalatable and rubbery. He used the rest of the cheese to make sandwiches for himself. He carried what he had prepared on a tray to the bedroom, accompanied by a bottle of Claret.

"Have you chosen a video?" he asked.

"I've found a film called *Reuben Reuben.* I've no idea what it's about but the title is intriguing."

"I can tell you what it's about. It's about a man who seduced his dentist's wife. The dentist gave the man a general anaesthetic and took all his teeth out."

"That's too familiar," said Anne. "I hear nothing but dentists' shop at home."

"Surely, your father doesn't do that sort of thing."

"That's only because none of his patients has seduced my mother."

"Do you want to see it, or would you like to watch another video?"

"I see you've got *Last Tango in Paris*."

"Would you like to see that?"

"I would. It's very erotic."

Anne was hungry and she appreciated the poorly-made cheese omelette. They were both stimulated by the video and got into bed.

"Have you got any butter?" she asked peremptorily.

"I beg your pardon?"

"Whenever I'm starting a new relationship, I like the man to use the tradesmen's entrance."

"You what?"

"I like it that way."

"Why?"

"Because I like the pain at the beginning. I like to be broken in like a horse and then treated with respect."

"Your request is absolutely extraordinary," said William. "No woman has ever asked me to do that to her, before."

"Are you very shocked?"

"Not really. I'm just baffled."

"Will you agree to it, then?" she asked as if she were asking a bank manager for an overdraft facility.

"I don't know if I'll be able to, Anne. I really don't want to."

"Please, William?"

William tried, but was unable to do so. He satisfied her in conventional terms, and to compensate for his inability to grant her request, he was particularly rough with her, as he had been with Sarah. He took some time to complete the act, and was relieved to have been able to gratify her.

"Are you going to mention this matter to your psychiatrist, William?"

"I'll have to. I'd be wasting his time and mine if I didn't."

"Well, William, my boy, what have you been up to with Anne, eh?"

William and Rowland were sitting in their customary places at the nursery table.

"She tried to make me bugger her," said William.

"She *what*?"

"Just as I said."

"And did you?"

216

"I couldn't, Father. It wasn't through want of trying."

"You mean you failed to give satisfaction to a young lady? Shame on you, boy!"

"I just couldn't do what she asked. I satisfied her in the normal way, though. She screamed her head off."

"Very well done, boy!" was all Rowland could think of saying. The degree of his love for his son was worrying him. He was beginning to feel physical attraction for him, but in the interests of decency, he suppressed it.

"Do you know that you were conceived in violence, William?"

"No, Father."

"I raped your mother in the back of a car. I was in a rage."

"Why?"

"I don't know exactly why. I can't remember, but judging by what a wonderful young man you are, it was the best thing I ever did."

"Have you seen *Last Tango in Paris*, Father?" asked William, suddenly.

"Yes, why?"

"Did you like it?"

"Not an awful lot. I found it rather boring. Time's up, my boy. Dolly's not feeling too well. She wants an early dinner. See you tomorrow,

217

at 7.00 o'clock."

William overslept the next time he was due to see his father. Anne failed to wake him because she wanted him to stay at home with her. He woke up at 6.45 in the evening.

"Why the hell didn't you wake me up at 6.00 o'clock, Anne?"

"I've only just woken up."

He put his clothes on, hurriedly. He was agitated because he was aware of the trouble his father was taking on his account. He thought it would be morally wrong to keep him waiting.

There was congested traffic in Wimpole Street. By the time he had reached Harley Street, it was 7.45. He was too late for his appointment with his father. He returned home.

Rowland was pacing up and down in the nursery, fearing that his son had come to harm. He dialled William's number from the dusty telephone by the television.

"Is this 589-7112?" he shouted.

"Why, yes," said Anne. "You sound hysterical. Is something wrong?"

"I'm worried about my son. Where the hell is he?"

"If I don't know who you are, how can I tell you where your son is? There's nothing to stop you being a bit more polite."

218

"Is your name Anne?"

"Yes. Anne Brenchley."

"My name's Rowland Rendon. I'm William's father," stated Rowland, his voice so loud that she had to hold the receiver a yard away from her ear.

"Oh, then you must be *Dr* Rendon."

"You're right. Where's William? I'm expecting him."

"He said he was going to see his psychiatrist. This is what he does at 7.00 o'clock every night of the week. He overslept, so he'll be a bit late for his appointment."

Rowland was in such an anxious state that he failed to keep his wits about him.

"It's me he sees every night at 7.00," he said.

"That's strange. He told me he had been seeing his psychiatrist at that time."

"I *am* his bloody psychiatrist!"

"You've just said you were his father."

"I *am* his father. I am also his psychiatrist. Does this make any sense to you?"

"No, it doesn't, Dr Rendon."

"Perhaps I should tell you this, as William doesn't appear to have told you," said Rowland, his tone more relaxed. "Some very inappropriate things happened to William when he was a child. I was unwell myself during those years. William suffers from a severe mental illness.

"I'm the only person who can help him because only I know him. He grew up in bizarre and unpleasant circumstances. His mother was mentally retarded. She also had a terrible, frightening-looking facial deformity and failed to relate to her son."

Rowland was exhausted by his obligation to explain the situation to a woman whom he had never met. "Oh yes, he runs into a lot of difficulties in relation to things which are red," he said vaguely, "but I'm working like a black to restore his sanity," he added, as an afterthought.

Anne thought Rowland was insane. She tried to turn the situation into a joke, to guard her from the confusion which was alarming her.

"Things that are red, Dr Rendon? What things in particular? He's exposed to plenty of blood in the hospital. That doesn't appear to upset him."

"That's because blood's dark red. It's bright red which disturbs him. That's why he walks about in dark glasses, to prevent him seeing bright red things."

"I was wondering about the glasses. They're very attractive. Why can't he tolerate bright red? Is it because he associates it with Communist flags? Maybe, he's rather Right-wing. That could explain it. I was also wondering if he'd been born under the sign of the Bull."

"What does that mean? I know nothing about

astrology," said Rowland.

"Is he Taurus? That's the sign of the Bull, isn't it? Some Taureans are quite averse to bright red."

"He's not Taurus. He's Aries," said Rowland. "His birthday's on April 12th."

"Do you know why he has this peculiar problem?" asked Anne.

"Yes, I do."

"Can't you tell me? I'd be able to help him. I could make him happy, in the same way as you are trying to."

"That's something I don't think I can do, Anne."

"Why?"

"Because, it's so terrible and shocking that I couldn't make myself turn the facts into words."

"Was he exposed to a major road accident?"

"No."

"Did he see a loved one bleeding to death?"

"No. It has nothing to do with blood. I'm sorry. I'll never be able to tell you the truth."

"Then how can I help him?"

"How much do you love him?"

"I've fallen in love with him. He means more to me than anyone. He's a kind, sweet, caring person, as well as being so good-looking, with his beautiful, big blue eyes. Perhaps, William will ask me to your house, so that I could meet you face-to-face and

221

find out what really happened."

"No, Anne, that can never be," he said, the hysteria in his voice returning.

"Might I ask why?"

"There's every reason why. The nursery area in this house, is locked up. It has not been used for a considerable time. Whenever William brings women here, he has an obsessive desire to take them to the nursery. If he took you there, your life would be in serious danger. Don't ever let him bring you to the house, for the sake of your own safety."

"Why?"

"I can never tell you exactly why. I'll look after William for an hour every evening. You look after him for the rest of the time, and give him all the love you have to offer. Between us, we'll cure him of his illness."

"What illness is it?"

"He has schizophrenia, Anne. It's a very severe case."

"Is he homicidal in any way?"

"Only when he brings women to the nursery. As long as they stay away from there, they're not in any danger."

"Has he ever killed a woman?"

"That is simply none of your business," said Rowland, angrily. "None of this is his fault. What he needs to aid his recovery, is patience, kindness and love. As he himself is a kind person, it will be easy for both of us to help him to recover from his illness."

"May I see you alone, one day, without William?"

"That could be arranged, but it would be pointless. What on earth do you think telephones were invented for?"

Anne replaced the receiver when she heard William coming upstairs. He came into the bedroom, looking anxious and flustered. She kissed him on the cheek.

"Shall I get you some whisky," she asked.

"Yes. I need it. By the time I got there, it was too late for my therapy. All because you failed to wake me."

"I'm so sorry, William. I wasn't awake myself, so I couldn't have woken you."

"I'm not blaming you. Let's lie on the bed and watch television. I've got to ring my father."

"Why?"

"Because I stood him up tonight."

"Rather a strange man rang me up. He said he was your father, and that you see him every evening at 7.00 o'clock."

William was undeterred.

"That's true," he said.

"You told me you saw your psychiatrist

at that hour."

"That is also true. My father and my psychiatrist are the same person. Only my father knows my own soul. Only he can help me, now."

"I hope I can help you, too."

"You do help me, more than you know. It's the fact that you're always there for me that protects me from horrifying thoughts."

Anne thought for a while, and wondered whether she would help him by confronting him.

"Are your horrifying thoughts about things which are bright red?"

"Why, yes, they are — and other things, events in my childhood. It's all rather nasty. I don't want to talk about it, now."

"Some other time, then?"

"All right, but I'll have to choose when."

"I've brought plenty of food home. Steak, salad, potatoes. I know you like simple food. What will you have?"

"You're such a sweet girl!" he said. "I'd like medium steak, a baked potato and peas, if you've got any."

"I have."

"I've also got rice crispies and cream. I know you like that for pudding. You said you had a particular liking for *Chardonnay*. I've got that, too. You lie down, watch the television, enjoy your whisky. It will take time to do the potato. Can you wait for about forty-five minutes?"

"I could wait for three weeks, and I still wouldn't mind."

Rowland was sitting at the nursery table, once more. There was no heating in the room and he was wearing Dolly's silvery seal-skin coat. In the role of psychiatrist, he looked staggeringly eccentric.

He and William refrained from speaking until they had consumed at least a quarter of a bottle of whisky between them.

"Been asked into her back-passage again, boy?" asked Rowland.

"No. She doesn't seem interested in that any more. She's content to do things the normal way."

"Do you compensate by being rough?"

"Yes. She likes it that way."

"What about you, what do you like? How do you like your French, dearie, as a prostitute might say?"

"I like my sex rough, Father," said the young man, rather shyly.

"You take after your father, then, for your sins! Do you remember when I told you you were conceived in violence?"

"Yes."

"Your mother was a virgin at the time. You should have heard the way she screamed. I was cruel in those days, but not now. Dolly has mellowed me and made me kind. I say, do you like to hurt your women?"

"No. Not hurt them, Father. I just like to make them happy. Nearly all the women I've taken, have wanted me to be rough. If a woman asked me to be gentle, I'd be so."

"There's something else I want to discuss with you, William. This time, it's about me. Are you, in any way, beginning to see me as a replacement for Nanny? If I were, surely you wouldn't need to see her in human form. That ought to put an end to your need to bring women in here, and murder them if they don't co-operate. Aren't you sitting with a real-life Nanny, now?"

William took another sip of whisky.

"It's true, some wonderful things have happened, since we became friends. You're not the sadistic father any more. You've changed into the significant other."

"Can you not just say, I've turned from a monster, into an adoring father?"

"Yes, I could say that."

"You love me to such an extent that you have decided to forgive me. Surely, you must see Nanny re-incarnated in me."

"I'd like to but I don't think I can. Nanny was a woman, a female entity. When I need security, I go to a woman for it, not a man."

"Suppose I were a homosexual?"

"A homosexual is still a man. Although I felt safe and loved that day you embraced me, I wept inside for days and wished you'd been born a woman."

"Do you not get on with other men?"

"No. I've never been able to. Women are more exciting because they are incomprehensible, and I love their delicate, soft skins. You're the only man in the world I can relate to, without feeling uncomfortable or bored. Apart from that, men repulse me."

"Why, William?"

"Because of something that happened on Remembrance Sunday, when I was eight. I'm not talking about what happened in this room that day. It was something after that."

"You must tell me, my boy."

"Do you remember that scruffily-dressed man who brought me home?"

"Of course I do. He was a damned impertinent fellow. What about him?"

"He brought me home the next day, the Monday. I was so disturbed and wretched after

Nanny died, that I ran away. I got on a bus to central London and got off at Piccadilly circus. I had no idea where I was. I walked round the streets. I was in Soho.

I found a place where there were rows of gaming machines with flashing lights. It was there that I met a man called Philip, the man who brought me home. He was so kind to me. He gave me food and took me up to his room.

"I was tired. He suggested I get into bed. I fell asleep straight away. I was woken up by him getting into bed beside me. He started touching me. I hated it. I kept saying, 'Please don't touch me, sir.'"

Rowland covered his face with his hands and sobbed convulsively.

"When you came home, you were terrified of telling your own father, who had been responsible for your running away. I was such an evil bastard! I don't deserve to live. Aren't you ashamed of me?"

"No, Father. You mustn't say these things. You're too hard on yourself. You've made up for what you did. You've repented. Isn't that enough?"

"This man, Philip, that is to say your experience with him, is that why you can't abide men? Is that why you hate members of your own sex."

"Yes, Father. I hate them all, all of them except you."

The two men got up and walked towards

228

the door.

"Just one thing before you go."

"Yes, Father?"

"Are you still having trouble with your red?"

"It's diminished a bit, but it's still there. I can handle it, though. There's nothing red in my house and when I go out, I wear dark glasses."

"I shall never rest until you can go out and be happy, without the glasses," said Rowland.

William felt sad. He did not anticipate being able to go out without them, but he wanted to reassure his father.

"That time will come, Father," he said.

Several years passed. William graduated and became a Senior House Officer, or SHO, as the term is known. His full title was SHO in Pathology. He practiced at the Hammersmith Hospital where he had trained.

It was not until he qualified that Anne invited him to her parents' house in Hampstead, one late July Sunday. Anne's two younger sisters, Margaret and Cynthia, were staying with families in France, as paying guests; their parents wanted them to learn fluent French.

William parked his Jensen outside the Brenchleys' house, which could be approached via a small, neatly-tended garden. Anne unlocked the front door with her key. Her parents were sitting in the living room, reading the Sunday papers.

Anne's mother was a very shy, but distinguished-looking woman. She had on a sleeveless yellow linen dress. Her long dark hair was heavily streaked with white and she wore it in a French roll.

The father, the Harley Street dentist, sat in an armchair, covered with cigarette burns. He had on an open-necked shirt and had rolled up his sleeves to his elbows. He had short grey hair and wore half-moon spectacles.

When William and Anne entered the room, the dentist and his wife rose to their feet, and forced themselves to smile.

"Daddy, this is my partner, William Rendon," said Anne with extreme tenseness.

"Brenchley's my name. David Brenchley," said the dentist, abruptly. "Are you Rowland Rendon's son?"

"Yes, that's right, Mr Brenchley."

The two men shook hands. Brenchley had a bone-crushing handshake, and confused William by failing to look him in the eye.

"I suppose you're wondering how I know who your father is," said the abruptly-spoken dentist.

"Well, yes, Mr Brenchley."

"Most of my patients go to your father, on their way to me."

"Oh?"

"Nearly all of them are afraid of dentists. They need psychological assurance, before seeing me."

"That's because Daddy's rather a rough dentist, or so I've heard," said Anne.

Brenchley was irritated. Mrs Brenchley, who hardly ever spoke, called everyone in to lunch. Very little conversation took place until after the first course, when Brenchley, an abysmal host, poured Claret into the glasses. William was alarmed by the sight of his host's shaking hands, and wondered how he managed to practice as a dentist.

At least, the dentist was well-mannered enough to fill William's glass on the many occasions it became empty. William felt artificially relaxed.

The dentist's sole topic of conversation was cricket, in which he had a passionate interest. He stated that he only kept a television in his house because of it.

William knew nothing about cricket, and had no intention of learning about it. He timidly introduced the subject of Medicine, once the coffee was being served by Mrs Brenchley, and commented about the high standard of teaching at the Hammersmith hospital.

"I trained at Barts," remarked the dentist,

suddenly looking conspiratorial and secretive. William was aware of this without being told, and felt that Barts-trained medics appeared slippery, sly and suspicious, as if they belonged to some clandestine, élitist club, run like an unwholesome Lodge of a Freemasonic society.

"I thought you were a Barts man, Mr Brenchley," said William.

"Oh, you did, did you? Why did you think that?" asked the dentist, defensively.

"Purely through instinct, sir. No logical reason."

"You're a strange, young man, Rendon. I'm bound to say I preferred the last man Anne brought to the house, some years ago. He was Barts-trained, and a splendid fellow he was."

William didn't answer. He looked forward to being able to report his meeting with Anne's parents, to his father.

"Mind you, young man, I feel that Barts-trained doctors are more successful with women, than doctors trained at what I consider to be lesser hospitals," said the dentist. "I can tell by looking at you that you are very much in love with Anne, although you look as if you've had innumerable women in your time. I know Anne dresses in rather a Bohemian manner, but what are your tastes in women's clothes, in general? How do you like them

232

to dress, ideally?"

William frantically stirred his coffee, first clockwise, then anti-clockwise. He hated this dentist whom he considered rude, boarish and typical of a Barts graduate.

"I personally prefer women when they're naked," he said, assertively.

The dentist rose to his feet.

"If that's your attitude, young man, I'm going next door to watch the Test Match."

William and Anne were married within the following few months. Anne was unable to forgive Brenchley's unwelcoming behaviour towards her fiancé.

The day before the wedding, William felt restless and went for a walk round the streets of London. He passed St Bartholomew's Hospital and found its front gates occupied by pickets. They were rattling tins to collect funds to prevent the hospital, threatened with closure by a Tory government, from fading into obscurity.

William deliberately walked close to the pickets.

"We're raising funds to protect Barts from closure," said one.

"I'm not giving you a penny!" shouted William.

"I hope this odious hospital is bulldozed down, and I'd like to stand here and watch it happen!"

William introduced Anne to his father and Dolly before their wedding. Rowland was friendly and flirtatious towards the bride-to-be, and cracked jokes to put her at her ease.

"You're so much easier to get on with than my father," she said.

"Your father? Oh, yes, Mr Brenchley, the dentist."

"That's right. He trained at Barts."

Rowland crossed and uncrossed his legs.

"Strange place, Barts. Strange doctors. Strange atmosphere, strange staff and a unhygienic, revolting mortuary!" he remarked with extraordinary heartiness, and slapped his thigh. "Tattiest of the mortuaries," he added as an afterthought.

Rowland, Dolly, William and Anne ate a heavy, three-course lunch. Rowland was generous with the *Chardonnay*, and by the end of lunch, all four of them were inebriated.

Dolly and Anne talked at length about dresses, and other women's matters. Anne found Dolly welcoming and humorous, and wished these qualities were shared by her own silent, unfriendly parents.

"It's been wonderful to meet you, Anne," said Rowland, as he rose to his feet, intending to go upstairs for his rest.

Dolly shook hands with Anne.

"William's lucky to have such a pretty fiancé. Any time you're coming this way, just ring the bell. You don't even need to say you're coming. You'll always be welcome,"

"Thank you so much, Mrs Rendon."

William put his arm round Anne's waist, and turned to his father.

"Do you mind if I show Anne the nursery?" he said.

"I thought we'd discussed this before, William. The place is being redecorated and there are loose rafters up there. It's not safe. Anne might fall over and break her leg."

"Oh, all right, Father. Perhaps, I can take her up there when the repairs have been done."

"Yes, yes, all right. If you'll all excuse me, I'm going up for my rest."

The young couple were sitting in the Jensen, which was still reliable, despite its age.

"It's a pity your father didn't allow you to show me the nursery," said Anne.

William's facial expression became one of

embarrassment, fear and secretive merriment.

"Perhaps, it's just as well. Father feels very strongly that it's not a safe place to go to."

"William, you suddenly looked awfully Bartsy just then. You looked so peculiar, not yourself at all."

"No. Probably not. You must be able to tell how extraordinarily drunk I am."

"That's not really the issue, is it, William?" Anne said, suddenly. They were driving down Harley Street, towards Cavendish Square.

William made a jolting movement. His foot bounced off the accelerator, causing the car to slow down.

"I don't know what you're talking about," he said.

"I hate to bring this up, but it's time I did. Some years ago, your father and I had a telephone conversation. He rang up the house. It was that evening when you overslept and were too late for your 7.00 o'clock appointment with him. Do you remember?"

"I remember I overslept, that time you didn't wake me up. It's true, I arrived too late to keep the appointment. What of it?"

"Your father told me you were a schizophrenic."

"Oh, did he?"

"Well, are you? Is it true? Are you over it, yet?"

"I don't know, Anne. Sometimes when I'm very disturbed, part of me switches off."

"That happens when you go up to the nursery, doesn't it?"

"It doesn't matter. Father said we weren't to go up there. You heard him, didn't you?"

"Why did he say we weren't to go up there? I'm sure it's nothing to do with the place being decorated."

The traffic lights at the bottom of Harley Street, turned green. William turned into Cavendish Square.

"It doesn't matter what Father's reasons are. I do everything he tells me, without questioning him. He knows, better than I do, what is good for me and what isn't."

"You're to tell me what's up there!" shouted Anne. "There's something red up there, isn't there?"

"Red, Anne?"

"Yes. Red. That evening, I asked your father if you had homicidal tendencies. He said you did, but only when you brought women to the nursery. He said, and these were his words, 'As long as they stay away from there, they're not in any danger.' Have you ever killed someone, William?"

237

"I don't think so. It's possible I might have done. It's best for you to ask Father. He knows me better than I know myself. If you thought there was something dangerous up there, why did you say it was a pity that Father said I wasn't to take you there?"

"Because I'm not afraid of you. I'm just sad that you suffer so much, sometimes, and you're not even able to say what's wrong."

William swerved to avoid a negligent pedestrian.

"I don't suffer as much as you think," he said. "As long as I've got Father in my life, and as long as I continue to see him every evening at 7.00 o'clock, I hardly suffer at all, and of course, I've got you."

"What's up there, William? I won't leave you alone until you tell me. If I'm to become your wife, I must be told."

William was exhausted. He pulled into the side of the road.

"It's no good asking me. I'm still on quite a heavy dose of Chlorpromazine and have been for several years. I genuinely don't know, not when I'm away from there, I don't."

William married Anne in an Anglican church in London's West End. Mr Brenchley, Anne's father, was in a furious mood at the time of the wedding.

As he escorted his daughter up the aisle, she felt vibrating waves of rage from his hand and arm.

When the time came for him to hand her over to William, he fixed the bridegroom with a hatred-ridden, homicidal stare, which was unnoticed, due to the younger man's failure to meet his eye.

They went to Florence for their honeymoon. William appeared happy and relaxed and developed an interest in Italian Renaissance painting. Anne decided not to mention the nursery again, and never to go to Rowland's house with William, for fear that he would try to take her there. She continued to fear for William's psychological pain, rather than her own safety.

William was waiting for her late one evening. As is the case with SHOs, the daily workload is colossal, and the SHO is lucky if he is able to sleep one night in three. The Chlorpromazine added to William's permanent drowsiness and he compensated for this with handfuls of Dexedrine.

Anne had made a decision not to go into medicine, once she had qualified, because of the long hours. Instead, she worked in a medical bookshop between ten and six.

The bedroom the newly-wed Rendons occupied, was on the first floor, and the staircase linking the ground floor to the first floor, was short, with only ten steps. Even a very elderly person could have

239

walked up it without discomfort.

Anne came into the bedroom, and was so breathless and exhausted that she could hardly stand.

"Whatever is the matter?" asked William. "You've had difficulty breathing for some time, now. It doesn't seem to be getting any better. How did you get here? Have you been running?"

She sat on the bed, trying to breathe normally but had to make an effort to suck the air into her lungs.

"I came by taxi. I got out just outside the door. I haven't been walking all day. I've just been sitting behind a counter."

"Have you seen a doctor? It seems as if you've got asthma," he said.

"I saw our family doctor, Dr Fox. He's done a battery of tests, and he also referred me to an Ear, Nose and Throat specialist. It's not asthma and all the allergy tests were negative."

"Why didn't you tell me all this, before?" asked William.

"Because you've over-sensitive. You never stop worrying, if not about one thing, about another. Whatever it is, I'm sure it will go away. The worst thing of all is that I can't sleep without pills. I lie awake until it gets light. At least, the pills I've been given, are working, now."

"What pills are you taking?"

"Chloral Hydrate."

"I see. That's not all that addictive but it's habit-forming if you take it for too long. Does it hurt when you breathe?"

"No."

Part of William suspected what was wrong with her. The other part assumed and hoped that her condition was self-limiting. The problem continued to plague the Rendons for nine months. There were no signs of improvement although William told himself that she was recovering. As more months passed by, the condition worsened.

William confessed his anxiety to his father, during one of his 7.00 o'clock consultations.

"Has she seen a specialist?" asked Rowland.

"An ENT specialist, yes."

"Which one?"

"Mr Stuart Groves. He's a Royal Free man with a private practice in this street."

"Oh, yes, Groves. I've never met him. He's well-spoken of. What did he say?"

"Just that it wasn't asthma and that all the allergy tests were negative."

"I know an excellent specialist, Dr Joel Zimmerman. Top consultant in Respiratory Medicine. 121 Harley Street. Trained at Guy's Hospital. I'm prepared to speak to him, personally but Anne's family doctor will have to refer her as a matter of protocol. What's her doctor's name?"

"Dr Fox. Dr Lionel Fox."

Rowland re-lit his pipe which had gone out.

"Never heard of him. Get him to do a referral letter, straight away. I'll speak to Dr Zimmerman. He's a nice man. We were students together."

Anne was sitting in Dr Zimmerman's consulting room. He was a friendly, affable person with white hair and a white beard. He was a devout man, and kept a copy of the *Talmud* on his desk, which he read whenever he had a spare moment.

"Do, please, sit down, Mrs Rendon," he said. "I suggest you use the armchair. It's much more comfortable."

Anne sat down. She was so short of breath that she could hardly speak.

"When did you start having problems, breathing?" he asked.

"Over nine months ago. It's been getting steadily worse."

"What stopped you reporting it at the beginning?"

"I was convinced it would get better."

Dr Zimmerman gave her a comprehensive examination. "Does it hurt you to breathe?" he asked.

"No. No pain. Is it lung cancer? I used to

smoke, but I gave it up about ten years ago."

"No. It's definitely not lung cancer," said Dr Zimmerman. "With lung cancer, you get a cough. As a medical graduate, I'm sure you know that, anyway. You sometimes bring up blood and there's associated pain. I want to take some X-rays, and I'll know more in a day or two."

William accompanied his wife to Dr Zimmerman's rooms. The doctor told them he suspected she had pulmonary fibrosis.

"I'm admitting you to the Brompton Hospital for a lung biopsy. Are you insured?"

"How long will that take?" asked William.

"The inside of a week. No more."

The lung biopsy was due to take place the following week, and a few days later, Zimmerman broke the tragic news to William, that his wife was suffering from advanced pulmonary fibrosis and that only a lung transplant could save her life. Anne was unable to go anywhere without carrying a heavy oxygen cylinder.

Her bleep went off while she and William were having dinner. A seven-year-old boy had just died in a car crash and his lungs were unharmed. William called an ambulance and held his wife's hand on the way to the Brompton Hospital.

The lung transplant operation was performed within a few hours. William felt relaxed and relieved, although his work had prevented him from sleeping for two nights in a row.

He went to a pub and drank several whiskies. His mood was happier and more optimistic than it had been for many months, and he laughed and joked with some SHOs working at the Brompton, before returning to the hospital.

Dr Zimmerman ran towards him in tears in the lobby of the Brompton.

"What's wrong?" asked William.

"Everything was going fine. Suddenly, the transplanted lung collapsed and Anne arrested.* She's brain dead, now. They can keep her alive for as long as you want, but she's a vegetable. I'm afraid it's for you to turn her life support machine off. I'm just so sorry! So terribly, terribly sorry."

The Hammersmith gave William compassionate leave. He went to stay in his father's house where Dolly and Rowland took it in turns to console and look after him. It comforted him to sleep in the bed he had occupied as a child, and he spent all day in the nursery, his Room of Love, sobbing.

He had forgotten about Sarah, perhaps because he had murdered her, and was vaguely reminded of

*In medical terms, if a person "arrests", it means the heart has stopped beating.

the incident, on seeing her skeleton in the alcove behind the armchair. Besides, Sarah meant nothing to him, because she had refused to dress up as the nanny, and apart from that, her once attractive body, had turned to bones.

William associated Anne's death with that of his nanny. Anne had never gone to the nursery but William was certain that she would have complied with his wishes, had he asked her to.

Anne was guiltless of offending him because he had loved her on a par with the nanny. The Chlorpromazine prescribed for him, almost stopped him from being able to think. Sometimes, Anne's death seemed to have taken place many years ago. Other times, he knew it was recent.

Rowland was terrified of him going into a catatonic* state, so he asked his son to come for his therapy twice a day. Rowland wondered helplessly if he could ever assuage him of his misery, and hoped he would find another girl to restore what there was of his mental health.

Rowland knew William had become a broken man, and cried in bed at night about his impotence and failure to rectify his son's condition, brought on since his childhood, by one severe trauma after another.

*Catatonia: a state of mental depression, so severe, that the sufferer cannot speak or move.

During the consultations, William's morale was so weak that he could only answer Rowland's questions in a whisper. He lay slumped over the nursery table, his head resting on its side, and his eyes so painful to look at, that Rowland looked the other way.

"Don't despair, my son, don't despair. At least, you're blessed with Anne's memory, and no-one can take that away from you. You are going to get out of this. Sometime, not long hence, you'll find another nice girl. I'm sure of that.

"How would you like to come downstairs and share Dolly's and my room? Dolly will sleep in the narrow bed, and you and I can be together. I'm going to put this right, William. I've dedicated my later life to atone for my cruelty, and to get you to be happy and normal. I will never accept failure. But if I cannot do it, I'm afraid I will have to do the honourable thing, because I will deserve to die."

"No! No! Father! You're the only stable influence in my life. You and Dolly, but you most of all."

"I'm an optimist, William. You'll get over Anne's death, and before long you'll find someone else. Surely, you don't want to sleep up in the nursery wing. By all means, sit there during the day, but sleeping in your old bed would be unwholesome and self-destructive."

William got up to leave. Rowland thought he might have to hold him steady. He was shocked and jolted by what he saw. The chair on which his son had been sitting, was soaking wet, so great was his shock, combined with his demented grief.

"Bring your things down to our room," said Rowland. "You mustn't get any funny ideas about incest, just because we'll be in the same bed. Besides, Dolly would love to have you. Remember, I'm not Philip from Soho. I'm a fully-blown heterosexual, just like yourself. All I shall do is comfort you when you get your nightmares. I've often heard them when you've been alone at the top of the house. Dolly is and always has been, devoted to you. She's told me she approves of our new arrangement."

Dolly did everything in her power to cheer William up. The more she did so, the more he cried. "I don't mind sleeping in the same room as Rowland and yourself," she said. "In fact, it's a good arrangement. What you need is love, and cheering up. Rowland and I are good at that."

The father and son occupied the double bed. Dolly read aloud some emotionally taxing short stories by Dylan Thomas. The stories were of a macabre and mysterious nature. They frequently described bizarre happenings outdoors, and introduced peculiar, surreal references to rivers and hills.

William was both enlivened and distressed by one of the stories, entitled *The Mouse and the Woman*, which contained obscure, nonsensical language. Alongside the strange prose, was the theme of a boy, escaping from an asylum to assess his father's whereabouts.

William was fascinated by the words describing what the boy found, *"the stains of death upon mouth and eyes and a nest of mice in the tangle of the frozen beard."* Somehow, the morbidity of the words, comforted him.

Dolly did not know the extent to which Rowland would despair, if William didn't recover. The presence of a demented young man, unhealthily dependent on his father, did not deter her from reading the story aloud, and it was only when William began sobbing again, that Dolly knew she had made a foolish decision in her choice of reading matter.

"Dolly, you really could have done a bit better than that," said Rowland.

"But he likes morbidity. I was trying to cheer him up."

"For God's sake, read something else tomorrow night! Who the hell wants to hear about nests of mice in someone's blasted beard?"

"What books do you like, William?" she asked

the sick young man.

"I like the pre-War Rupert Bear books. They're on a shelf in the nursery."

"Why, you big baby!" said Rowland.

William liked to look at the black and white pictures, as well as the verses in these books. Dolly sat on the edge of the bed, while Rowland lay on his back, smoking a pipe.

Despite Dolly's and Rowland's superhuman efforts to lessen William's tormented thoughts, he made no progress whatever. He had on average at least three nightmares each night, and deprived his father and stepmother of sleep.

They were eating breakfast.

"I don't think this arrangement can go on," said Dolly. "It's going to destroy us both. I don't know how much more I can put up with."

"I've been awake, thinking," said Rowland. "William's very severely ill and he should get admitted to that rambling white-washed House of Usher in Roehampton. It's called the Priory. He will need sedation, and access to nurses all day.

There's a lot of good about the Priory. Its rooms are lovely. They give you occupational therapy every day. They encourage the patients to draw, paint, do woodwork and other therapeutic tasks.

"The staff are kind to the patients, and William will have company all day. Arrangements are made for the patients to meet each other and share their troubles. Once William improves, all these things will help him recover.

"He'll be sedated most of the time at first, and there's a chance he may hardly remember Anne's death at all, once he's fit to leave.

"I will go to the Priory twice a day until his symptoms are relieved. He needs me more than anyone."

William was heavily sedated during his first week at the extraordinary-looking mental hospital. He hardly remembered Anne and associated her with just one of the few people who had been kind to him in the distant past.

The Chlorpromazine, administered in much heavier doses, was causing him clinical depression, which was so severe, that it deprived him of the luxury of being able to cry.

Rowland visited him and sat on his bed between 6.00 and 7.00 each evening.

"How are you feeling, my boy?"

William explained that the Chlorpromazine dose was so overpowering that it partially obliterated Anne from his memory. He said it had deadened his thoughts and made him wish to die.

"Don't despair," said Rowland. "I'm well-known here, and have rooms here. I admitted you as my patient, using another name. I'll alter the

Chlorpromazine dosage to 100 mg a day, a lower dose even than you've had in the past.

"As for your black mood, I'll see you're put onto a sedative tricyclic called Amitriptyline. The sedating effect of that drug works within a day or two, but it takes three weeks to reach its optimum effect. You won't suffer. It's so sedating that, when it is combined with Chlorpromazine, you'll be asleep most of the time it is building up its effect."

William felt that the end of the world had come. He was only able to lie flat on his back and speak with an effort. Rowland noticed the hopelessness in his son's eyes, and struggled to retain his tears.

William raised his right arm and grabbed his father's hand.

"Am I ever going to come out of this, Father?"

"Of that, there is no shadow of doubt. You'll return to your old self, go back to the Hammersmith, and find a nice new girl. Because of your work record, when you've not been off sick, I see you as being promoted to Senior Registrar in the near future.

"When you feel as you do now, it's normal to think that you'll feel like this for the rest of your life. However, it's not logical. You are going to be cured. I give you my word on that."

Rowland stood up abruptly. He had little faith in his own words and his feelings of self-worth were deteriorating each day. Once more, the option of suicide, as an honourable way out, occurred to him.

"I must go now, my boy," he said, and turned abruptly away from his son.

"Is he getting any better?" asked Dolly at dinner.

"No. There's no change. Not only that, he's convinced he'll never get right, and keeps asking me for reassurance that he will."

"Do you give him the reassurance?"

"Yes, of course, I do. The terrible thing is, I don't believe a word I say. I just tell him what he wants to hear."

The following morning, Rowland received a shock. The Charge Nurse of William's corridor, a loud-spoken, hysterical, thirty-five-year-old man, with a harsh, Scottish accent, thicker than a bowl of porridge, woke him with a 5.30 a.m. telephone call. Rowland was outraged by his incomprehensible Scottish vowels and held the receiver a yard away from his ear.

"God, your accent's heavy!" said Rowland. "Can't you take off an English accent?"

"Nay, I canna, but I ka geev ye a bonny fair try!"

"What's happened to my son?" bellowed Rowland.

The Scotsman was daunted by the peppery

252

psychiatrist's telephone manner. He explained that William had escaped during the night and that the police had been alerted.

"*What*? I can't hear a bloody word! Speak English, you slobbering, kilted halfwit!"

The same words were uttered a second time. Once more, Rowland bellowed "*what*?" The third time, he understood.

He remained demented for two hours, while Dolly held his hand, comforting him and spooning brandy down his throat.

The eventual arrival of the police put an end to his ordeal. A police constable, P.C. Lang, the only one dispatched to number 79 Harley Street, banged on the front door. Rowland, who, like his son, was stark raving, dragged the astounded constable, into the drawing room and pushed him into an armchair.

"Spill it, Constable!" he screamed.

"I beg your pardon, Dr Rendon?"

"Spill it, I said. Vomit it into an ash-tray! Where the hell's my son?"

"Your son's safe," said P.C. Lang. "We took him back to the Priory."

The colour came back into Rowland's face. "Where did you find him?"

"On a train from Waterloo to Portsmouth. He was lying in the luggage rack, menacingly reading aloud a story which he said was called *The Fall of the House of Usher.*"

"Oh? Oh, I see. I apologize for screaming at you and knocking you about. Have some brandy, my dear chap."

"Thank you, but no. In the interests of my own sanity, I'm getting out of this house as soon as I possibly can!"

Rowland drove to the Priory like a maniac, screaming with mirthless laughter, much of the time on the right hand side of the road, causing other drivers to swerve onto pavements and into ditches. He screeched to a gravelly halt outside the front door of the Priory and leapt from his car, leaving the keys in the ignition and the driver's door open. He ran upstairs to William's room and knocked over two lost-looking nuns as he did so.

William was dressed in white trousers and a white V-necked sweater. He had combed his hair and looked angelic, serene and childlike. He was working on a jigsaw puzzle.

"Oh, Father! I felt I was cured, so I walked out."

"Better, yes. Cured, no."

"Why do you say that, Father?"

This time, Rowland shouted with joy and relief, instead of pain.

"Because a man who lies in a luggage rack on a train, reading Edgar Allan Poe aloud in a menacing monotone to terrified passengers, is *mentally ill!*"

William's abrupt transformation from a sick man, to a charming eccentric, was seen by the staff at the Priory, as a miracle. Rowland was happy once more. When he wasn't laughing and joking, he was weeping with joy.

William's mood fluctuated and after another two weeks, it stabilized and he was discharged. Even then, his state of mind lacked the perfection which would have made Rowland completely happy.

William was no longer depressed, but he remained disturbed without really understanding why. He sold his house in Rutland Gate, and moved into a big flat in Vauxhall Bridge Road. He returned to the Hammersmith. Soon, he was promoted from SHO in Pathology to Senior Registrar and worked under an easy-going consultant, who cracked one morbid joke after another, about the dissection of dead bodies, and the diseases responsible for the deaths of their owners.

William shared his sense of humour, because of his belief that there is a funny side to all things grave. He knew that terrible things had happened during his life, but was unable to remember what many of them were. It seemed as if he were carrying a weight round his neck, but he had no idea what this entailed. He felt that only half his mind were functioning, and that the other half were closed down.

He wanted to know what was wrong. He thought of returning to his ageing father's house, and part of him craved the consultations in the nursery, because it was there, and there alone, that he could find out who he was, what he had seen and what had happened to him.

He wondered why bright red things outside the nursery tormented him but did not wish to know. He continued to wear his dark glasses to shield himself, and on the surface, he was affable, cheerful and popular with his colleagues.

He had avoided contact with Rowland, whom, he knew, would try to rekindle his awareness of the past, in an attempt to make him normal. He felt guilty about his having spurned the father who loved him and would have given anything to help him. Instead of seeing him every evening as before, he limited his visits to his father and stepmother to once a week, lunch on Sundays.

He was sitting alone in the Hammersmith Hospital canteen and was comforted by his short period of solitude. He did not like it when Sam Roberts, an SHO in his department, asked if he could join him.

"I won't mind if you don't want me to sit here," said Roberts. "Would you rather be alone?"

William was too polite to say he needed an hour to think and, if possible, to discover who he was.

"I don't mind. I'll move some of my papers to my side of the table," he replied, and hoped that Roberts would refrain from making conversation.

"Was it you who dictated that post mortem on the Barnett woman?" asked Roberts, as he crammed his mouth with hard bread and Cheddar cheese.

"Yes. Why do you ask?"

"I was impressed by it," said Roberts. "I know an SHO has no business to be talking to a Senior Registrar in this manner, but I'd like to, just to show my humble admiration. Not a single detail was left out. Mind you, a lot of medical secretaries edit the reports, through laziness. I know Juliet doesn't do that."

"Who's Juliet?" asked William.

"Haven't you met her? She's the brunette with the legs. She's an agency temp."

"How long has she been here?"

"Almost two weeks. I speak to her, sometimes. She's fascinated by the Barnett woman's post mortem. She said she'd never typed anything about a blot clot in the brain before. She seems to have a macabre interest in brains."

William wanted Roberts to go away but could find no tactful way of telling him.

"Why brains?" he forced himself to ask.

"No idea."

There was a silence. William picked up his copy of *The Daily Mail* and rattled it impatiently in the air.

"I say, William, you're awfully moody. Sometimes, you're full of life and laughter. Other times, you brood, as if you had something on your mind."

"Oh? I get these moods, sometimes," William said, non-committally.

"Can't you tell someone about them? It doesn't necessarily have to be a doctor."

"Who do you think I should go to?"

"It could be anybody. A clairvoyant, a counsellor, a priest."

"Maybe, I will. I can't stand having these moods. I wish they'd go away."

William drove his Jensen to Victoria Street and parked it on a meter. He fed the meter and walked towards Westminster Cathedral, bearing the facial expression of a man breaking out of jail.

As he had not had a devout upbringing, he had rarely entered a church and was intimidated by the cathedral's darkness and size, and the tables supporting row upon row of half burnt-out candles.

He walked towards an area in the back of the building, where an unhealthy-looking, pasty-faced woman of about sixty, was arranging piles of leaflets. She failed to look up, when she knew she was about to be approached and questioned. She was in a surly mood because she had been kept awake for five nights in a row, by dogs barking outside her house.

William's nervousness was intensified by her lack of friendliness. He leant across the table, dividing him from the woman, and although he thought he was whispering, he was shouting at the top of his voice. He wanted to leave the cathedral, once he had spoken to someone who could help him to find out who he was, and why the colour, red distressed him. If illogically, he was still unwilling to return to his father.

"Can I help you?" said the woman, her tone as cold as her features.

"I want to see a man of the Cloth! My father's a psychiatrist!" bellowed William.

"Would you kindly refrain from shouting," said the woman. "You are on sanctified premises. The fact that your father's a psychiatrist, is of no interest to me whatever."

"Where the hell can I find a man of the Cloth?"

"By queuing up in front of the church, like everyone else."

"I'm not prepared to do that." William was still shouting. "All I can see, is a lot of people on their knees. Where's the man?"

"I thought I told you not to shout in here. Besides, he's not 'the man.' He's a Minister of God."

"I don't care! Where is he?"

"In the confessional."

"Does that mean I've got to speak to him through a bloody grid?"

The woman was terrified of William because she knew, instinctively, that he was insane.

"Language, sir! It is only in the confessional that you will find a Minister of God," she said, avoiding eye contact with him.

"Look me in the eye, when you're speaking to me, woman! What do I say when I open the conversation?"

The woman continued to look away and lowered her head.

"When you've found the appropriate person, you say, 'Forgive me, Father, for I have sinned'."

"Who the hell do I say this to?"

The woman ignored his question and was silent for a few seconds before speaking.

"Are you a believer?"

William reached into his pocket for some Dexedrine which he chewed and swallowed. He suddenly had an agonizing yearning to hurl himself onto an unwashed Bohemian woman with mysterious, straight, black hair. He felt physically uncomfortable.

"Bloody hell, no!" he shouted.

The woman told William to wait. She disappeared to make a telephone call. When she came back, she looked paler and more drawn than when he had first met her. There was a tremor in her hands which took it in turn to clutch her fake pearls. She handed William a piece of paper, on which she had written the address of a house close to the cathedral.

"I have made enquiries," she said. "If you go to this address, you will find Father Wilson. He's at home, this afternoon."

"Wilson, you say?"

"Father Wilson."

"You're going to have to take me there. I don't know this part of London."

"Indeed, I will take you no-where," she said. "I'd be terrified of going anywhere with you outside this building."

"Terrified of what?"

"Never mind."

She gave William succinct instructions. The house was less than a five minute walk away from the cathedral. He lit a *Benson and Hedges* cigarette, and leaned against the front door of the house, with the palm of his right hand pressing the bell, for over a minute.

When the door opened, he overbalanced and fell to the floor in the hall. He inadvertently dropped his pill bottle. He had forgotten to secure its lid. The small white pills rolled about on the floor.

He rose to his feet, and was astounded by the sight of a petrified nun whose small, black eyes penetrated his head like screwdrivers.

"Would you please extinguish your cigarette," she said. "A description of you was given to me over the telephone. Father Wilson will be down from his rest, shortly."

"Am I to stand or sit?" shouted William. The nun pointed to an uncomfortable-looking, upright, wooden chair.

"You may sit down. Father Wilson does not like people shouting in his house. You were shouting in the cathedral, too, I heard."

"When's he coming down? I can't wait too long. I'm a doctor."

The nun ignored him. William had to wait for fifteen minutes for the priest to come downstairs into the hall. The priest had consumed four glasses of wine at lunch, and was feeling sluggish and depressed after his interrupted rest.

As he entered the hall, he failed to notice the

pills, sliding about like beads. He fell flat on his back. A crunching sound reminded him that he had put his back out, yet another time, and would need to go back into a tight, uncomfortable corset.

"What is the trouble, my son?" he forced himself to ask.

"I've got this ghastly problem in relation to things that are red," shouted William.

"Please do not shout. Red, you say?"

"Yes."

"You've had me woken up during my rest. You've frightened a lot of people in the cathedral. I'd appreciate it if you would explain yourself."

"Well, I don't really know what part of me is. I may have killed someone. I may have killed more than once, and on the other hand, I may not necessarily have killed anyone at all."

A wave of nausea surged through the priest. He was irritated by his visitor, whom he thought was an attention-seeking nuisance.

"Would you mind coming back again, when you know for certain whether you have killed someone or not," he said, trying to hide his irritability. He then went into auto-pilot and recited *Our Father*, with his hands gently resting on William's head.

William rose to his feet. The Dexedrine had reached his head. He wanted a woman so badly that he began to feel ill.

"Any chance of my using your bathroom?" he asked.

"Oh, do you require a bath?" asked the harassed priest.

"No," said William, failing to choose his words more carefully. "I lost my wife not long ago. Apart from our love, I miss the physical side of our relationship. If you'll pardon my ribaldry, I just need to get off."

The priest cleared his throat. "The lavatory is through there on the right. All I ask is that you don't make too much noise."

William was ready to leave. "Perhaps you might like to come back," said the priest.

"It's possible I might, although I'm afraid I'm not a believer. I say that because I wouldn't want to waste your time when genuine believers are waiting to see you."

"All right. Here is my butler's mobile 'phone number. He's trying to get a job somewhere else, so it's wise to fill up his recording space. Whenever you want to speak your thoughts to me, just ring the number, and say as much as you can."

William felt no better after the incident. He longed to go to his father's house and re-start the 7.00 o'clock consultations, because he knew that Rowland, and he, alone, could tell him who the unknown part of him was.

264

The yearning for his father's company, was replaced, within seconds, by fear. The idea of knowing who he was, terrified him. Although he retained a dependent, immature love for his father, he had no wish to be confronted by him in the Room of Love which was also the Room of Knowledge.

To compensate for not wishing to confess to his father, William rang the priest's butler's mobile 'phone number. He spat out the story of his wretched life, including giving an in-depth description of his failure to let his right hand and left hand meet. He also referred at length to his problem concerning things which were red.

He didn't expect an answer. After about a fortnight, he was examining an extracted brain, holding it Yorwickwise up to the ceiling light. His mobile 'phone rang.

"Yes?"

"Look here, you fuckhead!" shouted an American voice. "You've just filled up my whole tape, you no-good bum!"

"Oh, you must be Father Wilson's butler."

"You bet! Next time, I'll send you a carload of the boys."

William was in a mischief-making mood that day, and knew that only the most nonsensical of messages would infuriate his new enemy further.

265

He rang back.

"I say, how long did it take Mussolini to get over his mother's death?" he asked.

"Up your arse!" screamed the priest's butler.

"Hey, not so fast. I've something else to say. Do you know that Hitler's mother took trays of food up to his room, because he wouldn't get out of bed?"

The priest's butler had run out of expletives and was too exasperated to speak. He hung up.

William did not feel in a social mood that evening after leaving the Hammersmith. He took the Jensen to the Paddington area, where there were plenty of places in which to pick up a woman. He was aware that the shabbiness of the area was depressing. He was depressed already and he went there to become more so.

He saw a building near the slip road leading to the station. It was small, crudely lit and seedy, and displayed the word "hotel" in flashing neon lights.

He went to the bar, ordered a generous amount of whisky and sat down on a soiled, leopard-skin covered sofa. He drank the whisky slowly and became pleasantly sleepy. He leaned back and closed his eyes.

He dreamed he was having violent sex with a gentle, pretty woman, wearing silk, flowing robes. He had told her about his red problems and she had tried to help him. She said, "Come with me and I will take you to a place where there is no pain," and as he got up to follow her, he was happy instead of tormented. He was laughing and joking.

He felt someone tapping him on the shoulder.

"Excuse me, sir," said a provincially-accented man in a shabby, olive-green suit, laced with gold livery.

"What do you want?" asked William.

"This is a hotel, not a dosshouse. Would you please leave."

"It's not a hotel!" shouted William, "It's a sodding disorderly house!"

"Have you paid for the whisky?"

"I'll pay you once you've got me a woman."

"You'll pay up now or I'll call the police. The stuff has set you back seven quid."

William had plenty of money in cash but wished to confuse and upset the man who had woken him.

"I only pay by Access," he said. "I don't carry cash."

The waiter looked disgruntled and reluctantly produced a machine to make such payment possible.

"Sorry, Mister. The machine's not taking your card."

"Ring 'em up then. A dump like this should hand out liquor free of charge to someone like me. I'm a bloody doctor. I analyse dead bodies."

The waiter winced, and got the Access office on the line after a ten minute wait.

"I'll take your mother's maiden name and your date of birth," he said, unpleasantly.

"Cooper! April 12th, 1959!" shouted William.

"Aires, eh?" said the waiter. "Might have guessed."

William snatched the receiver from his hand. Loss of temper invariably dignified his misery.

"Standing me up, are we? Do you know who you're talking to? Let me tell you. I'm a distinguished member of the medical profession and my father's a consultant Harley Street psychiatrist, so I'd thank you not to treat me like Bill Sikes urinating into some doorway!"

The waiter was aghast. "There's no need to shout," he muttered.

He was puzzled by the behaviour of such a beautiful, blonde, male bombshell whom he secretly fancied. William had so much contempt for him, his kind, and the human race in general, that he snatched the card from the machine and stormed into the street, shouting, "Of course, it's only right for a doctor of my worth and distinction to be served on the house!"

As he drove home, he felt even more depressed than he anticipated he would be. For no apparent reason, his thoughts suddenly turned to Juliet, the medical secretary whom Sam Roberts, the SHO, had been speaking about.

William was intrigued by his colleague's description of Juliet, and, in particular, by his referring to her as "the brunette with the legs." He wondered what the most appropriate method of introducing himself to her, would be. He lay on his back in his Vauxhall Bridge Road flat, and after much serious thought, he decided to speak to her on a professional basis.

Juliet shared an airy, oblong office with another medical secretary called Sharon. Whereas Juliet was smartly dressed and vain, Sharon cared little about her appearance and habitually wore a thick, loose sweater, two sizes too big for her, and a pair of brown, cotton trousers.

William knocked on the door and came in. The two women peered at his thick, blonde hair and innocent, bloodshot blue eyes.

Juliet had on a black, silk blouse and a matching black mini-skirt. The first thing William noticed was her long, slender, bare legs. Her shoulder-length, copper-coloured hair was dragged back from her face in two gold combs. William felt a sudden fear of rejection, but he knew that once he was in the secretaries' office, he would be obliged to state the purpose of his visit.

Sharon continued to use her word-processor. Juliet looked up at William and smiled.

"Oh, Juliet," he began, "it is Juliet, isn't it?"

"That's right. Juliet Silverman. What can I do for you?"

"I've got a tape here. I'm afraid it's urgent. It's a post mortem report on Edward Conolly. It's very long. There's going to be an Inquest tomorrow as he died in suspicious circumstances."

Juliet took the tape from William's trembling hand.

"I'll do it straight away. Could you let me know your full name and what goes after it?"

"I'm so sorry," said William. "It's William J. V. Rendon, MA., DM., FRCP, Senior Registrar in Pathology."

Juliet put the tape in the machine and wound it backwards and found there was no speech on it. There are times when medical secretaries become paranoid if this happens, because they assume the doctors will think they have erased the tape by accident.

She turned it to its other side, and went through the same procedure, and found this side was also blank. She bleeped William.

"You've given me a two-sided blank tape, Dr

Rendon," she said.

"Oh, I may have made a mistake and given you another clean tape. I'll dictate the whole thing myself while you type it, and I can inhale your enchanting wafts of *Chanel 5*. Perhaps I shouldn't have said that. It was a bit familiar and disrespectful of me."

"I'm glad you like it, Dr Rendon."

William put his hands on her shoulders. "Don't call me Dr Rendon," he said shyly. "My name's William. Shall we get started?"

She loved his innocent, friendly, chivalrous conversation. The sadness shown in his bloodshot blue eyes made her inquisitive. She was insightive, and could tell that he had been in pain for most of his life. She became overwhelmed with maternal affection.

She turned her head and faced him, her facial expression pert. William wanted to kiss her. There were tears in his eyes because it was impossible for them to ravage each other on the floor.

"Well, William. Ready to start whenever you are."

William sat down beside her.

"'HISTORY'" in caps," he said gently. "New line. The deceased was a heavy drinker and had been to de-toxification centres in the past. He used drugs and on this occasion, had been in a fight and

271

had been badly beaten up. He was admitted to the Hammersmith Hospital on 1 August, 1991, suffering from a Morphine overdose, as well as an excessive alcohol intake.

"He was ventilated in ITU (Intensive Care Unit) where he had multiple fits. Despite all clinical efforts, he was pronounced dead at 2.48 a.m."

William ran his hands through Juliet's copper-coloured hair. Her extreme beauty made him feel ill. He continued,

"Under heading, Cause of Death, type,

(a)   Cerebral anoxia (possibly brought on by the blow he received to his head.)
(b)   Aspiration pneumonia.
(c)   Alcohol and Morphine abuse."

William continued to dictate the details of the cardiovascular system, respiratory system, abdominal system and endocrine system.

"We're nearly finished. We've still got to record the weight of the organs. Is this distressing you at all?"

"Of course not, William. I enjoy gore. Why else do you think I work in hospitals? It's we women who go for the gore. It's the men who run away from it."

"Good girl. Type the following, if you would,

272

you glamorous sexpot!"

This time, William quoted the weights, in a sleepy, liturgical manner, and sounded like a Russian Orthodox priest with a violent hangover.

"Heart 495 grams; (Oh, each organ on a new line, sexpot).

"Liver 955 grams;

"Spleen 170 grams;

"Left kidney 130 grams;

"Right kidney 225 grams;

"Brain 1555 grams;

"Right lung 650 grams;

"Left lung 580 grams.

"Am I going too fast for you?"

"No, of course not, William."

"Good girl. I'll have a look at it and sign it if it's OK."

Although smoking was forbidden, William lit a *Benson and Hedges* and read the report, while she leant against him."

"Not a single mistake, Juliet, you're a natural."

He wondered agonizingly whether to invite her to dinner that evening. He was terrified she would reject his invitation.

It was she who took the initiative.

"I fancy you, William. Will you take me out to dinner, tonight?"

"That's what I was going to ask you."

They kissed each other in the secretaries' office. Sharon was well-mannered and discreet, despite her frumpish appearance. She got up and left the room.

"Just wait till we get home," William said. "We're going to have a blockbuster, there. Why not bring a copy of the Barnett post mortem along? Sam said you were fascinated by it, almost to the point of being morbidly roused!"

"There's something about you I can understand," she said. "The linking of sex with death."

"It's not uncommon for them to go side by side," said William. "It is very often the case in anyone working in hospitals. The unpleasant work we have to do, forces us to see the funny side, and the stress entailed, makes us seek sex as a refuge."

They walked hand in hand to William's Jensen.

"I want to go to your place before dinner," said Juliet, with a brazenness which attracted him.

"So do I, you fast little hussy."

Once they reached Vauxhall Bridge Road, they threw themselves to the floor in the hall and had violent, disinhibited sex, which continued for half an hour. William and Juliet were nearly too exhausted to stand. They spent the next half hour, getting their breath back and eventually staggered upstairs to William's bed.

They romped again for another hour. Juliet was an exciting, original, and rare performer between the sheets. He had never felt so carried away with Sarah, the American woman, or even Anne, who had died, and who had treated him kindly and sensitively.

"You've got the Barnett post mortem with you, haven't you?" he said.

"Yes. Can I read some of it aloud?"

"You don't really want to do that, do you?"

"Yes. All this morbid stuff turns me on."

"I like to see you having pleasure. Instead of reading the whole thing, why don't I ask you a few questions, and we'll talk through yet another session?"

This time, he lay on top of her while she lay face downwards. Neither of them appeared to have breathing difficulties when speaking.

"So then, what was the cause of the Barnett woman's death?" he asked, once he had entered her.

" 'Twas a blood clot, 'twas a blood clot, 'twas a blood clot on the brain," she sang to the tune of *Clementine*.

"Do you usually break into song during the sex act?" he asked.

She didn't answer.

The act speeded up and became violent, but this

275

did not interfere with their conversation.

"What did the brain weigh, you incomparable, moribund little siren?" he shouted.

"One thousand, six hundred grams, exactly. Harder! Harder! One thousand, six hundred grams, William!"

"Here's a more difficult question," he said, still shouting.

"I bet I'll know the answer. I know the whole thing by heart. Ask me another question before I drown you. Hurry!"

"How much did the clot itself weigh, you fabulous, sultry, graveyard ghoul?"

"One ounce, I think. I don't know what that is in kilograms."

"And the liver?"

"Nine hundred and forty one grams! Hurt me, William!"

"And the heart?"

"Five hundred grams. Oh my God, I'm getting there!"

The lovers lay on their backs, exhausted. They got under the covers.

"Why are you morbid, Juliet?" he asked. "I'm not criticizing you. I'm asking out of curiosity. Both my other ladies were like that as well. Perhaps, it's a common trait in women."

"It's a gene. I get it from my grandmother. She

loved attending gruesome court cases."

"Is the lady still alive?"

"No. She died of a stroke, fifteen years ago. Both my parents are dead."

"Any brothers, sisters?"

"Just one brother. He lives in Jerusalem. We keep in touch by E-Mail. I'm not a very family-orientated person."

"You say you inherit your morbidity from your grandmother. Is there anything else contributing to it?"

"Well, there is. It was something which happened when I was ten years old. I didn't know all this about my grandmother, then. She gave me a camera for my birthday.

"I wasn't particularly interested in it until my mother threatened to take it away from me, because I wasn't using it. She said how lucky I was to have a camera. She put in a film and told me she would take it away from me, if I didn't use up the film by the end of the day.

"We were in Regent Street. My mother had parked her car there. She told me to stay in the car and recite *Sam, Sam, Pick up thy Musket* to traffic wardens, to make them go away."

"I've never heard that," said William, "How does it go?"

Sylvia recited it, using a rasping,

Yorkshire accent.

" 'Sam, Sam, pick up thy musket,'
Said the Sergeant Major with a roar.
'You knocked it down, so you'll pick it up,
Or it stays where it is, on the floor.'"

She attempted to recite the monotonous ditty in its
entirely, but it was too arduous for William. He
interrupted her, peremptorily.

"No wonder you drove the old bitches away,"
he remarked. "Then what?"

"My mother went into a shop to pick up some
dresses which had been altered for her.

"I waited and waited in the car. A whole hour
passed and there was no sign of her.

"On the other side of the road, a cyclist, a boy
of about fifteen, was hit and killed by a lorry. The
lorry had crushed his chest. I got out of the car and
crossed the street. I remembered my mother saying
that she would take the camera away if I didn't use
up the film.

"The boy was lying on his back, away from the
pavement. A crowd ogled his lifeless body.

"I got through the crowd and went as near to the
body as I could. I was fascinated. The boy's rib
cage had been crushed, and I could see his
motionless heart under the bones. It looked like a

278

sponge with a heavy weight on it.

"The camera was round my neck. I went as close to the body as I could. I knelt on the ground. I was only six inches away. I bent over the body and I started taking photographs. I kept getting up, moving and kneeling down again. I was taking photographs all the time. I just couldn't stop. My heart was going faster and faster. I got at least five close-ups of the chest. There was so much blood. I leaned forward and put my hand in it, to see what it felt like. It wasn't hot, as I expected. It was warm. I took some close-ups of the boy's lifeless face. His eyes were pale blue. They were like glass. They were staring into space.

"I could have gone on taking photographs forever. I heard my mother shouting and screaming from the other side of the street. She was calling my name. She was hysterical. Perhaps, when she came back to the car, and found I wasn't there, she may have thought I'd been in the accident, myself."

"I bet she did," said William. "Go on."

"I'd inadvertently left the passenger door open, because I was so excited by the sound of the lorry's screeching brakes and the screams the boy let out before he died.

"My mother crossed the street. She was still screaming my name. She was frantic. She forced her way through the gaping crowd. Oh, what nasty, horrible ghouls, they all were! They had no interest in trying to save the boy's life. They were such repellant *voyeurs*, I thought."

William laughed. Juliet continued.

"My mother caught me taking the photographs. She came up to me and dragged me to my feet. Oh, she was so livid! I'd never seen her so angry before.

"When I was taking the pictures, I was laughing. I just couldn't stop laughing. She slapped my face and took me back to the car. Her rage was not helped by the fact that there was a parking ticket on the windscreen."

"She must have thought you were the best thing that had ever happened to her," said William. "Continue."

"She got in and turned the engine on. She kept shouting the words, 'you wretched little brat! You odious, morbid, little monster!'

"'I only had one photograph to go before finishing the film, Mummy,' I said. 'You told me I was to finish the film. I could have taken that last picture, before you dragged me away.'

"For some reason, she looked so shocked. She was quite ashen and trembling, as if it had been I, who had been killed."

"Might that not have been a relief to her?" suggested William, in jest."

"I'm amazed by your ability to be so witty," she said, her tone sour, adding, "Her reaction to the whole thing was so unbelievably inappropriate, I thought."

William laughed a second time.

" 'I haven't yet fully taken this incident in,' my mother said. She wasn't shouting, this time. Her voice was quiet and cold. 'When we get home, I'm going to discuss this highly distressing and lamentable matter with your father.'

"I was made to go to my room and learn a passage from Shakespeare. My brother and I were always made to learn Shakespeare passages by heart when we were naughty. That's why I know so much of it. Do you like it, William?"

"Yes. I always have. I think he touches on just about every thought which passes through our minds, some time or another.

"What I like about him, is the way he describes, in detail, the psychology of highly intelligent people, who lose their heads because of their obsessions, and commit one thoroughly stupid act after another.

"He does it so well. Take Hamlet, Lear, Antony (in *Antony and Cleopatra*) and Othello. All these characters are different but they are all ruined, in the same way, by their compulsive obsessions.

"Incidentally, which piece were you made to

281

learn, the day you took the photographs?"

"That *Julius Caesar* speech, *O, pardon me, thou bleeding piece of earth.*"

"I adore those lines. I sometimes recite them to myself when I'm alone. It must be wonderful to have a hero, who's dead, because he no longer has to live up to your expectations. If he lives, he withers, in body and mind, and it's hard to go on worshipping him. When you find that your hero is not a god but a man, the disappointment causes something within you to die."

There was a silence, broken by Juliet.

"It's unusual to have a fantastic lover with a sensitive mind, as well," she said. "I've found both those qualities in you. Added to that, you possess physical beauty."

"I know that's true," said William. "Tell me, what happened to your camera, in the end?"

"It was confiscated."

"And you knew nothing about the morbid streak in your grandmother, at the time, you say?"

"No."

"Were you fond of her?"

"Yes. Very. My brother and I adored her. She used to tell us fantastic stories, some comical, some suspense-ridden, some just plain fascinating."

"No macabre stories?"

"None, whatever. She spent hours each day,

doing meticulous paintings of flowers. She never tired of this occupation and was incapable of boredom. There was a unique serenity about her. I always felt calm when I was with her.

"I remember, as a child, being deeply upset about Marilyn Monroe's suicide. I admired her and longed to bleach my hair and look like her when I was older.

"When I heard the news, I went into the room, in which my grandmother sat, painting. I said 'Have you heard about it?' She said she had.

" 'She's dead! She's dead!' I said. It was almost as if I had known her personally.

" 'She may be dead,' said my grandmother. 'But her films aren't dead, are they?'

"That statement has had an extraordinary influence on me. I've always thought that no-one can truly die, if they've created something to leave behind them. I so much want to be a writer, I know I will be, one day."

"You should," said William.

"I simply can't do it, yet."

"Why?"

"Because my will to do it is so overpowering that the intensity would crush me, and prevent me from doing so."

"Have you ever tried?"

"I will. I will" She suddenly looked haunted.

She changed the subject. "I know nothing about you, William. Are your parents alive?"

"They're both dead."

"Who was your father?"

"He was a doctor."

"What speciality?"

"Psychiatry," said William, abruptly.

"You don't really want to talk about your parents, do you? I can tell."

"Not a lot. I've got an idea."

"Yes?"

"Why don't you go to the kitchen and cook us both dinner? Then, you can bring it into the room on a tray."

"I'm afraid I can't cook," said Juliet. For the first time, she felt embarrassed and humiliated in William's presence.

"In that case, you'll have to learn. I'll teach you. If you move in here, which I hope you will, you will have to cook for me, because my hours are so much longer than yours."

There was something about cooking which terrified Juliet, in the same way that the prospect of writing books, daunted her. She could have written, had she disciplined herself. Indeed, she dedicated her life to the written word in later years. The idea of cooking was repellant to her, however, because she hated doing something she was no good at.

Neither food, nor its preparation, interested her, and she lacked the co-ordination required to cook. She could not even enter a kitchen without inadvertently dropping and breaking crockery. She also believed that women should no longer be expected to cook.

"You look worried," said William.

"I am. I've got a mental block about cooking. I suppose it's because my mother never stopped telling me that the way to a man's heart is through his stomach. It was a form of brainwashing, and the idea of being expected to cook, has always been an anathema to me."

"Your mother appears to have shaped your personality in more ways than one," said William. "Did you find her domineering?"

"Yes, I think I did," she said.

"I don't agree with the idea that the way to a man's heart is through his stomach. The way to a man's heart is through his cock.

"In other words, you have found your way to my heart, already, and whether you cook or not, makes little difference. I'm a rich man. I've inherited a lot of money. I'll hire a cook. I've already got a cleaner, so you don't have to do that kind of work, either."

They got out of bed and went into the bathroom. William turned on the taps and poured *Badedas* into the water. He sat at one end of the bath and Juliet lay back with her head between his knees.

She was feeling downhearted. She was ashamed of having told him that she did not wish to cook for him, and she felt even more inadequate on hearing that he would be happy to pay for a cook with his own money. He noticed a stray tear on her cheek.

"Who's your favourite poet, William?" she asked, her voice unnaturally raised.

"Edgar Allan Poe."

"He's one of my favourites, as well. In fact, he *is* my favourite. That stands to reason because of my experience in Regent Street, and my grandmother's genes. As a child, I used to attend the funerals of total strangers, for kicks. It was an activity which thrilled and excited me."

"Let me give you a word of advice," said William.

"What sort of advice?"

"I'm not saying this to hurt you, as I know that, under your exhibitionism, and apparently hard exterior, you are more vulnerable than you would let others believe."

"Well, what is it?"

"You talk far too much about yourself, Juliet. Every sentence you utter begins with the word 'I'.

It almost seems as if you think you're the only person in the world who exists."

"That's quite untrue," she said. "I tried to get you to talk about yourself, but you refused."

"That's because I do not care to talk about myself. Any more than I think someone would wish to hear it."

"What you've just said, suggests that I am not up to much," she said.

"You don't listen. I didn't say that at all. I love you and I have a very high regard for you. You're attractive, you're funny, and you've got a fine mind. Everyone has faults, and so do I. The only part of you, which is unattractive, is your tedious obsession with yourself.

"In order for me to continue to love you and find you attractive, you must stop these interminable monologues, regarding incidents in which you are the central figure.

"You're also very repetitive. You've said, not once, but several times, that morbid matters stimulate you. You're not talking to an idiot. You're talking to me. If you have something to say, you only need to say it once.

"When you described the incident in Regent Street, you didn't tell me what you thought was a humorous anecdote. You made a speech. You just went on and on and on, and through good manners,

I refrained from interrupting you.

"Also, you grossly exaggerated what you saw in Regent Street, stimulating you to take pictures. You couldn't possibly have seen a man's rib-cage, without lifting his shirt first.

"If the accident had been as terrible as you described it, not even you, aged ten, would have had it in you, to kneel by the body and take photographs, simply to convince your mother that you had been using the camera.

"You may indeed have seen an injured person lying by the road. I don't deny that you got out of your mother's car and peered at him.

"All this business about the crushed rib-cage, and your covering your hand with the dead man's blood, to see what it felt like, is ludicrous play-acting on your part. In short, it is rubbish.

"It irritates me, when you talk like this, because you not only make a fool of yourself; you demean my intelligence, by your assumption that I'll believe your anecdotes.

"As if to justify yourself, you blame your mother and your grandmother, both of whom are allegedly responsible for your attitude and behaviour. I can believe your attitude, but the acts you boast that you have committed, are bogus. They are pathetic. They are not even comical.

"If you want to tell a story, at least have the guts to take up pen and paper. Project your infantile fantasies onto paper, and not into the ears of people like me. You talk too much. You use too many words."

"I know you could write well, if you tried. You're articulate. You're imaginative and when you talk, you never appear to tire of your subject. You've got the mental qualities it takes to write a book, but you need to force yourself to have the courage it takes to start. Writing a book for the first time is very frightening, but you must be prepared to do the things you're frightened of doing because it will make a better person of you.

"Another thing you must do is grow up. Tell intelligent stories, not stupid, childish ones, and don't write about yourself. No reader likes to see 'I, I, I' on the page. Write in the third person."

The water was getting cold. She turned on the hot tap, feeling deflated and hurt.

"I suppose there's nothing an exhibitionist despises more, than being caught out," she said. "It's the same as getting high on a drug, and suddenly hitting the ground."

"I know I've hurt you," said William. "I didn't mean to. You would have been far more hurt if you'd heard it from someone else."

"No. The person who inflicts the greatest injury

is the person the victim loves the most."

They got out of the bath. William dried Juliet with a large bath towel with his initials embroidered on it, a gift from his father. She tried to disguise the fact that she was in tears.

"It's all right," he said. "So far, I've only told you about a fault you have, and we all have them. I haven't started on your virtues yet. That would take me at least a week."

Juliet moved into the flat in Vauxhall Bridge Road, the following evening. William took her to a Chinese restaurant in Wardour Street, ironically the same place that Philip, the paedophile, had taken him to when he was eight years old.

"I'm sure I'm not the first man you've been with," he said, smiling.

"You said only last night that you didn't like me to talk about myself."

"You are a silly girl. I'm not asking you about yourself. Just through interest, I'd like to know about your previous men."

She picked up a pair of chopsticks and tried to teach herself to use them. She realized there was no point in her learning. She dropped them onto the table from a height.

"The only men I've had, have been doctors from the London hospitals I've worked in."

"I see. Anyone from the Hammersmith?"

"Only Dr Roberts."

"You mean Sam?"

"That's him. Dr Sam Roberts."

"Oh, God, Juliet, not him! He's only an SHO, for Christ's sake."

"Whatever he is, it's finished. It was by mutual agreement. We'd been going out for three days."

William had a habit which many women find attractive. He was fascinated by the sexual and social behaviour of his predecessors, particularly if he knew them. He leant forward, across the table. His large blue eyes looked conspiratorial. He winked.

"What's old Sam like, eh?" he asked.

"Bloody conventional."

"Oh? What's his appetite like — in the bedroom, that is?"

"He's only got the energy for one session a night. He's not like you."

"Indeed? Mind you, an SHO is under so much pressure, he'd be too tired to satisfy a fanatic like you. Has he got a car?"

"He did have. He's been taken off the road for drink-driving."

"What sort of car did he drive before he lost his licence?"

"A Ford Capri. It was second-hand. It was white when he bought it. He had it sprayed turquoise."

"Jesus wept, Juliet! Vulgar tastes in cars, eh?"

"He never took me out in it. He'd already lost his licence, two months ago, he said. He told me, that when he drove, he liked to be fellated by his female passenger."

William let out a guffaw and slapped his thigh.

"Would you like to do that to me when I drive? I bet my Jensen goes faster than Sam's old bucket."

"I wouldn't say 'no'."

"Can you tell me anything else about him?"

"Yes. Before getting into bed, he likes to waltz."

"Waltz? Why?"

"That's just his preference. It gets him into the mood. He likes to do everything with the lights on. He even sleeps with them on."

"That's usually a sign of a man with a guilty conscience," said William. "Anything else?"

"Well, I shouldn't say this. Perhaps it wouldn't be fair."

"Go on, Juliet. I won't tell anyone."

"He needs a lot of manipulation."

"Good God! Poor old Sam. Why did the affair only last for three days?"

"He couldn't bear the pressure," said Juliet. "His workload was so heavy, he couldn't fit sex in as well. It was too much for him."

"I suppose that's as good an answer as any," said William.

Juliet and William were to live together for about two years. During that time, he told her nothing about his childhood or about any difficulties arising from it.

William casually suggested that they go to his father's house, one morning when he was seeing patients. He kept to his story that his father was dead, and to justify the fact that the house was lived in, he told her a friend of his father's had taken over the consulting room, and that he still had a key to the premises.

The lovers continued to have a lurid and outrageous sexual relationship. They were obsessed by each other. William had become deeply in love with Juliet. Apart from the physical side, he was emotionally dependent on her because she was funny, forthright, stable and strong, although she occasionally talked excessively about herself.

She, in turn, loved him but was not in love with him. She saw him as a good-natured, adorable child. Although she refused to cook for him, she looked after him, in a psychological sense, but he still remained too proud to discuss his history.

Inevitably, there came a time when he had to open a small amount of his psyche to her, if he were to put her through the ritual of visiting the nursery. He knew she had a penchant for eccentric and bizarre behaviour, so he was not nervous about raising the subject. He had already lied to her about his father's "friend" taking over the practice, and told her that he wanted to take her to the nursery wing, where he explained he had spent most of his childhood.

He took her to the house one Wednesday morning. As they approached the nursery wing, he put his arm round her waist, something he never did outside his living quarters. He charmed her by putting on a childish voice and by his repetition of the words "See Nanny, see Nanny."

"We'll go to my old room, first, because that's where we'll find a bed," he said, coarsely. They indulged in a number of sexual acts in his old bed, before going to the nursery.

Juliet was extremely amused by his request that she put on the grey wig and apron, and was happy to sit in the nanny's chair, simulating an act of knitting with the red wool which William gave her. She still knew nothing about events which had taken place in the nursery, and was flattered when William related to her as a "nanny" figure. He repeated the same words he had uttered to Sarah, and said how happy he was to see his nanny alive, her soul occupying a new, strong, healthy body.

294

They left the nursery and walked along the linoleum-floored corridor.

"I really enjoyed that, William," she said.

"I'm glad to hear it."

"You will bring me back here, again, won't you?"

"Yes, of course, I will."

"You're not just saying that to please me, I hope. I want to come as often as possible."

"We'll come as often as you like. What did you like most about it?"

"The place is absolutely alive."

"Alive? With what?"

"A wonderful projection of you. I don't know why, but there's more to you, here, than you've cared to show me. It's as if your very soul were trapped here, and wanted to get out but couldn't.

"As we leave now, it seems as if there were a side of you that you were being forced to leave behind. Whatever that thing is, it wants you to take it away with you, but you refuse. I had no idea there was so much pain in you."

William felt a slight jolt but it was not unpleasant. He felt warm and secure in Juliet's company. There were no warning lights in his brain, inviting him to harm her, for she understood him completely and entirely, while remaining devoid of factual knowledge. He continued to withhold the information stored in his father's memory, because Juliet's instincts were ethereal, with no leaning on rationale or intellect.

She leant against him and slept as he drove the Jensen down Harley Street. He took it to the bottom storey of the carpark in Cavendish Square.

The screeching of the car's brakes woke her. They got into the back of the car. She pulled up her dress and tore off his shirt before undoing his zip. "For Christ's sake, hurt me, William!" she shouted. They indulged in screaming, violent, brutal sex.

As their relationship progressed, they lived in perfect spiritual and physical harmony. Though they indulged in frenzied carnal activity several times each day, their souls were like those of an elderly, devout Russian couple, and their coitus like attendances of regular church services.

Juliet had given up her temporary status at the Hammersmith and became permanent. She wanted to be promoted from medical secretary to Administrator, which required training in management.

It was just after the beginning of the academic year. There were no colleges in London where she could begin her training immediately. The only institution available to her was the Princes' College of Business and Management in Oxford, which offered crash courses, lasting for two weeks. She arranged to stay at the Y.W.C.A.

"I can't live without you for two weeks," said William. "I can't do anything without you, dammit!" He poured a few Dexedrine tablets into the palm of his hand and washed them down with milk, which he drank from the bottle.

"What do those things actually *do* for you?" she asked.

"A lot of things. They stop my tiredness. They improve my concentration. They calm my nerves and make me work more efficiently. Sometimes, I use them to bomb my brains out, just for the hell of it."

"Aren't they bad for the heart?"

"Good God, no! They're only amphetamines. Dexamphetamine Sulphate's their full name. Or Dexedrine. Most people call them 'Speed'. I'm going to need them all the time when you're away. I don't know how I'm going to be able to bear it."

He was right. Being alone without Juliet grew more horrific for him as each day passed. He took Dexedrine daily and added to the dose each time.

Sometimes, he indulged in frenzied oninism, and when unable to ejaculate without a woman's touch, he rolled on the floor, sobbing and thinking about suicide.

297

Like Sam Roberts, whom he loved to ridicule, he was unable to sleep in the dark. He felt more secure with the lights on, but the drug prevented him from sleeping. He yearned for Juliet, and the fact that sex was being denied him, was destroying him.

It was 3.00 o'clock on a Tuesday morning. He got out of bed, cleaned his teeth, shaved and put on one of his casual suits. He eased himself behind the wheel of the Jensen and took another palm-full of Dexedrine which he chewed up and swallowed.

The roads were clear. He drove up Park Lane, reaching speeds of 110 m.p.h. The emptiness of the London streets had a calming effect on him, which, combined with the Dexedrine, gave him a temporary feeling of euphoria.

He took out a cassette of Russian folk songs which invariably caused him elation and sexual excitement. The songs had such a pleasant effect on him that he continued towards Marble Arch, driving like a raving madman, with the driver's window fully open and the crisp air whistling past his face.

He drove back down Park Lane, and round Hyde Park Corner once more, in the same abandoned manner. He repeated his route.

As he came down Park Lane a second time, he swerved to the left, mounting a pavement and brushed against some railings, as he headed for the

Shepherd's Market.

There were three prostitutes on the pavement. One was old and raddled, which may have explained her failure to attract punters.

Two other prostitutes, immaculately dressed in navy blue satin mini-skirts, and tight, bra-less sweaters, stood together, about fifty feet away from her. Both had thin, pointed faces and strawberry blonde hair, and were in their thirties.

William swerved the Jensen to a halt. The two young women advanced towards it. One leaned against the driver's door and rested her arms at the bottom of the open window.

The other leaned against the passenger's door.

"Do you two want a ride together?" asked William.

"Don't mind if I do!" said the one on the driver's side, whose name was Kessi.

"How much each?" he asked.

"Fifty pounds each, with condoms, Seventy without," said Kessi.

"Why don't you both get in the back?" said William. "What are your names?"

"I'm Kessi and this is Ruthie," said Kessi, pointing to the other woman.

"Jump in, Kessi and Ruthie. You look very alike. Are you sisters?"

"Twins," said Kessi. "You're a gentleman,

aren't you?"

"There's no such thing as a gentleman," said William, "certainly not on the streets of London at this hour. Are you fond of Russian music?"

"If that's the blooming stuff you was blearing when you pulled up, the answer is we don't. Where are you taking us?"

"Do you mind if I take you to Harley Street?"

"Up 'Arley, eh? Are you a doctor?"

"Yes, that's right. I'm a doctor."

William was anxious not to frighten the women, so he drove slowly, observing the 30 m.p.h. speed limit.

"Would you like me to shut this window?"

"Yes. It's bloody cold out there," said Kessi.

He drove the two women up Wimpole Street in silence, and turned right towards Harley Street. He got out of the car and locked the driver's door. He opened the back door to let the women out.

"This is where I live," he said quietly. "Can I ask you to keep nice and quiet, as there are other people in the house, and I don't want them woken up."

He opened the door and motioned to them to go in front of him. Their thigh-high, stiletto-heeled boots made a clattering noise on the marble floor in the hall. William no longer felt physically roused. All he wished to do now, was invoke his nanny, in Juliet's absence.

"I'm so sorry, ladies. I'm afraid I must ask you to take your boots off. You'll wake the whole household up."

Kessi and Ruthie did as they were told. William took each of them by the arm and led them up the flights of stairs. He unlocked the door of the nursery wing.

"Bloody 'ell!" said Kessi. "'Aven't you got a lift?"

"I'm sorry. There is no lift. Please keep your voice down. I've told you about problems with noise, before."

He took them through the nursery wing door, which he locked, and along the narrow corridor, into the nursery. The skeleton belonging to Sarah, the American, was still hidden behind the nanny's chair. William turned on the light.

"Where's the bed?" asked Kessi, aggressively.

"It won't be that kind of commitment," said William. "Because there are two of you, I want you to take this in turns."

"Take what in bloody turns?" asked Kessi.

"I did have something in mind, but now, I've got a better idea. I am going to ask you to do different things, and they will be extremely easy and quick. Just refresh my memory, please, ladies. Which is Kessi and which is Ruthie?"

"Me, Kessi. Her, Ruthie," said Kessi, impertinently. "All you do is talk. You're a right pompous git! Before we do anything, we'll both want fifty pounds up front."

William knew that the women sensed that he was feeling awkward and clumsy, because he was taking on two of them instead of one. He stepped backwards and handed them fifty pounds each. They counted the money out loud like professional saleswomen. Their long, manicured fingers flicked one note in front of the other at a speed which increased the diffident, upper-class doctor's unease.

"All right, Mister, out with it. What do you want us to do? Come on, we 'ain't got all night," said Kessi.

"It's very simple, Kessi. Would you please go to that cupboard over there. In it, you will find a grey wig, a plastic apron, two balls of bright red wool and some knitting needles. You only need one ball of wool. Once you've found all these things, I would like you to put the grey wig and apron on, and sit in that green armchair. Then, feed some wool onto one of the needles."

"Bloody blooming 'eck!" said Kessi. "I can't knit. I earn me living on me bleeding back, not making clothes."

"Oh, that's quite in order. Absolutely fair enough. All you have to do is go through the motions of knitting, provided the ball of wool is lying in your lap."

Kessi never questioned her punters about their reasons for bizarre requests. She had received her money and was satisfied. She moved the needles against each other but dropped the ball of wool.

"What's this ball of wool doing on the floor, Kessi?" asked William, in an unnaturally anxious tone. She bent over and picked it up.

"Sorry, Mister. It just fell. But it's OK, now, innit? How long do you want me to sit here?"

"Oh, not long. Now, Ruthie, this is where you come into it. Your task might be a bit more difficult than your sister's."

"No lesbianism. No incest, I hope."

"No, no. It won't be anything to do with sex."

"Get on and tell me, then," said Ruthie angrily. "Do you think we've got all night to sit on the top floor of a bloody freezing 'Arley Street house, messing about with balls of wool? We're flaming 'ookers, mate, and if you're not wanting S.M., we expect to get paid for decent, honest sexual intercourse."

"Ruthie," called Kessi.

"What's up, Kess?"

"You've forgotten we've both been paid, so you're to do as you're told!"

William's stiff reserve broke down. He had a

giggling fit. "Does your sister always order you about like this?" he asked.

"Only when there's a third person there, who'll give her an audience," said Ruthie.

William was suddenly reminded of Juliet's attention-seeking behaviour, which charmed him on some occasions, and irritated him on others. He wished she were with him, to comfort him, mother him, amuse him and service him with her aptitude, elegance and brilliance, during each carnal act between them.

He was becoming bored with the two prostitutes, and wondered whether they would talk about him, identify the house, and put his father's reputation at risk.

At the same time, he brooded about the lack of loyalty he would feel towards his nanny, if he failed to make them complete their performance. He had always associated the nursery with love, and suddenly felt guilty about asking two strangers, hard women of the streets, to remind him of those who had loved him.

He tried unsuccessfully to link the feeling of love with that which was cold, base and heartless. He did what he could to dispel his despair. He owed it to Juliet to revel in what sense of humour he had. Waves of absurdity and farce flooded his mind. He smiled, secretively.

"Come on, Mister! We're freezing our clitorises off up 'ere. Do you want me to do anything, or don't you?" snapped Ruthie.

"Don't be cheeky, Ruthie," said her sister, who was still pretending to knit."

"I'm rude because I'm pissed off! Come on, Mister, what do you want?"

"I'll tell you what I want, and by Christ, you'll get on with it, immediately!" shouted William. "You'll go over to the chair where Nanny, I mean your sister, is knitting. You will stand up straight and you will sing the National Anthem."

Both women were aware that they were in the company of a strong, fit-looking man in an advanced stage of insanity, a man whose path it might be lethal to cross. Ruthie's fear only increased her aggression.

"You want me to do *what*?" she spluttered.

"I've just told you. Go over to that chair and sing the National Anthem," he said, more quietly.

"Sing it, Roo," commanded Kessi. Ruthie ignored her.

"Do you mean, you want me to sing *God Save the* fucking *Queen*?"

"Oh, please don't use foul language," said William. "It's so disagreeable in a woman."

"I'm paid to screw punters. I'm not paid to sing."

"It's OK, sir," said Kessi. "Ruthie didn't mean it. Besides, she'd disappoint you. She's tone-deaf. I'll sing it for you. I'm sure a lot of the most respectable women sing it while they knit," and before she could be interrupted, she sang the first verse as loudly as she could.

William lay down on the floor and wept. "Kick me, Ruthie! Insult me! Order me to stand up! Just like my father did."

"I'm cold. I want to go," said Ruthie.

William realized the tragic shamness of the situation he had engineered. He knew that these women would be prepared to sell their story to the highest bidding newspaper, and his love for his reformed and repenting father was so overpowering at that moment, that he felt it suffocating him.

He loved him, just as much as he loved Juliet, but he needed Juliet more because of her magical technique between the sheets, and the abundance of sex he needed, to keep his body healthy and his mind as rational as his circumstances permitted.

Kessi got up.

"Me and my sister was wondering if we could go, now," she said, courteously.

William leant against the nursery door.

"Well, this is where there's a bit of a problem," he said, in the subdued voice of a man, tactfully cancelling a dinner engagement. "You both know

306

too much, now, so I can't let you. I fear that I am going to have to kill you. I don't want to do this, but I must. You don't have anything to live for, either of you, except the need to spend every day of your lives, standing in cold London streets. What sort of a life is that? I'm sure neither of you is happy.

"It's a good thing to die young. You'll be saved from the indignity of old age, and I have no doubt, you'll wish to lead this kind of life until one of you is dead."

Kessi, undoubtedly the only diplomat of the two, held William's hand and massaged it.

"It 'ain't true. We 'ave got something to live for. We live with our old mum in Bethnal Green. She's an invalid and we support her."

"I understand that, but surely she'll soon be dead. You won't have much money left because you've given most of it to her."

He paused, lifted his fist to his mouth and let out a genteel, little cough.

"I say, would either of you ladies care for a *Benson and Hedges*?"

Ruthie took the initiative. She squeezed William violently in the private parts. He fell to the floor. The sisters ran from the room into the corridor. Ruthie tried to open the outer door.

"Oh, my God, Kessi, he's locked this door! He

307

brought us up here to kill us. He meant to all along."

"We can still get away," said Kessi. "It's two of us against him. What do you think our nails are for? We can get his eyes."

William had recovered. He walked down the corridor towards the women.

Ruthie was standing with her back to him, banging on the door, screaming. William was carrying a hammer. He lifted it into the air and brought it down, with full force, on the back of her head.

Kessi raised her hands, intending to claw out his eyes. He threw down the hammer and clutched both her wrists.

"You can scream, if you want," he said. "This corridor's sound-proofed. No-one will hear you."

"Then why did you tell us to keep quiet?"

"Because I'd already decided what I'd do."

Kessi screamed, making a shrill, grating, carrying noise. William hoped that neither Rowland nor Dolly would hear it. His need to protect his father from pain was even greater at that moment, than his longing for Juliet to come home.

He covered Kessi's mouth with his left hand and hit her on the head with the hammer, with his right.

He dragged the dead women back to the nursery, one by one. He took their handbags from the table and laid them by Sarah's remains. He hid their bodies in the same place, and took a sheet from his bed next door, to cover them with. He pushed back the chair, making sure the sheet was out of sight. He sat in the armchair and dragged violently on a *Benson and Hedges.*

He left the room and let himself out at the end of the corridor, locking the door behind him. He went downstairs, through the hall and left the building.

The sun was beginning to rise. He had always loved the dawn. It took him ten minutes to reach his flat in Vauxhall Bridge Road. The sensation of driving up to speeds of 110 m.p.h. once more, and listening to blared Russian folk songs, caused him a temporary period of peace and wellbeing.

Rowland and Dolly had been woken by Mrs Dudley, who brought them a tray of filtered coffee and toast and marmalade. It was 8.00 o'clock in the morning.

Dolly poured coffee into the two cups. Neither spoke before the strong hot drink fortified them.

"You look worried, Rowland."

He turned, facing away from her.

"Did you hear it?" she asked.

"Hear what?"

"It must have been about 4.00 o'clock this morning. I'm sure I heard a woman singing the National Anthem at the top of her voice. Not long after that, I heard a shout."

Rowland felt his muscles go taut. His heart was beating so violently that he thought it was going to tear itself from his body.

"Oh, that," he said. "Yes, I think I did hear something like that. I thought it was a dream before you mentioned it."

She spread marmalade onto her toast.

"It sounded as if it were coming from this house, somewhere upstairs," she said.

Rowland took out a cigarette and lit it.

"That's where you're quite wrong. It was out in the street. Drunks larking about, that sort of thing."

"No! It *was* in this house. I swear it was."

"You're not making any sense. Who the hell would be upstairs shouting and singing at that hour?"

"I don't know. That's why I want an explanation?"

"Are you suggesting it was a burglar? When burglars break into houses, do you think they sing the bloody National Anthem?"

"Perhaps not."

"Well, do they?" shouted Rowland.

"I just *know* there was someone in the house.

Whatever it was, it wasn't outside."

"Perhaps it was Mrs Dudley. She may have been having a nightmare."

"No-one sings when they have nightmares."

"Sometimes, they do. It depends what they're dreaming about. This is beginning to annoy me, Dolly. I can't keep up with the taxing load of trivia with which women see fit to occupy themselves. To put your mind at rest, I'm ringing for Mrs Dudley. She may come up with something."

"You rang, sir?" said Mrs Dudley. Her personal appearance had not improved over the years, and she continued to look dishevelled and slatternly.

"I say, ever so sorry to have to get you back in here. We have a bit of a mystery to solve," said Rowland.

"Yes?"

"Did you sing the National Anthem during the night?"

"Sir?"

"I have reason to believe that you did indeed sing the National Anthem during the night."

"No, I didn't. What would I want to do that for?" asked the astounded servant.

"Would you mind telling us what you were dreaming about?"

"Oh, sir, I'm not mad like your patients. It wasn't me. I never have dreams."

311

"Did you hear any strange noises during the night?"

"I'm sorry I didn't hear you."

"I said: Did you hear any strange noises during the night?"

"Strange noises? No. My hearing's not what it was."

"All right, you may go. Thank you, Mrs Dudley."

Rowland was up and dressed by 9.00 o'clock. Dolly was sitting at the dressing table, blow-drying her hair. Her husband looked pale, drawn and ill. He crossed the hall and found his secretary sitting at her desk.

"Good morning, sir."

"Good morning. I'm not well," he said abruptly. "Can you please 'phone all the patients booked for the day, and cancel them."

"Yes, sir. Sorry to hear you're not well."

Rowland went to the drinks cabinet on the first floor. He took out an unopened bottle of *Bell's* whisky and drank it out of the bottle. He sat down and continued to drink until he had consumed almost half of it.

He felt anaesthetized enough to do what he had been dreading since 4.00 o'clock that morning. He carried the bottle to the top of the house, and unlocked the door of the nursery wing. He knew

312

William had been up there, because of the distinctive smell of his *Benson and Hedges* cigarettes which wafted from the nursery into the corridor.

He took another swig before going into the nursery. He noticed an unemptied ashtray and an empty cigarette packet on the table. He was feeling so unwell that he thought he was about to die. He took more swigs from the bottle, to prepare himself for the task of moving the chair.

Within two minutes, he pulled it violently towards him and lifted the sheet covering the three bodies. He observed Kessi's and Ruthie's clothes, and knew immediately they were street women, rather than women of William's class.

He picked up the hands of the two prostitutes in turn, in order to ascertain their approximate time of death. They were not yet in rigor which confirmed his suspicion that they had only died a few hours ago.

He covered their bodies with the sheet, and pushed back the chair to hide them. He sat down at the nursery table and sobbed, his heart completely broken and his mood beyond despair.

He drank the rest of the whisky and slept for about an hour, slumped over the table, before leaving the nursery wing and locking the door behind him. He went down to the bedroom and was

313

relieved by the fact that Dolly was not there. He got back into the bed, which had already been made, and fell asleep, hoping that he had swallowed enough whisky to kill himself.

"What's the matter, Rowland? Are you ill?"

Dolly had just returned from the hairdresser. It was 12.30.

"Yes, I'm afraid I am ill."

"You were all right at breakfast time."

"There's something I have to tell you but I'm afraid of losing you. I'm an accessory to the fact, you see. I've failed. It was my fault but I tried so hard to put things right. He's a serial killer, Dolly."

"Who is? Who are you talking about?"

Rowland turned onto his side, facing away from her.

"He's been up and done two more! I thought I'd cured him but he's started again."

"Who has, Rowland? Who's been up? Up where? Done what?"

"My William.... Oh, God, Dolly, help me! I love that child so much, more than I can say in words. I'd die for him if I could. It's not his fault!"

He continued shouting in short, tortured, staccato sentences.

"Don't you remember my cruelty to him? I've

mutated his sweet little soul. I've made him a paranoid schizophrenic, for my sins, a man who can't be let loose, a bloody serial killer. Oh, God, Dolly, what can I do now? I want to die! I want to do the honourable thing!"

He closed his eyes and sank into a noisy, gurgling stupor.

When William returned from the Hammersmith, he found Juliet sitting on a chair in the bathroom, waiting for the bath to fill.

"I thought you'd be gone another week," he said, baffled.

"I couldn't stand the course. I wasn't learning anything. The Y.W.C.A. at Oxford is full of vegetarians and ghastly lesbians, who sleep with their windows closed. God, I hate the company of women! Not only that, I didn't like being away from you."

"That's civil of you. I thought I'd go off my head without you being here."

There was a pause, broken by Juliet.

"Who is this woman, Dolly?"

William raised his head, startled.

"Dolly? She's an aunt of mine. What about her?"

"Why are you lying? She's not your aunt. She's

your stepmother. You also told me your father was dead. I've known all along he isn't. I've had other calls on quite a few occasions, from a caller identifying himself as Rowland Rendon. Each time, he asks if you're all right, and each time, he tells me not to mention to you that he called," said Juliet.

William turned away from her and looked out of the window.

"Oh, I see," he said, after a long silence.

"Why do you lie to me? Why can't you ever tell the truth when talking about yourself?"

"Because I am, and always have been, a liar. I was born a liar. I am still a liar and no doubt I shall die, a liar. I don't know the difference between truth and lies. There are times when I get out of the car, without even remembering where I've been. My right hand doesn't know what my left hand is doing. I don't allow the two hands to meet."

"Could you not arrange an introduction?" said Juliet. "It would make it much easier for those sharing your life, if you did. Have you, for instance, told your father who I am?"

"You said he already knows," he said. "You told me he rings you up. Incidentally, you just said Dolly had rung up. Did she leave a message?"

"No. She sounded in a hurry."

"Did she sound as if something was wrong?"

"I don't think so, no, just in a hurry."

"I'll ring her later this evening."

William tried the Harley Street number repeatedly that evening. No-one answered. He switched off his mobile telephone, and turned it on the next morning.

He had the usual, unpleasant, familiar feeling that he might have done something of which he had no knowledge. An eerie instinct told him that something of a potentially horrifying nature was either happening or was about to happen.

William and Sam Roberts, the SHO, were dissecting the organs of an exceptionally overweight man who had died of a heart attack. William was clutching the heart, its aorta and surrounding arteries in his right hand, and squeezing with all his might to ease his tension.

He thought, fleetingly, that he was wringing out a water-logged sponge, and was surprised to see the yellowish-brown fat, like rancid butter, coming out from the aorta and surrounding arteries, in unsightly rubbery lumps. He pretended he was strangling the person or parties responsible for his inability to know who he was.

The mobile 'phone in his pocket rang. It played the first few bars of *Molly Malone*. He grabbed hold of it with his right hand, which was covered in blood and fat, while Roberts stared at him, aghast.

"Hey, what have you got against that heart,

William? Whatever has it done to you? That's not pathology, that's butchery!"

"Shut up, Sam! Who's that? It's a bad line. Is that Dolly?"

Dolly was speaking from her car telephone. Her voice sounded steady and gave William the initial impression that nothing was wrong. She was driving from London to High Wycombe to pick up hers and Rowland's daughter, Kate, from Godstowe School.*

"It's a bad line, William. Can you hear me?"

"Yes, are you all right?"

"It's tragic news, I'm afraid, William."

"Oh, my God!"

"It's about your father. He's taken his life," she said nervously and abruptly.

William leant backwards and sat on the slab, on which the heart attack victim's body lay. He perched awkwardly on its arm, which had fallen over the edge of the slab while its heart was being removed.

"Why?" was all he could think of saying.

"We both heard the sound of a woman singing the National Anthem and screaming in the nursery wing. Your father went up there and found two recently murdered women, as well as the body of a woman whom you had killed quite some time ago.

---

*Godstowe: A girls' preparatory boarding school, known for its strict discipline and academic excellence. The Author herself attended the school.

"Whom *I* had killed?"

"Yes, whom you had killed. He'd kept the first murder secret over all these years. He'd treated you so badly as a child that he thought the least he owed you was protection. He was convinced that his long talks with you had cured you.

"When he found the two recent bodies, it hit him hard. He thought he'd failed you. He said all his work had been in vain and that he no longer deserved to live.

"When I rang you last night, I was with him at the Royal Free Hospital. He'd taken an overdose of Nembutal. He died half an hour ago. I wanted you to know so that you could come to the hospital.

"I'm sorry to have to tell you this, and this will be the greatest shock of all. I'm not covering up for you, the way he did. I don't see why I should, considering the fact that I never treated you badly as a child. Once I've picked Kate up and brought her home, I'm reporting you. I'm taking the police up to the nursery wing and I'm showing them the bodies of the three women you killed."

"Oh, I see," said William, adding "Do you really think this matter would be of any interest to the police? On second thoughts, they might be grateful to me."

"Why ever should they?" asked Dolly. Her vision had become blurred. She suddenly felt faint and giddy.

319

"The answer's obvious," said William. "If no-one ever did this sort of thing, they wouldn't be able to earn their living, would they?"

He gripped the mobile 'phone as savagely as he had gripped the heart. He heard the sound of an ear-piercing scream, accompanied by the screeching of breaks.

Dolly's feeling of faintness had reached a climax. She veered to the right hand side of the road where she had a head-on crash with a lorry. She died instantly.

William looked as if he were close to death himself.

"Are you all right?" asked Roberts, as he lay his dissecting instruments onto a white marble surface.

"No. My father is dead." As he spoke, he fell flat on his back over the heart attack victim's body. The two forms, crossing each other at right angles, were sufficiently undignified to appear comical.

Roberts went into the secretaries' office. Juliet was there. Dolly had rung her up once more before getting through to William. Juliet had taken a taxi to the Hammersmith, knowing that William needed her.

Roberts contacted Accident and Emergency.

"This is Pathology," he said, his tone phlegmatic. "Dr William Rendon has collapsed in a state of shock." In a lame attempt to provide comic relief, he added, "He's fallen backwards over a dead body."

Two Accident and Emergency nurses covered William with blankets and lifted him onto a stretcher. Juliet followed. He regained consciousness. His blood pressure was taken and found to be dangerously low. He was injected with adrenalin and given hot, sweet tea. Juliet helped him raise the cup to his mouth.

"It's all right, William. Juliet's here," she said. "We're going home. I'm going to look after you. Today's Thursday. You'll be able to get plenty of rest. You know that French restaurant in the King's Road, called *Thierry*'s, the one you say is your favourite?"

"Yes. What of it?"

"We can go there for lunch on Sunday. Would you like that?"

"Yes."

Juliet had gone out late on Saturday night to buy whisky and cigarettes. She had only been out for ten minutes, and when she came back, William had disappeared.

She had never been prone to worrying, and she knew the extent to which he doted on her. She had made a decision to leave William, once he was restored to an acceptable degree of normality and had recovered from Dolly's, and, in particular,

Rowland's death. She would have left him immediately, had Dolly told her about the murders.

She had started to fear him when he told her, in hysterical fits and starts, that there were times when he did not remember where he'd been and that he wasn't prepared for his right hand and left hand to meet. She had formed her own conclusion that William was suffering from a form of schizophrenia, and, unless he were cured, she decided she couldn't take the responsibility of looking after him.

In a way, she hoped he would never come back and that she would receive a 'phone call in about two days' time, informing her that his body had been found in the Thames. There were times when he was too great a responsibility for her to bear.

At 1.00 in the morning, she turned out the light, and fell asleep after about an hour.

It was at least 5.00 in the morning, when she saw William, standing by the bed, his eyes wild. bloodshot and staring.

His appearance frightened her.

"What the hell are you doing?" she asked.

"Nothing serious. I was going the wrong way up Harley Street. I was called into the side. I got done on a charge of D and D."

"Is that drunk and disorderly or drink driving?" asked Juliet impatiently.

"Drink driving. I'd taken a lot of Speed. I was almost smashed to pieces by it."

"Why were you going the wrong way up Harley Street?" she asked, bemused.

"I had to, Juliet. I had to go up to my Room of Love in order to be with my beloved Dead, including my father. It's not as bad as it seems. Once they slung me down the nick, I had a long discussion about who Jack the Ripper was. I insisted it was Queen Victoria's personal surgeon, Sir William Gull, and by God, I was right! It's known it was a Freemasonic plot to cover up for the indiscretions of the Duke of Clarence."

"You need rest," said Juliet. "We'll go to *Thierry*'s, tomorrow. We can go every Sunday, if you like."

William cried for a lot of the time on his first visit, and was cheered up when he saw the welcoming, good-natured, waiters, all of whom were French. William had a fluent knowledge of the language, and he felt more at ease speaking French than English. He had thought and spoken about his tragic life so much in his own language, that the speaking of a foreign language refreshed him and set him free.

It was mid September 1993, which coincided roughly with his motoring offence. For the next two months, Juliet was happy to continue to go to

Thierry's every Sunday. The rich *Bouillabaisse*, which William asked for each time, and the friendly waiters, calmed him and even enabled him to smile. Juliet decided she would stay with him.

The date was 14th November, 1993. It was Armistice Sunday and William had been looking forward to having lunch with Juliet at *Thierry*'s.

William was in their sound-proofed bedroom, drinking cups of filtered coffee.

He poured out his fourth cup and came into the living room. Juliet was ironing and watching the Remembrance parade.

He bellowed at her to turn the television off. She was so shocked because he had shouted at her, that she did so without question.

"All right, I've turned it off. I had been thinking of leaving you, but I know that's something I could never do.

"Why can't you ever tell me what is troubling you so much? I know how badly hit you've been by your father's death, and I understand why that's upset you. It's a grief that you will overcome in time."

"I'm already taking steps to overcome it," he said. "I go to Harley Street and I sit in my glorious Room of Love, where I see my father all the time.

I sit surrounded by the souls of my beloved Dead, and, oh, what a cheer and comfort they are to me!"

"I only wish you'd tell me about all the other things which seem to have traumatised you throughout your life," said Juliet. "Why do you need to go on these drinking benders? Why do you drown yourself with Speed, which you appear to need as a religion?"

He knelt down on the floor at her feet. "Mr D. keeps me alive."

"Who's Mr D?"

"I'm sure I've told you before. If I have, why do you keep asking? Mr D. is Dexedrine, or Dexamphetamine Sulphate. Some people call it Speed.

"When I take it, something transports me from hell to Paradise, in about fifteen minutes. I'm in hell when I don't take it and it's so bad, I want to die. Why should I allow myself to want to die? Naturally, I need to take more."

Juliet pushed the ironing board to the corner of the television room. She had just finished ironing her favourite woollen emerald green dress.

William remained kneeling, as if unaware what graven image to direct his prayers to. Juliet knelt by his side and put her arms round his waist.

"Come on, William. There was something about the Remembrance parade that haunted you, almost to the point of killing you. You had that terrified and terrifying look in your eyes. Perhaps, something dreadful happened when you watched the parade, a long time ago in the past.

"For God's sake, William, was it that, and if so, what *did* happen? I want to look after you until one of us dies, and I have the right to be told."

William lay, front downwards on the floor, and wept. Juliet lay down beside him.

"I can't, Juliet, oh, would that I could! I've been raised as an upper class Englishman. I want to tell you the truth but I can't. Experiences and emotions are so difficult to express. It would be like ramming a stomach pump down my throat."

He started crying piteously, again.

"Can't you tell me next time you take Mr D?"

"I'd like to, but I don't think I could. The drug's a personal friend to me, and like a friend, it holds me back, if there's a risk my confessions will hurt me."

Juliet got up. She had finished ironing one of William's shirts and folded it.

"We've made progress," she said. "At least, I'm going to do what I can to see what horror lies at the back of your poor soul. When you knock back as much Speed as you can hold, your story will come flooding out, and you'll feel as if the shackles had been torn from your feet."

326

"It's got to be done, Juliet. I know that," said William.

"Anything I can get for you while you're lying on the floor?" she asked.

"Man-size bottle of whisky. Bring it, quick! It's not strong enough to make me drag up my demon-drenched bile, but it will make me a bit more open than I'm otherwise capable of being."

Juliet poured out two brimming beakers of neat whisky. She was only able to get a small quantity of it down. He drank all that was in his glass.

He got up from the floor, and staggered to the sofa, where he lay on his back. The whisky had removed the mental stiffness, for which his Englishness was responsible. He felt slightly more comfortable and, although he tried to keep his conversation away from the Remembrance parade, he felt overwhelmed by a sudden, reassuring spontaneity.

"This will make it easier," said Juliet. "We'll play the word game. I say a word and you say a word. Or it can be just an expression. I won't force you. You can stop any time you want."

"I don't see why not," he said.

Juliet started.

"The Queen."

"Kick me! No, that's not what I meant. Oh, yes, corgis."

"Wars."

"Of the Roses."

"Funeral marching music."

"Brave, bold, unselfish men who fought for the freedom we now enjoy."

Juliet laughed. "This isn't the easiest thing I've ever done, but I'm going to conquer it, because I want you to be happy. Only, use brief expressions. Don't make a speech."

"OK, go ahead. The whisky's anaesthetized me a bit."

"Queen going up to Cenotaph, putting down wreath," said Juliet in staccato bursts. "You've got to respond with a word or a phrase, the first thing that comes into your head."

"I wish I could bend over like that without cricking my back," he said.

"I'm not going to stop, William. And you're going to co-operate with me. Here's some more whisky. I'll go on.

"The old veterans, unable to accomplish military feats any more, who fought for our freedom. Don't stop to think. Answer straight away."

"'They threw in drummer Hodge to rest, uncoffinned, just as found.'" screamed William.

Juliet raised her voice suddenly, on what could

have been a telepathic impulse, as if an unknown force within William, were trying to break out, like the life-loving young of a wild creature.

"The two minute silence," she said assertively. "Come on, William, spit it out!"

William felt that his right hand and left hand were being tied together. Juliet's words automatically reminded him of his nanny, wishing to observe the two minute silence.

This was the first time William had remembered his treacherous childhood, away from his nursery, and his facial features screwed up as if he had toothache.

"Come on, William, the two minute silence," repeated Juliet.

There was a pause.

"I order you to throw it up. No woman who loves you as I do, wishes to be disappointed by you. You're gentleman enough to refuse a woman nothing."

William thought of Rowland. The memory he had of the former monster, and the loving, reformed saint, overwhelmed him so much that he sobbed once more.

He savoured some of the kindest of Rowland's words. He couldn't bear to say a word against his father at that time.

"Come on, William, I'm waiting," said Juliet.

329

"The two minute silence. No, he wasn't good to me at the time," said William, "but he became saintly later, over so very many years. I'm glad in a way, to have some good memories. After all, it's less comforting to hate the dead than it is to love them. I loved him so much that his death is a comfort, not a pain."

"Let's go back to the Silence," said Juliet.

"OK. My father came into the nursery and sacked the nanny, just before the Silence on Remembrance Day when I was eight," he said in the dead pan voice, of a news commentator, saying that Tony Blair had spent his Sunday, fishing.

"Why?"

"I can't say."

"Then what?"

"My nanny died on the nursery floor."

"Of what?"

"Heart," he said brusquely, adding, "No, Juliet, that incident doesn't hurt me because I adored my father from adolescence to the day he died. I've tried to produce so much for you and it hasn't been easy. Perhaps, I, or another, will tell you the whole story one day.

"I had two previous non-blood cousins. I married a girl called Anne Brenchley, the dentist's daughter. Anne misguidedly told her cousins the whole story, of my childhood and my inability to be normal."

William was blind drunk by now. A sudden surge of love, coming from his memory of his father, passed through him, causing a pleasant warming sensation in his stomach.

William's comforting memory of his father turned to a feeling of despair. The fact that he wasn't present at Rowland's death, made him guilty and disappointed. He wished he could have been with his father when he died, and sensed the pain of parting without saying "goodbye".

His thoughts turned back to the time when Dolly had read to him. He remembered the story in which a phrase occurred, a phrase, both fascinating and moribund. He savoured it without speaking out loud.

He poured himself some more whisky and drank three measures of it. He was resting his head on the back of the sofa, feeling happy and sad at the same time.

Juliet held his hand, on seeing his wet cheeks. "Is there anything else you'd like to say about the grief you suffered on Remembrance Day as a child?"

William did not answer.

"What are you thinking about, William," asked Juliet.

"Oh, the stains of death upon mouth and eyes,

*and a nest of mice in the tangle of the frozen
beard!"* he screamed, and rolled about on the floor,
repeating the words with pleasure mixed with grief.

"What you need is a rest. Then we'll go to
Thierry's. You do want to go, don't you?"

"Yes."

Thierry's, the French restaurant in the King's Road,
was more crowded than it had been on the previous
Sundays.

One of the French waiters ushered William and
Juliet to an unoccupied table close to a wall. Juliet
had on a leopard-skin coat over her emerald
green dress.

"May we take your coat, *madame*?" a waiter
said, a tone of obsession in his voice, as if he were
morally offended by customers keeping their
coats on.

"Ah, *monsieur et madame*, my most favoured
customers. Are you keeping well?"

"Yes, we're both well, thank you, and
yourself?" said Juliet.

"On Sundays, we are always well," said the
waiter. "We are the better for seeing you here. A
bottle of your preferred *Chardonnay*?"

Chardonnay, a mild, gentle, unassuming wine,
was William's and Juliet's favourite. Once it was

brought to the table, and poured into their glasses, they felt more relaxed, and ate the garlic-covered olives, already on the table.

They had both drunk two glasses of *Chardonnay* before they had ordered.

Service that day was slow because the restaurant was crowded. William felt tetchy and edgy. He took his bottle of Dexedrine from his pocket, and emptied a copious amount of the drug into the palm of his hand. He washed it down with the wine. Juliet watched him, disapprovingly.

"William, are you addicted to this stuff?"

"I suppose I am addicted to it," said William. "When I get these nervy moods, I assume it's because the last dose is wearing off. When I take another lot, I feel at peace with myself, and everyone I have contact with."

"What worries me is the effect it has on your heart," said Juliet.

"My heart is the last thing I care about. I've got so many conflicting thoughts, all harder to bear than I can say in words. I've got to get my mind right. Once that's done, I'll get someone to take a look at my heart."

The waiter eventually brought the food to the table. William's Dexedrine had not started working. He felt disappointed, and was unable to enjoy his cheese and walnut salad.

The table they were sitting at, was not ideal. Juliet sat by a wall, enabling her to watch the other diners, and William faced inwards. This suited him because the only person he wished to see was Juliet, with her coiffed, copper-coloured hair and the clothes she wore, to enhance it.

Another ten minutes passed. William's Dexedrine had still not taken affect. It was at that time that a middle-aged woman entered the restaurant, wearing a bright red, buttoned-up maxi-coat. William had his back to her and couldn't see her.

She was alone and sat down at a table, close to him.

The pernickety waiter went over to her.

"May I take your coat, *madame*. We do have fine central heating in here. It's not that I mind. It simply gives other customers the impression that the customers keeping their coats on, are freezing."

The middle-aged woman was irritated. She said she was cold, and that she had the right to keep her coat on, and added vehemently that she was not living in Caligula's Rome.

"*Madame*, you either take your coat off, or you leave!"

"I'll leave! I'll go to the Chinese restaurant next door. The food's better there, anyway."

She got up, facing away from William. They

had been sitting back to back. William was amused by the fact that the woman had refused to surrender her coat.

The woman found his thick, fair hair attractive.

She went closer to his chair and stood in front of him, ogling him.

"Piss off, you old boot!" said Juliet.

The woman turned to William, intending to flirt with him. It was the first time he noticed that she was wearing a bright red overcoat.

He started to shake and whitened as if he had a fever.

"Whatever is the matter, William?" said Juliet.

William took more Dexedrine which he washed down with the *Chardonnay*. His heart was beating so hard that it hurt him.

"Have I done anything to offend you?" asked the woman.

William felt as if his stomach were being tied up in knots. He no longer had any inhibitions. He jolted himself to his feet and pointed menacingly at the woman:

"Take it away, it's red! Take it away, it's red! Help me, Juliet! Only you can help me, now."

"What *are* you talking about? Are you going to make these psychotic scenes every time you see someone in red?"

"I know the names and whereabouts of the two

cousins of my late wife, Anne Brenchley.

"I'll write them a note, and ask them if we can come to tea. They're quite pleasant, both men."

"You've landed a new one on me, William," she said. "I had no idea how much red things distressed you."

"I know full well you had no idea. The red is a part of the horrible whole. I don't want to tell you about red, as well. I haven't the strength. My wife's cousins found out, because in some ways, Anne, was very indiscreet. She knew what red did to me and why. She knew because I told her. There's nothing I left out."

"In that case, I want an introduction to your cousins as soon as possible," Juliet said, adding, "I was planning to leave you the odd six weeks ago, but the more I've got to know how much you need me to look after you, the more I've realized it's something I could never do.

"When we first met and started living together, it is true that I loved you very much, but I was not in love with you.

"The situation has changed. I am hopelessly in love with you. Your pain is my pain. I know how much you miss your father."

"I do miss him. I think about him all the time. When my grief is at its worst, I go back to 79 Harley Street, and I sit down in my Room of

Love," said William. "I feel my father's presence and Nanny's presence very very strongly. I weep but my tears are not of pain, but of peace and love."

"I've got an idea," said Juliet.

"What idea?"

"Will you take me back to the nursery this afternoon. I'd like to go through the ritual we went through before."

"Why, yes. We should go as soon as we can because, as Dolly and my father are both dead, the house will be re-occupied, sooner rather than later."

"I want to. I'm not just saying that to please you. I'm worried about the nursery, though. Can you not reconstruct an identical room in a part of your flat? That way, whoever buys or rents the house will keep the old nursery, and the identical replica will be in your own home. It may even be necessary to sell your flat."

"I'll think about that," said William. "When would you like to come to the nursery?"

"Can we go, now?"

"Of course, we can."

They took the Jensen, let themselves into number 79 Harley Street and mounted the stairs. William unlocked the door to the nursery wing, occasionally muttering "See Nanny ..." in a childish voice.

"Oh, Juliet?"

"Yes."

"Would you mind waiting in the bedroom for five minutes? There's dust on the chairs which would spoil your beautiful clothes."

"I can wait."

She lay down on the bed he had slept in as a child, and waited.

"OK! You can come in, now."

William had checked that the bodies of the three women he had murdered, were securely hidden in the alcove behind the armchair. The sheet was in place. Rowland's determination to cover up for the son he had once molested, had a profoundly moving effect on William.

He was concerned about the unpleasant smell, permeating the nursery. It was the smell of Kessi's and Ruthie's decomposing bodies. He knew he would be able to deceive Juliet in some way, if she questioned him about it.

She came into the room, smiling. She hugged him.

"I hope you don't mind my mentioning this, but there's a very unpleasant smell in here," she remarked.

William spoke nervously, in fits and starts.

"I know. I'm sorry about that. I should have told you earlier, but I feared it would put you off

338

coming here. This room has been in a state of disuse for quite some time. There's been a problem with rats. In fact, just before my father died, he came in here and said there was a dead rat under the floorboards."

"Oh, oh, I see."

"We can leave, if you want. That is, if this puts you off going through the ritual."

"That's all right. I don't mind. Can we get it over and done with, quickly?"

William took the bright red wool, needles, grey wig and plastic apron from the cupboard. Juliet dragged the wig and apron onto herself, without speaking, and sat in the armchair. She forced herself to go through the motions of knitting, and suddenly rushed into the bathroom.

"You are all right, aren't you?" asked William.

She knew he was insane but it gave her pleasure to do anything he asked her to. So intense and selfless had her love for him become, that she would have been prepared to commit murder, had he requested it.

"I feel fine, now. There's still something I don't understand."

"Oh, yes. What's that?"

"It's about the wool, William. You were quite happy to take it out of the cupboard last time, and you were happy again to take it out this time.

Surely, you can see it's bright red, but it doesn't bother you to see it. At the same time, when you saw that woman's bright red coat, I thought six men in white coats were about to stretcher you off. You must explain this senseless ambiguity. When you handed the wool to me up here, you behaved quite normally. "That scene at *Thierry*'s — did you do that to attract attention in your drug-induced state?"

"No, no, Juliet. You won't understand, yet. If there's something red up here in my Room of Love, I can and love to accept it, because this is where my soul belongs. "Outside, I cannot look at bright red, which is why I so often wear dark glasses. Dark red things like blood, don't bother me so much."

He paused for a few seconds and continued, "The red business. This is the one thing I can't tell you about and will have to leave that to Anne's cousins. It's something to do with my father when he was young."

"Can't you confess it, now? We're alone. No-one will hear what you say."

"The reason I can't and won't, is that I would rather die than betray my beloved father. I guarantee my cousins will tell you about red. They'll tell you everything. I've got to leave it to them, and cannot allow the words to come from my own lips. "Tomorrow, you'll know. You will wait till then, won't you?"

"Yes, if that is what you want. Now, there's another question I wish to ask."

"Oh, yes?"

"It's about the smell. Whatever you say, I can't believe it's only a dead rat which is causing it. It's all coming from behind this chair."

William had it in mind to kill Juliet in the way he had killed the others. He feared the risk of being jailed, and banned indefinitely from his Room of Love, if she broke loose and reported him. He knew that his attractively innocent looks would enable him to find any woman he wanted, and get her to fall in love with him, because of his polite, humorous, kindly manner, and erudition accompanying it.

He went over to the window and watched the one-way traffic moving down Harley Street, which was almost empty on a Sunday afternoon. All he could see were two unoccupied taxis, and a solitary ambulance, turning off into the Harley Street Clinic.

He wondered whether he should strangle Juliet, before hanging himself from the beam on the ceiling of the sanctuary which would soon be taken from him.

He turned round and walked towards her.

"What is that dreadful smell, William? Please tell me."

His hands were outstretched and his fingers bent. He was looking at her throat.

341

"Is there something the matter?" she asked.

He suddenly noticed she was still wearing the wig and apron, and realized that everything about her was the epitome of the nanny he had lost.

His hands were still outstretched but another force within him was holding him back. The dominant part of his personality wanted to save her.

"Take those off, straight away! Run away from here as fast as you can! Get out into the street!"

"What are you talking about, William? Why are you shouting at me like that?"

"Because, if you don't get out, you're going to be killed, and I may not be able to stop that happening."

His behaviour was incomprehensible to her but she did as he asked. She went outside and waited by the Jensen. William came out ten minutes later, opened the door for her, got in and started the ignition.

Neither spoke for several minutes as the car moved down the street with unusual slowness. William was the first to break the silence.

"*'The skies, they are ashen and sober,'*" he remarked in a depressed tone, quoting the words of Edgar Allen Poe, his favourite poet. "I've always hated this time of year."

"I don't understand you, William. First, you shout that I'm about to be killed. Then you start talking about the bloody weather, as if nothing had happened."

"I'm sorry if I confused you. It might be better if I didn't take you up there, again."

"I don't want to go up there, again. What *was* that smell?"

He laughed and kissed her on the cheek.

"Oh, that. That sort of generally relates to three murders I committed," he said in a strangely elated voice. "The first was an American woman called Sarah. The two others were prostitutes called Kessi and Ruthie. I did the last two quite recently. One of them sang *God Save the Queen* before I topped her."

Juliet laughed with relief.

"You've got a superb sense of humour," she said, "so dry, so wonderfully macabre!"

He continued to stare at the street unfolding before him and smiled enigmatically.

"I say, let's motor down to the Ritz and have some afternoon tea," he said. "There's always a man playing the piano in there. He can even strum out part of Rach III if you ask him nicely."

He increased his speed. Without saying anything, and without indicating, he swerved to the side of the road and screeched to a halt.

"Oh, for God's sake, William, what is it, now?" asked Juliet.

"Go down on me, will you," he said.

"What, at the edge of Hyde Park Corner? You're joking."

"Just do it! I order you to do as I say! I'm absolutely desperate!" he shouted, vulgarly.

A waiter brought a pot of tea and sandwiches to the table.

"I'm not all that happy about the events of this afternoon, William," said Juliet. "I want to meet these two cousins of your late wife's as soon as possible. I demand an explanation for your extraordinary eccentricity, and for your dotty attitude towards things that are red. How old are they?"

"How old are who?"

"Your late wife's cousins, of course."

"Nineteen and twenty one. They share a flat in Battersea."

"Can't we see them, now?"

"No. It's too short notice. I'll ring them and ask them if we can see them after work, tomorrow."

"Do they know the whole of it — about you, that is?"

"I told Anne everything there is to know. She felt she had to tell them because she couldn't take the responsibility of being the only person who knew."

"Did Anne know why you behave so bizarrely when you see things which are red?"

"Yes, she knew."

"Why can't you tell me?"

"Because I don't want to."

"Why?"

"It's too painful. I'd prefer them to tell you, not me."

William parked the Jensen in Vauxhall Bridge Road. He was about to open the door leading to his block of flats.

"I'm not coming in," said Juliet.

"Why? Have I upset you?"

"No. I want to be alone for a few hours. There's a film I want to see."

"What film, Juliet? Where is it showing?"

"It's called *Naked*. It's in Tottenham Court Road."

"Oh, don't see that! It's a horrible film. It's absolutely nauseating."

"Someone told me it was quite good. What is it about?"

They were standing in the doorway under the arch. It had started to rain, and there was a harsh east wind.

"It's about this really sordid, professional bore, with this Manchester accent, positively awash with grime," said William. "He bores the entire population of Manchester. Then he comes South and bores the entire population of London," he said.

"I'm told it's meant to be funny."

"It's not funny at all. There's not a single joke in it. There's a scene showing a seedy hophead of a woman being sadistically buggered by her landlord in a kitchen. If you still want to see it, I'll drive you there."

"No. I'll walk."

"All the way from here to Tottenham Court Road? Have you any idea how far that is?"

She started crying.

"I've got to walk, as far as I possibly can. I'm so upset by your terrifying behaviour in Harley Street this afternoon, that I need all the cold and the rain I can get."

It was already dark. William was exhausted, now that the Dexedrine had worn off. He got into bed, wearing his clothes, and went to sleep.

Juliet sat through the film which depressed and disgusted her, but she was too tired to get up and leave.

It was 8.30 p.m. She went to a public house near the cinema where she sat for a few hours, getting systematically drunk on Vodka and Coke.

346

She made up her mind that, irrespective of what she would hear from Anne's cousins, William suffered from a dangerous form of mental illness. She still loved him but knew there was a risk that he might easily kill her. She was going to leave him, and in doing so, kill part of herself.

The combination of the film, the alcohol and the nursery visit, made her physically sick. She sat on a public seat with her head between her knees, weeping. She got up and wandered aimlessly about the streets for a while, before returning to the seat and crying one more.

It was long past midnight when she let herself into William's flat in Vauxhall Bridge Road.

William woke up at 11 o'clock that night. He, too, felt depressed and exhausted. He wondered where Juliet was and was afraid that he might have killed her in his father's house that afternoon.

He thought of driving there to see whether Juliet's was among the bodies of his victims, but remembered she had left him to go to the cinema alone.

He went to his medicine cabinet and filled the palm of his hand with his beloved Dexedrine, and returned to the bedroom where he lay on his back.

Over an hour passed, and the Dexedrine still

showed no sign of calming him and elevating his mood. The knowledge that he was heavily addicted to it, depressed him further.

He rolled onto his stomach and opened a book of Edgar Allan Poe's poems. He considered *Annabel Lee*, the most popular of his poetic works, embarrassingly "soppy". His disillusionment with one of the poems of the man he referred to as "the Divine Edgar", sharpened his pessimism and disappointment with his life, and increased his fear that Juliet would leave him, following his uncontrolled episode in the nursery.

He reached for the pill-bottle and took at least two more palmfulls of Dexedrine, and waited.

About half an hour passed. He felt the drug working and almost wept with joy. He rolled onto his stomach once more and read *Ulalume*, the poem he had quoted a line from, as he had driven down Harley Street, after his psychotic episode.

The nobility of the language and metric structure elevated his mood further. He turned onto his back and read the whole of *The Raven* out loud.

Because of his view that images of bereavement and sex, were often united, he yearned for a woman, but preferred not to go out, for fear of finding another prostitute, and taking her to the nursery. He was hoping that Juliet would soon be back. He planned to recite *The Raven* to her during an act of torrid, disinhibited sex.

He noticed that his heart was beating harder and faster than he had experienced before, and the sensation had become unpleasant. He felt very cold and anxious, so he instinctively took more of his best and only friend, in the vain hope that it would restore his calm.

The previous effect it had had on him, turned dramatically from being peaceful and pleasant, to nightmarish. He was terrified without being able to assess the cause of his fear, and the idea of his being alone was an anathema to him.

He put on his overcoat over his clothes to keep out the icy cold which had descended on him. He found he could not stand still. He jumped up and down like a jogger, to drive out the cold, and shake off his all-embracing agitation.

He lit a *Benson and Hedges* and paced up and down the room, his body temperature changing from stiflingly hot, to cold.

He went into the kitchen, by now in a drugged and disorientated semi-stupor, alternating with pangs of unbearable panic. He went to the stove, and turned on all four gas rings, forgetting, in his altered state, to light them. He assumed they would heat the kitchen and blow away the neo-Siberian cold which had got into his blood and his bones.

It was only then that he felt a pain in the centre

of his chest, radiating to the left and to his left arm. He was so giddy that he felt he were at sea in a Force Ten gale. To make his suffering worse, he found it difficult to breathe and his whole body seemed awash with faintness and nausea.

It was only because he was a doctor, that he realized that his heart was failing, but he forced himself into denial.

The pain in the centre of his chest was worse, and was so acute that he thought he was being stabbed. He slid to the floor and lay on his back. The telephone was out of his reach.

In his delirium, and slow drift into death, he heard the crude, tuneless sound of a vulgar brass band, playing *God Save the Queen*. He felt someone kicking him sharply in the ribs. When he looked up, he saw his father in his cruel, young days.

"Leap to your feet when the National Anthem is being played!" shouted the psychiatrist.

WILLIAM'S POEM TO JULIET

The lost Mortician

A wicked mortician called Cupid
Said, "I think seat belts are stupid.
Now, they've become law, my libido is poor,
And the meat feels ancient and putrid.

"For a stiff which is thrown through a windscreen
Is the necrophile's sacredest daydream
Its skin is still fresh, there is warmth in its flesh,
And its cock is as hard as it had been

"When a young marble stiff's on the table,
With a fresh cunt to ram in your cable,
She might *not* fuck you back; but, by God, you could jack
Off your rocks like a skunk in a stable.

"Why are laws incommoding and stupid?"
Wistfully wailed wicked Cupid.
"Why be saddled with wizened cocks, withered and old,
When the youthful cadavers were blisses untold?

"Why be left with the cocks like slack, wintry vines
Because they'd been belted at earlier times?"

351